remember

Also by

EILEEN COOK

What Would Emma Do?

Getting Revenge on Lauren Wood

The Education of Hailey Kendrick

Unraveling Isobel

Used to Be

The Almost Truth

Year of Mistaken Discoveries

remember

EILEEN COOK

Simon Pulse

New York London Toronto Sydney New Delhi

SIMON PULSE
An imprint of Simon & Schuster Children's Publishing Division
1230 Avenue of the Americas, New York, New York 10020
First Simon Pulse hardcover edition February 2015
Text copyright © 2015 by Eileen Cook
Jacket photograph copyright © 2015 by Shane O'Donnell/Getty Images
All rights reserved, including the right of reproduction in whole or in part in any form.
SIMON PULSE and colophon are registered trademarks of Simon & Schuster, Inc.
For information about special discounts for bulk purchases,
please contact Simon & Schuster Special Sales at 1-866-506-1949
or business@simonandschuster.com.
The Simon & Schuster Speakers Bureau can bring authors to your live event.
For more information or to book an event contact
the Simon & Schuster Speakers Bureau at 1-866-248-3049
or visit our website at www.simonspeakers.com.
Jacket designed by Karina Granda
The text of this book was set in Adobe Garamond.
Manufactured in the United States of America
2 4 6 8 10 9 7 5 3 1
Library of Congress Cataloging-in-Publication Data
Cook, Eileen.
Remember / Eileen Cook. — First Simon Pulse hardcover edition.
pages cm
Summary: Harper, whose father's company trademarked the "Memtex" procedure for
wiping out bad memories, is surprised when her father objects to her having a treatment
but afterwards, she begins having strange flashes about her own life and she joins forces
with Neil, one of the company's protesters, to find the truth.
ISBN 978-1-4814-1696-2 (hardcover) — ISBN 978-1-4814-1698-6 (eBook)
[1. Memory—Fiction. 2. Fathers and daughters—Fiction. 3. Protest movements—Fiction.
4. Best friends—Fiction. 5. Friendship—Fiction. 6. Love—Fiction.
7. Science fiction.] I. Title.
PZ7.C76955Rem 2015
[Fic]—dc23
2014012808

To Laura Sullivan for answering my thousand questions about horses and for being my friend all these years.

chapter one

It's not clear if Saint Thomas More had murder on his mind when he fell from his alcove in the north stairwell and onto my friend Win. It's far more likely that over the years the vibration of hundreds of high school students thundering up and down the stairs finally shook him free. The statue did a huge swan dive that would have made an Olympian proud and clipped Win right over her eyebrow. She caught him, saving the statue from crashing to the floor. It can be hard to help someone see the bright side of things when they are nearly taken out by a religious icon.

"Sod it all, I'm bleeding." Win looked at her face in the mirror above the nurse's sink. When Win was really ticked, she sounded even more like her British-born mom.

I handed Win a wet paper towel. "Look on the bright

side—saving a saint is going to earn you some valuable karma points."

"Harper, I'm not Catholic." Win winced as she pressed the towel to her forehead. "And it's not like I had a choice; the stupid thing basically fell into my arms. If it had been up any higher, it probably would have killed me."

"I can't see Tom holding your lack of religion against you." I leaned over and patted the plaster statue of the saint on the head as he sat innocently on the floor. Our school, Saint Francis, was one of the highest ranked in Washington State. This meant the student body was made up of people who wanted their kids to have a religious education and also those who didn't mind forcing their kids to wear the most hideous mustard-yellow and navy-blue uniforms ever created as long as they went to a good school. "Having a saint who owes you one is nothing to sneer at. You could club a seal or something and it still wouldn't be enough to land you eternal damnation."

"Stop trying to find the silver lining in every situation." Win squinted at her reflection. "Look at that: It's going to leave a scar. That's it. I'm disfigured."

"You're fine. The nurse doesn't even think you need stitches."

"She's a school nurse. Do you really think I'm going to leave the destiny of this face in her hands?" Win continued her self-inspection. Only she could get clocked by a statue and still look great. It would be annoying if she weren't my best friend.

"Fair enough. But we got out of going to chemistry; you

have to admit that counts as good luck," I pointed out.

"Seems to me you're the lucky one. You weren't nearly decapitated *and* you still got out of class."

The nurse bustled back into the room. She handed Win an ice pack. "You'll want to keep this on to reduce the swelling."

Win blinked. "Ice. Don't you think I should have a CT scan or something? I could have brain damage."

"You'd want an MRI," I said. "CT is more for orthopedic injuries."

Win shot me a look.

"It basically grazed you. The only part of the statue that hit you was the hand." The nurse pointed, and I saw that Saint Thomas More had lost a finger in the accident. It looked like his blessing days were over. I wondered if the finger would count as a holy relic if someone found it on the stairs. The nurse yanked a folder out of her desk. "You'll be fine. Just keep the ice on there." She scribbled something in the file and then glanced up at the clock. "You two are free to go. If you hustle, you won't be late for Friday assembly."

We were barely out of the door before Win said, in a voice loud enough to carry to the nurse, "If I die of a brain aneurysm, my dad will sue this place."

"Getting hit on the head won't give you an aneurysm," I pointed out as we moved down the hall. "They're usually caused by a weakness in the artery since birth. High blood pressure could cause one too."

"Having you as a friend is like having my own personal WebMD. Handy and terrifying all at the same time," Win said.

"You're welcome." Having a neuroscientist as a dad made me more knowledgeable on brain function than the average high school senior. It also meant that I was more likely to kick the bell curve's ass in anatomy.

We were among the last people to get to the auditorium, but the assembly hadn't started yet. My boyfriend, Josh, yelled out my name and waved us over.

I tugged on Win's arm. "He saved us seats." We moved down the row and plopped into our chairs. Josh squeezed my hand and I fought the urge to pull mine back. Josh was only happy when we were constantly touching.

"Heard God tried to take you down." Josh motioned toward the Band-Aid on Win's forehead.

"Ha-ha. Maybe as official class president you should figure out if any other parts of the building plan to crush a student. I'm no lawyer, but that seems like a lawsuit waiting to happen."

Josh saluted. "I'll get on that on at our next council meeting."

"It could have been worse—what if it had been that statue of Saint Sebastian in the cafeteria, the one with all the arrows? You would have lost an eye," I said.

"Thank you, Mary Poppins." Win grabbed gum out of her bag and offered it to the both of us before jamming a piece in her mouth.

"It wouldn't kill you to see the positive side," Josh said.

"It might. Besides, that's why I keep her around." Win chomped on her gum with a smile.

We were unlikely friends. People called us yin and yang. She was half black; I was pasty white. I got nearly straight As, and she was happy with Cs. Win was the ultimate social butterfly, and I tended to be shy. Win vowed she wasn't going to be bothered with a relationship until she was at least forty, and I'd dated Josh for two years already. I always looked for the positive, and she had honed being cynical to an art form. There was no reason for us to get along, but we did.

Our principal, Mr. Lee, was on the stage waiting for everyone to pay attention. He did this sort of Zen thing where he would stand in silence with his eyes closed until we all shut up. You wouldn't think it would work, but it did.

"There's your dad," Josh whispered.

I followed his finger. My dad stood at the side of the stage, fussing with his tie. He almost never wore one. At work he got away with jeans, T-shirt, and lab coat. There are some benefits to owning your own company. Other than wealth and not having a boss, that is. I shifted in my seat. My dad liked to be goofy, which was bad enough at home, but I had no idea what he might pull at my school. I sent up a silent prayer that he didn't do one of his impressions.

"What's he doing here?" Win asked.

Saint Francis had a mandatory assembly every Friday with

various speakers. The school promoted it as a chance for us to gather as a "community." "Community" sounded better than what we suspected, which was that the teachers liked having the last hour of the week free.

"He agreed to do a talk on the importance of science," I said.

Win pretended to snore.

"How can you say that? Science impacts everything," Josh said.

Win held up a hand. "Spare me. I'm going to have to hear the talk from her dad; I don't need to hear it from you, too." She flipped her hair over her shoulder. "Also, for the record, having a bromance with your girlfriend's dad is creepy."

Josh was ready to argue with her, but Mr. Lee was already introducing my dad, so we had to be quiet.

I'd heard Dad's science talk before. It was fairly interesting. He managed to connect all these major scientists like Darwin and Einstein to random things like punk rock and winning World War II. My prayer must have worked, because so far he'd managed to avoid doing any of his lame Dad stand-up comedy routine.

"Now, some of you know that my company, Neurotech, recently received approval from the FDA to offer our revolutionary Memtex treatment to teens and children." Dad stood with a Neurotech logo projected onto him and the screen behind him.

"Holy shit, we can go for a softening now?" someone hissed a few rows behind me.

I turned around to hear who had said that. My dad hated when people called it a softening. He thought it sounded too woo-woo. He was not a fan of anything that smacked of being new age.

"I thought you guys might like to be the first group to see our new commercial. Sort of like a movie screening, only without the hot movie stars—unless you count me." A few people laughed. It's a well-accepted truth that everyone else will find your parent's feeble attempts at humor funnier than you will. My dad spotted me in the crowd and waved. I scrunched further down in my seat.

The auditorium lights dimmed, and my dad stepped out of the glare of the projector. The commercial was well done. It showed a bunch of perfectly airbrushed teens in what adults must think of as ideal moments: dancing at a prom, laughing with friends over a bonfire on the beach, crossing the finish line at a track meet. No one had acne or bad hair. I recognized the main actress from some cable show.

"Are bad memories holding you back from doing everything you want and enjoying the life you deserve?" she asked. Her eyes stared out of the screen as if she personally felt bad for us. "You don't have to be bogged down anymore. Ask your doctor about Memtex today—and imagine what you could accomplish tomorrow!" Her face split into a wide smile and just a hint of a wink.

The lights went up, and people applauded as if it had been an Oscar-winning performance. I wondered if Mr. Lee was ticked that my dad had managed to sneak a commercial into his talk. I could have told him he should have known better; my dad never missed a chance to promote his business. Once he slipped our dentist a brochure in the middle of a root canal.

"Well, thanks for having me today and letting me share with you why I find science so important, and how I think it can impact your life. I'm excited to have Neurotech providing services to teens. To mark that evolution in our company, I'm pleased to announce we'll be offering a part-time internship for a deserving high school student with a passion for the sciences. Applications are available on our website. At the end of the year the lucky recipient will also receive a grant to assist with college costs."

Josh jolted straight up in the chair next to me, vibrating with excitement. I couldn't believe my dad hadn't said a thing about this to me. He winked at me from the stage. That made me wonder what other surprises he had up his sleeve.

chapter two

I can't believe you didn't say anything." Josh was practically bouncing off the lockers in the hall. He'd left being excited behind, had blown through thrilled, and was now hovering in an enraptured state. People who discovered they had a winning lotto ticket in their pocket were calmer than Josh at this moment.

"I told you, he didn't tell me anything about it." I grabbed my history and math books out of my locker. I smiled when I saw the picture of my horse, Harry, taped to the inside. Other girls might have pictures of hot actors hanging in their lockers, but I preferred Harry. He was arguably better looking, and certainly more loyal.

Win took the books out of my hands and put them back on the shelf. "You're not going to have any time. You have a riding lesson on Saturday. You know you'll end up spending the rest of the afternoon at the barn."

"That's Saturday. I can study on Sunday."

She shook her head. "You might think that, but Sunday is actually reserved for coming over to my place and hanging out. Enough with all the studying. Live a little."

"Do you have any idea how many applications they might get?" Josh acted like he hadn't heard a word we'd said. "It's a huge opportunity, but you'd have to be local. The job is here. I can't imagine anyone is going to let their kid move for an internship. That should cut down on the numbers. Plus, it's a short turnaround time. There are only a couple weeks to get an application together." He bounced on the balls of his feet.

"Chill out, Mr. President," Win said.

"Call me that, and I'll call you by your real name," Josh threatened.

Win's eyes narrowed. For reasons that eluded everyone, her otherwise cool parents had burdened her with her grandmother's name, Winifred. If you really wanted to piss her off, you would call her that. "Fine. Chill out, *Joshua*. My point is that you're a shoo-in for this internship. You're in the house of the guy who founded the entire freaking company almost every day. You're dating his darling daughter. Of course he's going to choose you. He probably came up with the program so he could give it to you while still making the whole thing tax deductible."

I made a point to roll my eyes as if I thought what she'd said was absurd. My stomach was in a tight knot. There *was* a chance he had come up with the program just for Josh. I was an only child, and it was pretty clear that my dad didn't know what to do with me. It wasn't that he didn't love me, but he didn't get me. My dad was into computer games, every tech gadget you could imagine, and boring science shows. Josh was the son my dad had always wanted. They liked the same movies, read the same science fiction books, and got each other's obscure jokes. They'd both been raised by single moms, had a passion for science, and were willing to work insanely hard for what they wanted.

It wasn't that my dad and I didn't get along, but they got along better. Josh made sense to him. I knew my dad worried about how Josh was going to afford college next year. Most of the time I liked that my dad and Josh got along, but lately it felt too close.

I grabbed my history book back out of my locker and stuffed it in my bag.

"If making out with the boss's daughter doesn't give you a better-than-average chance, what's the point of doing it?" Win teased him.

Josh leaned over and kissed me. "The point is I like making out with the boss's daughter. Even if she wasn't the boss's daughter."

"Hey, no PDA in the hallways." Win slapped the two of us apart. "You think I want to see that? I had a big lunch."

Josh made giant kissing noises near my face while Win pretended to gag. I did my best to ignore both of them.

"That's going to cause me trauma. 'Course now I can just soften that nightmare right out of my head," Win said.

"Memtex," Josh and I said in tandem.

"Thank you for the correction, groupthinkers. I can Memtex that vivid image out of my brain." She slung her Coach bag over her shoulder as we headed down the hall. "Don't you think it's a bit creepy? The whole 'dial down a memory that bugs you' thing."

"Are you kidding? Do you know how much Memtex has done for people with PTSD? The impact of past trauma is huge. The ability to . . ." Josh searched for the right word.

"Soften?" Win offered with a raised eyebrow.

Josh sighed. "Fine, the ability to *soften* those memories is a game changer."

"Look, I'm all for helping war vets or some crime victim move past what happened to them, but people go for treatment for everything now. Lose a job? Get a divorce? No problem, just soften the heck out of it until you don't care."

"For some people getting a divorce can be as traumatic as war," Josh said.

Win snorted. "Please. People need to ball up. Life isn't all sunshine and unicorns. Now they're selling it to people our age? What, because not getting into the college of our choice is crushing? No date for prom causing premature PTSD? It's not trauma; it's real life. Life is hard sometimes. It doesn't mean you don't face it."

"You realize the irony of you saying life is hard, don't you? You live in a house the size of a hotel and you spent your Christmas vacation in Venice."

"We didn't go to Venice," Win protested. "We went to Florence. Venice is too damp that time of year." She smirked at Josh. "I still stand by what I said: You have to learn to deal with life. Whatever it throws you, good or bad."

"But if you can make it easier, why shouldn't you?" I said. "Isn't that the point? Life is hard, but if there's a treatment that can make it less difficult so that you can focus on other stuff, positive stuff, that is dealing with it."

"And if you happen to run a pharmaceutical company, you can focus on making a few billion off the whole process." Win waved off what I was about to say. "Don't get me wrong. I'm for capital gains. Especially if it means we can use some of your dad's money to pay for a trip to Europe this summer before college. All I'm saying is that I wouldn't do it. No one is messing with this head." Win knocked on her skull.

"Don't mess with perfection?" I said sarcastically, as we walked toward the door.

"Exactly." Win stopped short after a few steps. She stared straight ahead. "Whoa."

I looked through the open front door. There was a crowd of people standing on the sidewalk. "What in the world?" I slid past her and closer to the door so I could see. Josh tried to grab my hand, but I stepped outside.

A group of about thirty protestors were milling around, holding signs. One said NO VOLUNTARY LOBOTOMIES; another said NEUROTECH—STAY OUT OF OUR CHILDREN'S HEADS! I drew back when I saw one woman in a neon-yellow tracksuit holding a sign that was a picture of my dad with a Hitler mustache drawn above his lip. NEURO-NAZI was printed in bright red letters underneath the photo.

"How did they even know your dad was here?" Josh whispered as we stood on the top steps of the school.

I scanned the front parking lot. My dad's car was gone. Company security must have whisked him out of there before the protestors arrived. The protests were getting worse if they were starting to follow him around. They usually stayed outside his office. No wonder he wanted to put a new security alarm on our house. "There may have been some kind of announcement on the company website that he was coming here for a talk."

"Or some eejit in this school tipped them off." Win scowled. "We should go."

"Who the hell do they think they are?" I asked. Didn't these people have jobs or someplace to be? Did they have nothing else to do but hang around yelling at people? I hated that they made me feel vaguely ashamed of what my dad did. "The treatment is voluntary. If they don't want it, no one is forcing them."

One of the protestors, a young woman in a business suit with bright red lipstick, broke from the group and approached us. "Harper Bryne?"

"Oh, shit," Win said. "She knows who you are." Win grabbed my elbow and started to hustle me toward her car.

"I'm Lisa Gambel, a reporter, and I wondered if I could ask you a few questions." She pulled out her phone to record our conversation.

Win kept pulling me toward her SUV. "Don't talk to her. Whatever you say, she's going to twist it all around. Trust me, I've seen how they've turned around what my dad said in interviews, and they were sports reporters. God only knows what she'll cook up."

Josh walked behind me, shielding me from Lisa as we moved quickly. The pack of protestors swarmed around us, yelling to get my attention. I felt closed in. Why couldn't my dad do something boring like work in a bank?

"What are your thoughts on your dad's company offering the Memtex treatment to teens?" When I didn't respond, the reporter kept firing off questions without even pausing to let me answer. "Do you worry about the possible negative side effects? Have you heard rumors about serious complications? If there's even a chance of those complications, is it worth the risk?"

My heart raced. I knew the only reason they were hassling me was because they couldn't get a quote from my dad. The reporter wanted something in time for her deadline. She shoved the phone closer to me, and I pushed it aside. I wondered if this was how animals felt when they were being hunted, as if the world were collapsing around them. I stumbled on a loose piece of concrete, my foot catching in a pothole. I started to fall. Someone reached forward and grabbed me before I hit the ground, then pulled me up. He was tall and broad-shouldered, but loose-jointed and gawky, like one of those puppies that grew large before it knew what happened.

"You okay?" He held on to my elbow to make sure I had my balance. His touch was warm and chased away some of the chill. His eyes locked me into place, creating a focal point in the midst of all the screaming and noise.

I opened my mouth to thank him when I noticed he was wearing a T-shirt that said PEOPLE NOT CORPORATIONS! He was one of the protestors. Perfect.

"She's fine; please back off." Josh was at my side and guided me toward Win's giant SUV.

"Your father is a monster!" a woman yelled, inches from me. A fleck of her spit hit my cheek, and I recoiled.

The guy who had kept me from falling put a hand on the woman. "Hey, take it easy. She's not responsible for what her dad does."

His words hit me like a slap in the face. My fear sucked out like a wave, and in its absence rage rushed in. I lunged forward so that I was in his face. "I'm proud of my dad. At least he does something with his life. You think it's so easy to make the world a better place? Why don't you do something rather than bitch about what other people do?" I jammed my finger into his chest.

Josh wrapped his arm around my middle and pushed me into the open SUV door. Win was already behind the wheel. She gunned the engine, and it roared to life.

"Let's get out of here," she said.

Josh was right behind me, and he slammed the door. The silence inside the SUV seemed somehow louder than all the shouting outside.

chapter three

I leaned forward on my horse and whispered in his ear. I could feel Harry's excitement. It was clear in every twitch of his ears and the way the muscles in his back tensed. He was ready to go. I pushed my heels down in the stirrups and felt the stretch in my calf muscles. When I rode for fun, it felt as if Harry and I were connected in some way. Like I could read his mind and he knew what I wanted from just the slightest tension in my legs. My trainer, Laura, was always telling me I needed to go to that headspace in competitions. My jumps in practice were almost always just a bit cleaner and higher than in competition.

Harry had been there almost my entire life. My parents had given him to me for my sixth birthday. They'd thrown me a horse-themed party, and we'd gone out to a stable so that all my friends and I could have pony rides.

Some of the girls had been scared, but I remembered being excited. The groom brought out small ponies for each of the girls, but when it was my turn he led in this giant, beautiful creature. Its mane was braided with pink roses, and I thought he was the most beautiful thing I'd ever seen. The groom whisked me up and into the saddle and led me around the ring, telling me how to hold the reins and how to sit. I took the whole thing very seriously. When we went the full way around, my parents were there with their camera.

"How do you like your present?" my dad asked.

I didn't get it for a beat. I looked around the arena, and then I realized what he was saying. Harry was my present. I burst into tears. There wasn't enough room in my entire body to hold how happy I was. I flung my arms around Harry's neck and inhaled his horse smell. It seemed that in that moment he knew he was mine, too.

Now, Laura took the reins and checked over Harry. I'd braided his mane that morning. She tucked a loose piece so it was tighter. She pulled on one of the buckles on his bridle, the leather creaking as it stretched.

"He's looking good." She glanced at me. "You, however, look like shit. You overthinking things?"

I laughed. I yanked on the chinstrap of my helmet. "Right now I'm overthinking how I tend to overthink."

"I'm not sure if that's progress or not." Laura patted my leg. "You did great in the first round. All you need to do is exactly what you did before. Now take a deep breath."

I filled my lungs and held my breath for a beat. Harry let out a snort, tossing his nose in the air. Horses aren't too great at yoga breathing.

"Remember, you're supposed to be having fun out there. Trust your instincts."

I nodded and pulled on the sleeves of my velvet jacket. The fact that our first round had been nearly perfect now seemed like a fluke. I could feel sweat pooling in my lower back under my jacket.

"Representing Hampton Mews Stable, Harper Bryne." The announcement rang out over the PA system.

My heart began beating like crazy. Laura gave me a crisp nod. I tapped my heels into Harry's side, and we entered the competition space. The ring held twelve fences. I mentally traced the route we'd take one more time. The crowd in the stands gave polite applause. The judges sat at a long table, watching. I closed my eyes and forced myself to focus and block out the distractions. Some people like the smell of fresh bread or flowers, but for me there is nothing more relaxing than the smell of leather and fresh hay and the musky scent of horse. I opened my eyes.

"Let's do this," I whispered to Harry. We'd be judged on if we cleared each of the fences and made our turns in the time allotted. Points would be deducted for any knockdowns or refusals. Harry almost never refused. He loved to jump. He was a flyer. His registered name was Hermes of Caelum. He was named after the Greek god with the winged feet. I called him Harry, after Harry Potter, another great flyer.

I kicked my heels, and Harry thundered out into the ring, his hooves sinking into the soft-packed dirt. We approached the first fence, and I stood in the stirrups, leaning forward, my knees tightening around the horse. His muscles coiled as he leaped forward. We cleared the fence with no problem. I pulled the reins to make the sharp left. The course had three jumps in a row. I could faintly hear the applause as we cleared each one, but my entire concentration was on the next fence. I made the next two fences, but on the second to last I heard a clang as Harry's back hoof hit the bar. Shit. I yanked my head around to see if the bar fell. It rattled in the metal berth, but held. If it fell, I'd be out. My glance back meant I lost my focus, and I missed the last turn. I had to turn Harry around and make another attempt. I kicked myself for compounding one mistake with another. Harry and I crossed the line. I checked the clock—we'd made it.

Harry walked out of the ring, his legs high stepping, and I pulled off my helmet. Win was waiting with Laura.

"Nice."

"We almost blew that one fence." I shook my head, annoyed.

"I had three knockdowns," Win said. "I dream of having a run with only one near miss. I didn't even make the second round. Clean runs and I never seem to go together."

"Instead of dreaming about better runs, you could try more practice," Laura suggested. She was Win's trainer too. Win jumped in a different group than I did. If she'd put her mind to it, she could have jumped in the elite class too, but she wasn't interested. She joked she only rode for the great outfits and the chance to meet guys in tight jodhpurs.

I jumped off Harry and patted his side. I could tell he felt bad. The mistake wasn't his fault; it was mine. My hand ran down his back leg, making sure the bar hadn't cut him.

"You want me to have the groom walk Harry?" Laura offered.

"No, I've got his cooldown." It would do me good to have something to keep me busy while waiting for final scores. I couldn't watch other riders. It made me too nervous. If I was ever going to make the Olympic level, I was going to need serious antianxiety medication.

"I'll come with you," Win said. We walked around the back to the barn. It was early spring, and the cold air felt good. I took a deep breath to clear the tension in my chest. There were rows of dust-covered horse trailers and trucks parked along the road. Some were painted with the names of their stables on the side.

"I should have worn my lucky jacket," I said. I kicked a rock with my polished black boot and watched it skitter down the road.

"Your old jacket isn't lucky; it's just old. Once you win in this jacket, it will be your lucky jacket," she said.

"If I win."

"You will." Win pulled off her jacket and unbuttoned the top few buttons of her white shirt. She smiled at the off-duty police officer who was guarding the end of the road. She tossed her braids over a shoulder. His mouth fell open when he realized she was smiling at him, but he recovered in time to give her a wide smile back.

I nudged her in the side with my elbow. "He's at least in his midtwenties, maybe thirty."

"Don't get your knickers in a twist; I'm not planning to marry him." She smirked. "And if I run off with a cute man in a uniform, it will be your dad's fault." She put an extra swing to her hips as she walked. Win's dad was an elite athlete and her mom was distantly related to some type of royalty and had done some modeling when she was young. Win was genetically destined to have natural rhythm and grace. Her ass didn't sway so much as waltz. The cop didn't stand a chance. He turned and watched as we strolled past.

Since the incident at school almost a month ago, my dad had hired off-duty police officers to provide security whenever I was out in public. So far the protesters hadn't bothered me again, but he wasn't taking any chances. It was a toss-up which I hated more, having police follow me around or the risk that I'd be mobbed by a group of sign-waving protestors. Win, on the other hand, didn't mind the police protection at all. She kept calling it the badge buffet.

"Hey!" We spun around to see who was yelling. Josh. With

all the people at the show, he'd had to park down the road. He jogged toward us. The cop looked ready to tackle him and stepped between us. Maybe he thought it would impress Win if he pulled some ninja moves. Josh held up a hand. "Easy, I know them," Josh said.

"Never saw this guy in my life," Win said. She couldn't keep her expression neutral and started laughing. I waved off the officer so that Josh could jog closer.

"Could you try not to get my boyfriend shot?" I asked.

"Did you see how he was ready to leap into action? I like that in a guy." Win winked at the cop.

"Premature trigger action is not attractive," I pointed out. Josh ran over and spun me in a circle. I whacked Josh on the back. "Put me down."

Josh backed up and pulled a small square of white plastic out of his pocket. He held it aloft and looked disappointed that I didn't fall over in shock.

"What? You have a pretend credit card? Call me when you get the real thing," Win said. "Provided it's platinum, of course."

"It's not a credit card; it's a key card," he said.

That's when I saw the small NT logo in the corner. My stomach tightened. "You got the internship."

Josh pumped his fist in the air with a whoop. Harry tossed his head as if he were celebrating along with him. "I got the call this morning, and then the company had a package couriered over to my house. I got a lab coat too."

"Way to go, nerd boy," Win said. She smiled at me. We both knew what a big deal it was for Josh even if none of us would expressly say it. Win liked to give him a hard time, but she was happy for him. This wasn't a part-time job at a coffee shop; it was his ticket out of his life. Josh was a scholarship student at Saint Francis. Most everyone at our school lived in gated communities with full-time gardeners. Josh lived in a small house in a neighborhood that was decorated with chipped garden gnomes from Walmart. He'd been accepted to Stanford. He'd applied for all kinds of grants and scholarships, and there were always student loans, but he'd been sweating how he'd cover everything. Going out of state was expensive, and he wanted to go all the way to med school, so he had a lot of years to cover. With a wave of my dad's laser pointer, those worries had just gotten a lot easier.

"So are you going to be washing floors?" Win asked. "Do you have to wear a hairnet, polyester uniform? Ooh, is your name sewn on your fancy lab jacket?"

He smirked at her. "No. The internship is designed to give me some practical experience. It's going to be great exposure to the business. I'll be checking people in who come for the procedure at the clinic, recording their vitals, sending out follow-up surveys, and doing a bunch of data entry."

"Look, he's getting a data boner," Win said. Josh laughed.

"I'm happy for you," I said, convincing myself. I was glad

he'd gotten the position, but I didn't like that he'd be spending more time with my dad. It wasn't that I wanted to break up with Josh, but lately it felt like even if I did, it wouldn't be possible. It was if our lives had become enmeshed and everyone expected us to be together forever. How do you break up with someone who is also one of your best friends? Who works with your dad? He pulled me close and we kissed. I pushed the negative thoughts out of my head. Expecting fireworks with someone I'd been dating for two years was ridiculous. I should have been happy that we got along as well as we did.

The squawk of the PA carried out to the field.

"They're announcing the winners," Win said. "Let's go get you a first-place ribbon."

"Then we're going out to celebrate. Dinner is on me," Josh said.

"He's got a job for a day and he's already a big spender." Win pulled her jacket back on and turned to head to the arena.

I leaned against Harry's warm flank and turned my face up to the sky, letting the spring sun beat down on me. I wanted to enjoy the moment.

The groom loaded Harry into the trailer. I stepped up on the wheel, and Harry poked his head into the slot so that his nose bumped me.

"Good job, big guy." I stuck my hand through the slats and rubbed him.

"You're giving that horse a better good-bye than you gave Josh," Win said. "Hurry it up, I want to go to dinner. I'm starving."

I jumped down and brushed my hands off on my pants, ignoring what she said. "I got lucky taking first place with that missed gate."

"Even for you perfection might be asking a lot." She put her hands on her hips and rocked back. "Good news about Josh, huh?"

"Mmm-hmm."

She arched one perfectly plucked eyebrow.

"It *is* good news. I'm happy for him," I said. Win couldn't stand when there was any tension between Josh and me. She said our relationship was the only proof she had that true love existed. No added pressure or anything.

"It's a good thing your dad likes him. Dads are programmed to hate their daughters' boyfriends. Don't worry. The two of them working together will be fine." She smiled. "C'mon, I hear onion rings calling my name."

I *was* happy for Josh. I just wished I could sort out how I felt about our relationship. It seemed I should either want to break up with him or be happy we were together, but I felt like I was stuck in the middle and unable to commit to either side. It was going to take more than onion rings to sort it out.

chapter four

The sound of the phone ringing woke me up. I pushed the covers down to see the clock. It couldn't have been for me, because no one I knew would have been up that early. Win always said I slept like a prairie dog. I liked to burrow down under all the covers, pulling them completely over my head. It wasn't even seven a.m. Who called that early on a Sunday morning? Even God wasn't up at that hour.

I reached over and touched the giant first-place blue ribbon I'd won yesterday. Later I'd take it down to the stables and mount it on Harry's stall door. I could tell he liked them; he knew he was a winner. He had this way of strutting into the barn with a LOOK AT ME NOW! trot. Maybe I'd take him out for a ride, too, a chance to stretch his legs.

There was a rustle outside my room. My mom popped her

head in. Her face was pale without any makeup. She looked sur-prised when she saw me awake. She stood outside my room as if she was reluctant to come in. It wasn't that my mom and I didn't get along, but there wasn't any risk people were going to confuse us with those moms and daughters who were best friends.

"You're up," she said.

"I'm hoping it's a temporary condition." I yawned. "The phone woke me."

She crossed the room and sat down on the edge of my bed. She picked up one of the throw pillows that had fallen to the floor and pulled off some lint. Her lips were pressed into a thin pale line.

"Is everything okay?" I should have known a call this early was bad news. I couldn't think of what it would be. My grand-parents had died either before I was born or when I was really little. Both of my parents were only children, so there weren't groups of cousins or aunts and uncles to worry about. There are some advantages to having a small family. I wondered if the protestors had done something to the Neurotech office.

"That was Laura on the phone." She placed her hand on my leg.

My heart seized in my chest. I wanted to ask what had happened. A fire at the barn? A break-in? I couldn't pull any air into my lungs to speak. It was like they'd turned to lead.

"Oh, honey, I'm so sorry, but Harry died."

I heard the words. They slid across my mind, but I refused

to let them stick and start making sense. I took short shallow breaths, the way I did when I had the flu and was afraid I might throw up.

"What—" My voice cut off as my throat tightened, squeezing off the words before they could come out.

"They're pretty sure it was colic. Laura found him this morning."

Colic kills horses all the time. They can't vomit, so if something doesn't digest well, it goes bad quickly. The pain in their gut causes them to thrash around. Their intestines twist and then burst. It's an ugly and awful way to die. If you catch it early, you can walk them around to keep them from rolling and a vet will give a huge dose of castor oil, but if it's not caught, it's deadly. My throat hitched picturing him in pain and all by himself with no one around. He shouldn't have had to be alone.

I flung the covers off. "I have to go to the barn." I knew it was ridiculous, but I couldn't shake the feeling that the whole thing must be a mistake, or some kind of horrid joke. I knew horses died of colic, but this wasn't just a horse; this was Harry. *My* Harry.

Mom backed up so I could get out of bed. My legs were shaking as I stood. I yanked on a sweatshirt over my tank top. I didn't bother to look for my jeans. No one would care if I went in my pajama pants.

"You don't need to go. It might be better if you remember him the way he was."

She didn't know me at all if she thought I was going to stay here. I ran my hands through my hair and hoped it wasn't sticking up too badly. My hands were shaking. Harry. My sweet Harry. "Can I take the car?"

She sighed. "Give me two minutes; I'll drive you."

"You don't have to."

"I want to. You don't have to do this alone." She stepped forward and hugged me. I held stiff for a moment—we weren't a big huggy family. Then I buried my face in her cashmere robe. She smelled like toothpaste and the jasmine perfume she always wore. I started to cry, and she squeezed me tighter. "Your dad will want to come too."

I pulled back and looked at her. My dad wasn't great with emotion. It wasn't that he didn't care, but he was a total engineer. He wanted to fix things. I wasn't ready for him to launch into how I could get another horse and start planning on how to make that happen in the most efficient way possible.

Mom saw my expression and must have known what I was thinking. "I'll talk to him. We'll meet you downstairs in a few minutes."

Neither of my parents were horse people. My mom was afraid of them, but my dad just wasn't much of an outdoorsy guy. He preferred sterile labs to barns. He claimed he had all kinds of allergies to grass, hay, and flowers. We all knew they were excuses to avoid being outside. My dad liked that I rode. He had a picture of me in my riding gear on his desk at work and would tell anyone who would listen that I was going to be in the Olympics someday. Me having a horse was sort of like his Rolex, a sign he'd arrived. Show riding wasn't cheap, and the only thing my dad liked more than money was other people knowing he had money.

We didn't talk at all on the way over to the stable. My dad turned up the news radio he liked so the silence didn't seem so suffocating. I boarded Harry at Hampton Mews. There was another stable just a bit closer, but Hampton Mews was known as second to none. Their trainers were nationally ranked, and they decorated the best barn with brass nameplates on each of the stalls, and the floor was covered in fake bricks that were made of rubber, which was better for the horses' legs.

The car crunched over the gravel drive, almost coasting to a stop in front. I stepped out of my dad's BMW. The smell of fresh-cut grass and horses filled my head, and I started to cry. Laura was standing by the barn door. I could tell she'd been crying too; her eyes were red and swollen.

"I should have walked him longer," I said, putting my biggest fear into words. What if I hadn't given him enough of a cooldown? Somehow all of this must be my fault. I'd let him down.

Laura gave me a fierce hug. "Don't you dare blame yourself. He must have gotten sick after we left last night. This happens. It sucks and it's awful, but it isn't your fault."

"Can I see him?" I searched my memory, trying to recall if

there had been anything out of the usual yesterday. Why hadn't I come back to the stables after the competition? I'd gone out for dinner with my friends instead. I'd been laughing and joking when he died, and I hadn't even known.

Laura nodded. She put her arm around me and led me into the barn. There were a few grooms there, polishing tack and mucking stalls. When they saw us enter, they stood silently off to the sides, like an honor guard.

I stopped just outside his stall. Harry lay there, completely still. It seemed he'd always been in motion. If there had been any doubt in my mind this was real it, was gone now. I reached out and touched his side. He was cold, and whatever life force had made him Harry was long gone. I knelt down by him and placed my head on his side. His hair prickled my skin. I'd known that someday he would die, but it had seemed like something remote and almost impossible. Horses can live thirty years, so I had just assumed I would have him much longer. I understood that at some point I would need another horse for jumping when he got too old, but I'd been so sure we had more time. I'd thought that when he eventually died, I would be ready in some way. I'd thought I would see it coming. I'd thought he would slow down and get older and give me time to get used to the idea. I'd never pictured him going this way. It felt like a knife in my gut. Sharp and unexpected.

It was as if a trapdoor had opened under my feet and I just kept falling.

chapter five

I pushed the food around on my plate. The idea of eating made me nauseated. It wasn't the pasta; my mom's roasted red pepper and ricotta ravioli was one of my favorites. She made the noodles from scratch. I had no doubt this was a bribe to get me to eat. The past two weeks the house had been full of my favorite things: mint chocolate chip ice cream, fresh bagels from Bagel Oasis, and bags of SunChips. My mom wasn't part of the food police, but she was big on eating healthy. She'd never met a meal that wasn't improved by adding quinoa, broccoli, or flaxseed. Our house was normally a processed food/white bread–free zone. The fact that she'd bought a bunch of snacks was a sign that she was worried about me.

I was worried about myself. I couldn't focus on anything. I'd catch myself staring into space and realize that I had no idea what was going on in class or on TV. It was like I was in my own bubble, which didn't connect with the real world. The worst part was I couldn't sleep.

That wasn't completely true. I didn't *want* to sleep. I had nightmares. At least I guessed they were nightmares: I didn't remember a thing about them, but I would jolt awake in the middle of the night, sweating, with a racing heart. I was afraid, terrified, but didn't know why. The dream would vanish the instant I woke up, but I could feel it lurking inside me, waiting to come back as soon as my eyes closed. I would stay up as long as possible, hoping that if I was tired enough, the dream would give me a break. Sometimes it did, sometimes not.

"Can I be excused?" I asked. Both of my parents looked down at my almost-full plate. "I'm not hungry," I said.

Dad sighed. "Sit down, pumpkin." He pushed his plate away, and I could see him mentally organizing his thoughts into something that would be helpful. "I hope you're aware that if you want to talk, or if you need anything, you just have to ask. I know how hard it's been for you to lose your horse."

I wondered if he was going to tell me that Harry would want me to go on with my life and be happy.

"Harper, is there anything else?" Mom leaned forward on the table. "Is something bothering you besides Harry? You aren't yourself."

I felt a flicker of annoyance. Wasn't Harry enough? Win was the only one who came close to understanding how I felt.

Even Josh didn't get it. It was like he and my parents felt there was a reasonable amount of grief I should feel over the whole thing and I was acting unseemly by still going on about it. "No," I said. "It's just Harry."

"Maybe you need to get back to riding," she suggested. "Laura said you could ride Dallas anytime."

"Or you could take up something new," Dad said. "You liked sailing when we went last summer. There's a sailing club in Ballard. Summer's coming—we could take it up together."

If I didn't say something soon, I would come home tomorrow and discover a giant sailboat parked on a trailer in our driveway and matching life jackets for the whole family with our names embroidered on the back in navy blue.

"I don't want to start sailing. Or play guitar, or learn Bollywood dancing." I tried to find a way to explain it. "It isn't that I need something to do; I'm just sad." I chewed the inside of my cheek. I felt like I could cry again. It was like I was trying to keep my head above water, but each time I tried to take a breath, a wave of crushing sadness would push me down again. I was exhausted. I wouldn't be able to keep fighting much longer. I wanted to feel like myself again. "There is something I've been thinking about that would help."

Both of my parents nodded, their faces serious. We didn't always get along, but I never doubted that they loved me. They were ready to do whatever I needed, from buying me a small dog that came with an entire designer wardrobe to flying out some pet psychic who could help me connect with Harry in the great beyond. "I want to go in and have the Memtex treatment."

My dad pulled back, shocked.

"Oh, Harper, I don't know," Mom hedged. "It's a medical procedure. You should give yourself more time before you do anything drastic."

"I don't want to spend any more time feeling like this. That's why Memtex exists, isn't it? To keep these kinds of things from making your life miserable? I'm not asking for special treatment. I can ask Dr. Cale to make a referral."

"Absolutely not," my dad barked.

My mom and I both spun our heads to look at him, surprised at his vehemence. He was acting like I'd asked for permission to run off and join the circus.

"Why not?" I asked.

"Isn't it enough that I said no? You don't need the treatment. You'll get over this. I forbid it." He tossed his napkin down on the table.

Forbid? I looked at Mom, waiting for her to back me up, but she was staring at her plate as if the pasta sauce were going to spell out an answer.

"Because you said no?" I stared at him in disbelief. He never pulled the because-I'm-the-dad-and-what-I-say-goes card. Ever. Even when I was little and did things like jamming Legos up my nose, he would take the time to explain how the nasal system worked while I sat there with a blue building brick sticking out of one nostril. "You're always talking about how great Memtex is, how it's changing the world, and you won't let your own daughter do it? Why? Are you afraid it isn't safe?"

His face flushed red, matching the pasta sauce. "Don't even say that. Do you know how much that group of protestors would like to hear you talking about how you don't trust Memtex? That's all I need at this point."

Mom put her hand on his, clearly trying to get him to calm down, but he yanked his hand back and pointed at me across the table.

"The procedure is one hundred percent safe. I don't want you to have it because there are plenty of people who would jump all over that fact. They'd say I was doing it for promotion. They'd point out what perfect timing it is that Neurotech is moving into the teen market just when my own daughter happens to need the treatment." He shook his head as if I had argued with him and he couldn't believe the things I was saying. "That would play great in the press. That stupid reporter is already sniffing around, looking for any possible negative thing to say. Imagine how she would spin this—Dr. Bryne treats his own kid like a lab rat."

"No one would have to know," I said. I thought it went without saying that I hadn't planned on sending out a press release or appearing in a commercial.

Dad pushed away from the table, his chair squealing its

protest on the hardwood. "Don't be naive, Harper. Ever since Neurotech went public, we've had the press all over us like ticks on a dog. You're not going in for the treatment. That's it. End of discussion." He walked out of the dining room without looking back at either of us.

Tears ran down my cheeks. I wiped them away with a swipe of my hand. I felt the return of the headache I'd had for days from crying too much and not getting enough sleep.

Mom passed me a clean napkin so I could blow my nose. "He's not mad at you. He's grumpy and frustrated. Things at the office are complicated." Mom fidgeted with her fork. "He's used to being the golden boy, the new Einstein. He's finding all this criticism hard to take."

"I didn't know it was that bad," I said.

Mom took a sip of her wine. "That reporter is leading the charge, trying to dig up stories where the treatment has gone badly. Your dad thinks she's trying to push the FDA into doing an investigation. That could take years, knowing the government."

What she didn't say was that if Neurotech couldn't offer the treatment, it would put them in a huge financial bind. Neurotech did a few other things, but there was no doubt that Memtex was what paid the bills and kept the company afloat.

"I had no idea," I said.

Mom stood and grabbed some dishes and motioned for me to help. "Everything will be fine. Your dad wouldn't want you to worry about his work. We don't want you to worry about anything if we can help it."

I scraped the food off the plates into the disposal and tried not to think of starving kids in some third-world country. I had enough guilt already without picturing them with their distended stomachs. I told myself they could be lactose intolerant and cheese ravioli wouldn't be their thing anyway. "Have there been cases where the treatment went bad? Is that what's bothering him?"

She took the plates out of my hands. "No. Or, to be more precise, there have been a few cases where people have had issues after the treatment, but there's no research to back up the idea that the treatment had anything to do with what happened to them." She filled the sink and pulled out the bright yellow rubber gloves she wore when she did the dishes so her manicure would last. "The problem is that there's nothing journalists like more than a fanciful theory—gives them lots to talk and write about. Scandal sells."

I wiped down the black granite counters with the organic cleaner my mom got at Whole Foods. Mom leaned over and kissed my cheek. "It'll all work out. He's not upset with you. You've got to make a leap of faith and know we're doing what we think is best. We know you're going to be okay; give yourself some time. I'll finish up tonight. Consider yourself dish-duty paroled."

"Thanks." I felt bad that my dad was having a hard time, but the thing was, I was having a hard time too.

chapter six

"You're unnaturally attached to that key card." Win motioned to Josh's hip, where he had the card hooked on a lanyard that clipped to his jeans. "You realize wearing that thing makes you look like a janitor."

Josh spun the card around like it was a watch on the end of chain. "Don't hate me because I'm fabulous."

"Your boyfriend is delusional." Win wove through the crowd in the cafeteria and sat at our usual table. She nodded to a couple of our other friends who were deep in a conversation about some band.

"Delusional, huh?" Josh put his bagged lunch on the table. "Guess that means you aren't interested in the conversation I had with Kyle Vais in history class."

Win froze. "Did he ask about me?" She looked around to

see if anyone else was paying attention to what we were talking about.

Josh shrugged and made an elaborate production of unwrapping his sandwich, smoothing out the foil. "I'm not sure I can remember; I have all these delusions . . ."

Win whipped a cherry tomato across the table, and it whacked Josh right in the center of the forehead. If she used bullets instead of veggies, it would have been a kill shot.

"Somebody has a crush," Josh said in a singsong voice. He picked up the tomato from the floor, brushed it off, and popped it in his mouth. "Five-second rule."

I spun around to face Win. "You've got a crush on Kyle?" I asked loudly. The news hit me like a slap, breaking me out of the fog I was walking around in. Win flirted madly with everyone, but she never fell for anyone.

Win glared at me, and I lowered my voice. "Sorry. You like Kyle?"

Win smoothed her braids. "He's in my art class. We've talked a few times." She feigned great interest in organizing her salad. "It's not a big deal."

I shared a look with Josh. Win wasn't usually the one to get crushes; she was more commonly the object of affection. Her mom had cheated on her dad a few times, and it drove her crazy that her dad put up with it. She'd always vowed she wasn't going to give her heart to anyone because then she didn't risk getting it broken.

"Sort of a shame it's no big deal," Josh said. "Kyle was curious if you were going to the dance."

Win leaned across the table. "Are you serious? Did he actually ask that?" Her eyes narrowed. "If you are making this up, science boy, you will find that key card you love so much in a very painful location."

"Does Kyle know about this violent side of you?" Josh teased her. "I'm not judging. He might like it. Lots of guys are into tough women. It comes from playing all those video games."

I smiled weakly at the two of them. I wanted to tease Win too, but my brain still felt like it was operating at a slower speed compared to real life.

"Yes, he really asked if you were going to be at the dance." Josh poured some Cheetos in his mouth. He nudged me with his elbow. "We could all go, and then Win could accidentally-on-purpose run into him."

"I don't know," I hedged. I didn't feel like going out. All I felt like doing was crawling into bed. I was tired all the time. Everything seemed to take so much energy. By the end of the day it felt like I was dragging a thousand pounds around on my back while walking through quicksand. There were times when blinking seemed to be almost more than I could cope with; going to a dance seemed like an impossible feat.

Win grabbed my arm. "We have to go. You can be sad there, but we have to go."

"C'mon. We have to go—young love is on the line," Josh said with a smile.

I opened my mouth to protest.

Win held up a finger. "Don't decide now. You'll just say no. Think about it. We could go for a couple of hours. That hardly even counts as going to the dance; it's more like a drive-by." She looked at my expression. "Or even just an hour. I'm going to grab you a cookie while you think." Win bolted up and joined the food line.

I watched her. "When did all this with Kyle happen?"

"Never thought I'd see it myself: the Mighty Win, felled by Cupid's arrow. She started talking about him a while ago. I noticed she kept finding excuses to bring up his name, that kind of thing. The two of them have been exchanging meaningful glances for like a week or two. Maybe getting hit by that statue knocked something free."

It felt like that statue toppling had happened in a different lifetime. It wasn't just me who was different; Win had changed too, and I hadn't even seen it. If Josh had noticed, then Win's feelings must have been obvious.

Josh put a few of his grapes on my tray. "I think she really likes him."

I leaned back in my seat. How did Josh know this and I didn't? "I should go to the dance. Win liking someone is a big deal, but I don't feel like doing anything." I picked at the bread on my sandwich. "She'd go for me."

"That's so weird you would say that—I was just thinking how what you really needed on top of everything was an extra helping of guilt."

I sighed.

"If you're not up for it, you're not up for it. Or maybe you could try and see how it goes," Josh suggested.

"It isn't that I don't want to," I said. My eyes started to fill with tears. Great. Now I could start crying in the cafeteria. "I'm trying to be normal. I told my dad I wanted to get Memtex." I turned in my seat so we were face-to-face. "He won't let me to do it. He actually used the word 'forbid.' He says people will use it against him in some kind of media propaganda war."

"Everyone at Neurotech is hypersensitive these days about the press. I had to sign some kind of twenty-page form detailing how I won't talk to anyone about what I see at the clinic." He smiled. "If I'm honest, it was kinda cool. I felt like I was signing up to be a spy."

I bit back that this wasn't about him. "But my dad has to know I wouldn't talk to anyone. It's not like I'm going to take out a full-page ad in the paper talking about how I decided to have the treatment."

"I'm sure it's not that your dad doesn't want you to go through with the procedure. It's that he's afraid it will cause trouble. I'm telling you, people come in every week, and when they leave, you can see the relief on their faces. He's afraid to risk it. He's going to do what he thinks is best; you have to know that," Josh said.

I didn't want Josh to stick up for my dad. I wanted him to take my side. The point was my dad was doing what he thought was best for his company, not for me. "Too bad you aren't really a spy. You could help me get a secret identity so I could get the procedure that way."

Josh sat up straight. He put down his sandwich. I could practically see the gears turning in his head.

"What?" I asked. He stared out the window. "What did I say?"

He tapped the key card against his thigh. "The thing is, your dad doesn't really care if you have the procedure, right? It's just the media attention he wants to avoid."

"Yeah. What's your point?"

"I think I thought of a way where you'll want to go to the dance. Where you'll be ready to move on, and your dad can stay out of the whole thing." He smiled. "I've got a plan."

It took a few days before we could put Josh's plan into action. He tried to back out the next day, saying the whole thing was a big mistake, but I wasn't giving up that easily. Win and I sat outside the Neurotech clinic, hunched down in her SUV, watching the front door while I willed my cell phone to ring.

"This is a bad idea," Win whispered.

"You realize no one can hear us, right?"

"We're probably on a security camera." Win's gaze swept across the parking lot.

"Of course we are. Do you have any idea how much equipment they have in there, not to mention the value of research?" I said. "It doesn't matter if we're on camera. There's nothing wrong with being parked in the lot, no reason for anyone to flag that we were here. You're my best friend. My dad works here. If anything they'll be watching the protestors." There was a small group across the street from the front door. They looked tired to me. No one was waving their signs; they milled around as if they were at a bus stop instead of trying to make some kind of political statement.

"You can say nothing will go wrong, but trust me, when the shitstorm rains down, somehow I'm going to get at least part of the blame." Win sighed.

I jabbed her in the side with my phone. "Don't worry. It will go fine. You can take off as soon as Josh calls."

It was Josh's plan, even if he wished now that he'd never told me his idea. He didn't want to run the risk of getting in trouble. I wore him down, pointing out that the chances we would get caught were small and that all he was really doing was showing confidence in my dad's work. Part of Josh's internship duties included checking in patients who were there for the treatment. Every day there would be at least one or two people who wouldn't show up for their appointment. They were either sick, decided they didn't want it after all, or maybe forgot the

47

appointment altogether. Since the treatment had just opened up to teens, they made up the bulk of new patients. Josh's idea was that we would wait for a day when a girl around my age didn't show up for her appointment. He would check me in under her name, and I'd get the procedure. No one would have to know my real identity. My dad wouldn't be any wiser, and I'd get over this funk.

"Someone is going to recognize you," Win said, her finger tapping on the steering wheel.

"I doubt it. Some people in his office know me, but the medical staff doesn't. I doubt anyone in the clinic will look at me twice. They're not expecting to see the owner's daughter. Even if there's a chance they've been in his office and he pointed out my photo, the only picture of me that he has in there is at least five years old."

Win rolled her eyes. "Yes, clearly you're a master of disguise. No one would ever think, 'Hey, I thought that was Harper, but she looked just a bit older so it couldn't have been her.'" She reached over and touched my arm. "You don't have to do this."

"It's the only option. There's no way my dad is backing down."

"You know I'm not a keen believer in parents and rules, but he might be right. What if something goes wrong?" Win chewed her lower lip.

"Nothing's going to go wrong," I said.

Win slapped her forehead. "Of course, I'm being ridiculous—

what could go wrong? You're simply having someone shoot lasers into your brain under an assumed name. I'm just being barmy."

"Your craziness is irrelevant to this discussion. The point is I'll come out of there back to my usual self. Isn't that what everyone wants?"

Win snorted. "You assume that means we like the real you."

I smiled. "You love the real me." My phone buzzed with an incoming text. This was it. A rush of adrenaline hit my system. Whoever was supposed to check in was still late. I was going to take her spot. "Meet me in a couple of hours?" I stepped out of her truck.

"I'll be here. Last chance—you sure you want to do this?" Win's face was scrunched up in concern.

"Positive."

chapter seven

I walked past the main lobby of Neurotech, ignoring the calls from the protestors, who yelled whenever anyone came in or out of the main door of the building. I went to the side door that most of the employees used. I tapped on the glass. The security guard looked up from his newspaper. He sat at a long desk that blocked the hallway beyond. I pulled off the giant sunglasses I'd borrowed from Win so he could see my face. He pushed the buzzer to unlock the door when he recognized me.

"Hi, Mr. Epstein." I held up a paper bag. "I'm dropping some cookies off for my dad."

"What would the guy do without you?" Mr. Epstein laughed. "Let me get you a visitor badge." He went to pull out the log-book, the dark hair on his arms peeking out from his sleeves.

"Nah, don't bother. I'm just going to run these down to

him and then I've got to go." I mentally crossed my fingers. Officially they were supposed to log everyone in and out of the building, but I was counting on the fact that since he knew me, and it was a hassle, he wouldn't want to bother. It was unlikely my dad would ever check, but I wanted to avoid a record that I'd been there if I could.

"You want me to page your dad? He could come here and save you trying to hunt him down."

"It's okay. I'll leave them in his office. It'll just take a minute." I stepped into the hall, holding my breath.

"Wait a second."

My heart slammed into my chest. He wasn't going to let me in. Our plan was falling apart already. I turned around slowly, but Mr. Epstein was smiling at me.

"I wanted to ask you a question about horses. My daughter wants to go horseback riding for her birthday. I thought you'd know some place we could go."

The irony of him wanting to talk about horses when I was trying to sneak into the clinic to soften my memories of Harry wasn't lost on me. It had been my experience that the universe had a wicked sense of humor. "Um, sure. You could call Hampton Mews; that's where I ride." I fired off their number from memory, and he jotted it down on the message pad on the desk.

Mr. Epstein pursed his lips. "I thought it would be more fun to do something like a trail ride. Nothing against the kind of riding you do, but we don't have all that fancy gear, the funny pants and all."

"Jodhpurs?"

"Yeah, those. I was thinking something like a dude ranch."

"I can send you a list of those around here," I offered. "I don't know the numbers by heart, but I can find them for you."

He pretended to swing a lasso over his head. "That would be great. We're more the cowboy type."

I pressed my mouth into what I hoped passed for a smile while he blathered on about cowboy movies he'd loved as a kid. The clock above the security desk ticked loudly. Josh was going to freak out if I wasn't there to meet him. In the meantime Mr. Epstein was giving the blow-by-blow about why he thought Hollywood never made a good western after Clint Eastwood hung up his spurs.

"I'll look up some places tonight," I said, cutting him off midsentence. He looked surprised that I'd interrupted him. "Yee-haw," I added, trying to sound enthused.

"Well, thanks. That'd be a huge help." The phone rang, and he looked down to see if it was his line.

I waved, then walked quickly down the hallway before he could suck me into another conversation. I fought the urge to run. Unless someone yelled "Fire!" first, running down an office corridor tended to attract attention, which was the last thing I needed. I slid past a few office doors and turned the corner where we'd planned to meet. Josh wasn't there. Shit.

There was a door that led to the clinic side of the building with a swipe card reader on the wall. I tried the door just in case, but it was locked. A couple of lab technicians walked past me. I couldn't hang out in the hall; it looked suspicious. The floors were done in a bright white tile, and the walls were blank, so I couldn't even pretend an interest in something. I bent over and fidgeted with my shoe.

Still no Josh.

It was just a matter of time before someone who knew me walked by. I hated when Win was right. I was never going to hear the end of it. I leaned against the wall and acted like I was checking a message on my phone and started to fire off a quick text to Josh.

There was a soft click, and the door opened. Josh's head poked out. There were voices coming; they would round the corner in a second. I dashed across the hall, joined Josh, and pulled the door shut behind me.

"Where were you?" I thumped him on the chest with the palm of my hand.

"Where was I? Where were you? I opened the door three minutes after I called like we planned, and you weren't there." Josh rubbed his hands on his pants. The air-conditioning was up high, but I could tell he was sweating. "I walked down to the staff room and back," he said.

"I got held up." I glanced at my phone to check the time. "Let's go."

"Okay, come with me."

I followed Josh down the hall, my shoes clicking on the tiled floors. I'd been at Neurotech thousands of times visiting my dad's office and the labs, but I'd only been to the clinic side of the building once or twice. The good thing about not knowing this part of the building was that the chance of running into anyone who knew me went way down. The clinic had the same white floors and walls as the labs, but black-and-white photography prints hung on each wall, spaced exactly in the center and an even distance apart. It was like someone with a serious case of OCD had decorated the place. The photos were pretty, but the lack of color made the space feel even colder.

We slipped down a couple of corridors, and then Josh motioned to a small exam room. "Change into the robe in there. No jewelry. Put all your stuff in the plastic bag on the shelf. You're technically almost an hour late for your appointment, so the staff is slipping you in. I had to wait at least a half hour to make sure the real person didn't actually show up. I'll be back in five minutes with a nurse who will check your blood pressure and temperature. Your name is Emily Ludka. Got it?"

I pulled my sleeves over my hands. "Are they going to think it's weird my parents aren't with me?"

Josh shook his head. "The real Emily's parents signed a consent form when they booked the appointment. It's not that unusual for people to drop someone off and pick them up later. A lot of parents don't want to sit around."

"Must be kinda creepy to be here alone."

He smiled. "You're not alone. I'll be waiting for you." Josh looked around quickly to make sure no one was watching, then kissed my cheek.

I pressed the paper bag into his hand. "These are the cookies."

"Okay, I'm going to drop these in your dad's office so if someone saw you in the building the story jibes. The security guard that let you in is off shift in fifteen minutes, so it won't seem weird that he doesn't see you leave. Odds are he'll forget he saw you unless someone specifically asks."

Josh left the room and I shut the door behind him. The room was small, with just an exam table with the white paper cover, one of those tall scales with the sliding weights, and a blood pressure monitor attached to the wall. I grabbed a plastic bag that was marked PATIENT BELONGINGS off a shelf of supplies. It had an adhesive strip on one side of the opening that you peeled off so you could seal your things inside. I shimmied out of my clothes and shoved everything in the bag along with my ring. I didn't have much; I'd left my school bag with my driver's license in Win's SUV just in case. I didn't think anyone would go through my stuff, but I didn't want to take a chance. There was a washed-out, pale green hospital gown that tied in the back and a thin robe that I pulled on so that my ass wasn't hanging out. The tile floor felt cold through thin paper slippers. I glanced down at the picture of Harry I'd brought with me.

A rush of hot tears came to my eyes, and my lower lip

shook. Just when I thought I was doing better, I would slam into a wall of emotion and find myself crying again. I hoped that wherever Harry was, he knew how much I loved him. As much as I wanted to believe there was a horse heaven, or a heaven in general, I wasn't sure. I would have done anything to save him from dying the way he did. I couldn't escape the feeling I'd let him down.

His loss had left me feeling like someone had scooped out my heart with a rusty spoon: raw and gutted. Not that I'd expected to bounce right back, spouting things like how he was in a better place or how the circle of life took us all eventually. Instead his death had made me feel like someone had whipped off my blinders and I could see this entire ugly side of the world that I hadn't known existed. There was this heavy feeling of dread that followed me around. As if there were something else, just out of sight, that I instinctively knew I didn't want to see. I hadn't been completely honest with Josh or my parents. I did want the treatment because I was sick of feeling so depressed all the time, but it was more than that. I wasn't only depressed. I was scared. I shoved his photo in the bag and sealed it.

"Okay, Emily." I jolted when the technician touched me. For a second I'd forgotten that's what she thought my name was. "We need you to think about the memories that upset you," the technician said. She pushed the table I was on inside a huge machine. She patted my foot. I shifted slightly on the metal table. There was a thin blanket underneath me, but I wasn't at any risk of getting so comfortable that I would fall asleep, even with the shot of something they'd given me that was meant to relax me. How someone could be relaxed when they were tied down was a mystery. Velcro straps ran across my chest and legs, ensuring I stayed still. The straps were covered in a soft white fabric designed to make you forget you were lashed down. I wondered what memories the real Emily wanted to soften and why she'd missed her appointment. I hoped it was because she'd decided things weren't so bad.

"Try to stay still." The technician's voice seemed to float out of nowhere. I couldn't see her. It was dim inside the machine, with just a soft blue light. It felt very science-fiction-ish, like the equipment was talking to me. *I'm sorry, Hal, I can't do that.* This was what came from watching too many sci-fi movies with my dad.

"Sorry," I said to the technician. Now that I needed to think about Harry, my brain refused. I'd been obsessed with his memory for the past few weeks, stuck thinking about him over and over, but now my thoughts were racing. I swallowed and made myself remember what he'd looked like lying in his stall. The suffering must have been horrible, and he'd been alone. He would have been scared, his eyes rolling, his heart seizing as the pain he felt became unbearable.

There was a metallic whir above me, a soft breeze of cool air as the robotic arm moved. I smelled a hint of rubbing alcohol.

"You're doing great, Emily. We're going to walk you through a couple sensory memories to help us get a lock on things. Don't try and force anything; let yourself free-associate."

I was going to nod, but remembered I wasn't supposed to move. "Okay." My voice sounded funny to me, as if it were coming from someone else. Clearly whatever had been in the shot had had more kick than I'd thought. My lips felt funny, almost electric. I bit my lower lip, but it didn't hurt. It was like my entire head was full of Novocain. I fought the urge to reach up and touch my face to see if it was my own. I had this fear that my features wouldn't be mine and instead I would look like Emily.

"First think about scents associated with your memory."

I inhaled, recalling the smell of fresh-cut hay, how Harry's flesh smelled almost earthy when he'd been out in the sun. The warm tangy smell of the leather saddle and tack.

"Now think about the images that go along with your memory."

I saw Harry run through a field, his mane and tail whipping in the wind. I pictured how he'd toss his head when he was excited. Images of Harry flipped through my mind like a slide show on slow speed.

"Great. Now I want you to think about anything associated with how your memory might physically feel." There were more clicking sounds as the machinery spun around me.

I closed my eyes and pictured myself running my hands down Harry's flank, his soft fur that felt prickly if you ran your hand the wrong way. I felt the burn in my thighs when I'd been riding for hours.

"Okay, last step, Emily. We're almost done."

I jolted slightly on the table. I'd nearly fallen asleep. I'd been sure that would be impossible. I took a deep breath. I felt light-headed, almost a bit drunk.

"Can you think about some sounds that go with your memory?"

My mind shifted, hearing Harry snort. The clang of the metal bar when we didn't clear a fence, and the soft thud of his hooves as they sank into the soft dirt.

There was another whir from the machine above and a soft buzzing sound. I felt myself starting to drift off. I couldn't tell where the buzzing in my head stopped and the buzz of the machinery started.

Then I heard the sound of a woman gasping, followed by a loud crash. My eyes flew open. Something was wrong. I tried to sit straight up, but the straps on the table held me in place. In less than a second I realized that no one else had heard the sound. It had been in my head. Everything was fine.

The lights came up, and the technician slid the table out of the machine. I blinked in the harsh light. She undid the straps, the Velcro giving a loud tearing sound. Her fingernails were painted a bright pink. "We're all done. We're going to have you rest in the recovery lounge for a bit, and then you're good to go home."

"That's it?" I looked around as if the room should be different.

The technician laughed. "Everyone says that, but yep, that's it." She winked. "Miracles don't have to be loud and splashy. It's not all dividing the Red Sea." She helped me off the table and into the wheelchair.

I was going to tell her I wasn't sick and I didn't need a wheelchair, but then I realized I wasn't very steady. My feet and ankles didn't feel connected to the rest of my legs.

"It's normal to be a bit woozy. It's the medication. It will wear off soon. How do you feel?"

I paused and realized that the tight band that had been around my chest, the feeling of dread, had disappeared. I forced myself to imagine Harry. He was there, but no giant tsunami of guilt or sadness went along with him. I felt lighter. A laugh bubbled out of my lips and I clamped my hand over my mouth.

The technician patted my back. "I'm going to take that to mean you're feeling better." She rolled me toward the recovery lounge.

I took a huge breath, my lungs expanding like a balloon. "I feel like myself again."

chapter eight

There are few people who can carry off wearing spandex, a cape, and a hat made out of crushed tin cans. Thankfully, I was one of those people. Win was not.

"No way." She held the tin can hat with two fingers like it was something that had been found at the very back of the fridge with an expiration date from a few years ago.

"It's part of the skit," Josh said. He was wearing bright green pants and a blue shirt.

"How come you get to be the earth and the rest of us have to be recycling fairies?"

"You said you didn't want to memorize a bunch of stuff," Josh said. "The earth is the one who gives the speech."

"Besides, we're not fairies; we're environmental superheroes." I thrust my fist in the air.

Win's look told me that she didn't rank environmental superheroes as any better than recycling fairies. "Just because you've lost your mind doesn't mean I have. Community volunteer credits are not worth my pride."

Saint Francis required students to do fifteen hours of community service every year. Josh had talked us into helping a local environmental group that was trying to raise awareness. We were supposed to do the skit at the mall, then for a group of elementary classes, and next week at one of the local old-age homes.

"Who came up with this skit idea anyway?" Win asked. "No wonder the planet is going in the shitter if this is the caliber of public relations it's got going for it. These outfits make me want to leave the lights on to avoid nightmares."

"Do your best not to mention that when we're onstage." Josh passed her a cape. Win crossed her arms and refused to take it. Josh pulled out the big guns. "Did I mention that Kyle is on the environmental committee at school? He's the one who spearheaded the no-plastic-cutlery-in-the-cafeteria idea. He's a huge fan of this program."

Win tapped her foot, staring at Josh.

"I think it's so nice when couples have things in common," Josh added.

Win yanked the hat out of Josh's hand and shoved it on her head and then took the cape. She and Kyle had gone out only a few times, but they were on their way to being one of the "it" couples at school.

"Great! I'll let the announcer know we're ready." Josh slid behind the curtain into the mall's main concourse.

"What happened to your dignity?" I adjusted my own hat.

"Have you seen Kyle's abs? He took his shirt off in gym class. I can live without a bit of dignity." Win raised a finger in my face. "However, if someone takes a picture of me in this outfit, I will remove their spleen through their nose. Besides, I'm not doing it just for him. Don't laugh. I'm saving the planet here."

I couldn't help smiling. Win with a crush was too much fun. She'd actually been nervous around Kyle at the dance, downright giggly. Josh and I watched them as they swayed together for the last slow song. Josh commented how when Win was no longer sarcastic and bitter, it must be a sign of the end of times. I laughed so hard the fruit juice I'd been sipping came out my nose, which made me laugh even harder. It felt good to be back to myself. Or almost myself. I was still having trouble sleeping. I would jolt awake in the middle of the night, but at least now I could fall back asleep. Even the annoyance I'd felt with Josh lately seemed better.

I felt bad about lying to my parents about the whole thing. Both of them had commented on how they were happy I was acting more like myself. I thought about telling them the truth now that it was over, but I backed down when my dad went off on a tirade about the protestors getting bolder and intimidating patients. I'd tell them someday. I wanted my dad to know that what he'd made had helped when I needed it most. Josh poked his head behind the curtain. "Ready to go?"

"Truth, justice, and clean drinking water for all!" I cried. I waited for Win.

She rolled her eyes. "Fine, fine, don't get your knickers in a wad." She struck a pose. "You too can be a superhero for the planet by doing your part. Recycle."

"Try to put a bit more excitement in your voice," Josh coached.

Win flipped him the bird. The mall PA announced our show.

We stepped onto the stage in the mall atrium. A few shoppers glanced over at us but didn't stop wandering on to the next store. Never get between people and their consumer quest. A small boy squealed in excitement and ran toward the stage. It wasn't clear if he was excited by what we were wearing or if he was happy to have escaped the stroller he'd been strapped to a moment before. There were a few people watching from the food court, but I was fairly sure they were only paying attention because it was better than noticing what they were putting in their mouths.

"Did you know that with only four percent of the world's population, North America consumes twenty-five percent of the world's resources?" Josh boomed out so that his voice carried out into the mall. He turned and glared at Win when she didn't speak.

"But we can make a difference," she said finally.

"Recycling even one aluminum can could power a television for three hours," I announced. No one in the food court looked impressed. Win was right; we shouldn't have let Josh talk us into this.

The toddler who had rushed the stage was bouncing up and down. He loved the show. Clearly, he was a future earth warrior.

"C'mon, Benny. It's time to go." His mom tried to pull him away. Benny demonstrated zero interest in leaving. We were like a rock show as far as he was concerned. He was moments away from taking off his diaper and throwing it at us on stage. "Step away from there. I mean it. I'm serious. Come here right now." His mom's voice grew louder.

Win was launching into her next line about the value in buying local, but there was a buzzing sound in my ears. I could still hear the mom yelling at her toddler, but her voice was high and far away. The smell of meat burning filled my nose.

My breath was coming hard and fast. I let out a whimper. I saw Win turn to look at me. It seemed as if she were moving in slow motion through a fog. I heard a woman gasp, followed by a sickening thud. I flinched; it sounded like something thick and wet hitting the floor. The smell of burned meat grew even stronger, searing into my sinuses. Then I heard a scream and I realized it was coming from me. I backed up and fell off the small stage, landing hard on my ass. My teeth slammed together, and there was a hot, sharp pain as I bit my tongue. I had a flash of the Saint Thomas More statue falling at school, only unlike that, no one had been there to catch me.

Josh leaped down and knelt at my side. Win was there a beat later.

"Are you okay?" Win's hands hovered over me as if she expected to see a bone sticking out of my leg.

I swallowed. The coppery taste of blood was in my mouth from biting my tongue. I felt nauseated, but I could feel my breathing returning to normal. I nodded.

"What happened?" Josh asked.

"I heard that woman make that sound, and that smell," I said. I saw Josh and Win exchange a glance. "The woman with the little boy. She startled me, that's all."

"She didn't make any sounds," Josh said.

I opened my mouth to disagree with him, but then I realized he was serious. This wasn't the kind of thing he would joke about. I sniffed the air: The mall smelled of popcorn, greasy pizza, and cookies. The burning-meat stench was gone, if it had ever been there at all. I could see a crowd from the mall pushing closer. They hadn't been interested in our environment skit, but they wanted to be sure to get a front-row seat for me falling apart. I could hear them talking about me, speculating what my problem might be.

"Help me up," I said.

"Maybe you should lie there. The mall administrator went to get their first-aid person," Josh said.

"I'm fine." I pushed away a sense of irritation with Josh. He always had to act like he was forty. Win pulled me up. My tailbone throbbed, but I was pretty sure I hadn't broken anything. "I just sort of blacked out for a second."

People leaned over one another, trying to get a better look at me. I wanted to scream at them to back off. It was like being in a zombie movie with all of them closing in.

I slid my tin can headdress back on. There was a slick of oily sweat on my skin. "Want to start at the beginning?"

"I should get you home." Josh's forehead was all bunched together in concern. I knew he was trying to help, but it annoyed me. I fought the urge to whack his hand off my shoulder.

"I'm fine. I overheated there for a second. I didn't eat enough at lunch." I tugged my costume back into place.

Josh rubbed my shoulder. "You're the only person I know who can forget to eat. I've got a protein bar in my bag. Eat that with some water and then we'll give it another go. As long as you're sure."

I smiled as if the idea of having a protein bar filled me with glee. "I'm sure."

Win's headdress was tilted. Her mouth pulled up at the side.

"What?"

"You ate lunch." Win's eyes never left mine.

"Apparently not enough. I'm fine, just a bit light-headed."

"Then why did you whisper 'let her go' before you fell? Who were you talking about?"

My throat seized. A bead of sweat ran down the small of my back.

"I heard you," Win said. "Who were you talking about?"

"I don't know."

chapter nine

I jogged down to the entrance to the subdivision. Our neighborhood had an elaborate wrought-iron gate that stretched
across the road, complete with an intercom. In theory this was
for safety, although it didn't take a criminal mastermind to realize that if you went three feet to the side of the road you could
go around the fence. I suspected the real purpose of the gate
was so that everyone in our subdivision could picture themselves as important enough to require a locked gate between
their house and the rest of the world. Next best thing to having
your own drawbridge. Each house had a box mounted inside
near the front door that allowed you to talk to whoever was at
the gate and buzz them in. Our intercom worked, but not the
buzzer. My dad refused to call for a repairperson because it was
the kind of thing he could fix himself, not that he ever did.

Now I was stuck running down to the main gate to sign for some stupid package.

The tulips the home association had planted last fall were coming up, like an extra line of defense along either side of the fence. I pressed the release for the gate on my side and stepped toward the waiting car. I'd expected a UPS truck, but it must have been a private courier, unless UPS was downsizing to beat-up Toyotas.

"I can sign for the package," I said. The car door opened, and I took a quick step back when I recognized him. It was the guy from the protest, the one who was around my age. He unfolded out of the car. He looked almost too big to fit inside, like someone climbing out of one of those clown cars. I turned and pulled the gate shut between us, liking the clanging sound it made as it clicked.

"Wait," he called out.

"What the hell are you doing here? This is private property." I felt somewhat better standing behind the gate, despite the fact that it didn't really offer any protection. I wondered how long he'd been at the gate, staring at the giant houses that made up our subdivision. Each house had a perfectly manicured lawn, some even with fountains. I felt awkward, the way I always did when someone saw my house for the first time, and I became hyperaware that it was huge. Like mansion huge. It wasn't that I wanted to live in a trailer, but there were times I wished we just had a normal house. I could only imagine what he thought of us now that he'd seen where we lived. If he was anticorporation before, seeing our house wasn't going to change his mind.

"I wanted to talk to you." He held out his hand. "I'm Neil, by the way."

I stared at his hand through the gate and left it hanging there.

He took his hand back. "Fair enough. We didn't get off to a great start."

"We haven't gotten off to any start," I clarified. I crossed my arms over my chest. "You need to leave. If you don't, I'm going to call the police. You have no right to protest here." My dad had only arranged extra security for when we were at any events. I guessed he'd thought the gate would stop any possible threats. When he heard about this, we were going to end up with guards patrolling the subdivision like a mini SWAT team ready to swing into action.

"I'm not protesting." He held up both hands and waved them. "Look, no signs." He smiled.

He had an infectious smile. It made me want to smile back, which made me want to smack him. "What are you doing here?"

"I didn't know how else to reach you. I know showing up at your house is a bit forward, but everyone knows your dad lives here. I don't have your number. I don't go to your school, and hanging around outside waiting for you is kinda creepy. I'm a freshman at Seattle Central Community College; I can't exactly hang around a high school without looking like I've got issues."

I stared at him. Did he expect me to congratulate him on his educational achievements? "How do you know who I am?"

"The reporter used your name, and I'm a bit obsessed with Neurotech, so I knew a bit about your dad and that he had a daughter. I put it all together."

Community college was teaching him some fine detective skills. I kept my arms crossed.

"I wanted to talk to you about something," he said.

"So you came to my house? You think because you want to talk you can show up at my home?"

"Technically, I came to your gate, not your house." Neil smiled again. His top lip was crooked. "I'm simply pointing out that it's not like I'm leering at you through the window or anything. I just want to talk to you."

This conversation was doomed. Who knew what he wanted. He might be taping what I said, trying to find some quote he could share with that journalist to make my family look bad. He might be cute, but he was bad news. "Anything you have to say to me you can say to my dad's lawyers." I spun around and started walking back up the road.

"I saw you collapse at the mall," he called out. "And I know you had the Memtex procedure. The two things are connected."

My jaw locked. *How could he know?* I turned to face him and did my best to look uninterested. "You're wrong. You've made a mistake."

He shook his head. "I'm not mistaken."

I marched back down to the gate and tore it open, the metal screeching. I got up in his face. "You have a lot of nerve showing up here and spouting off about my personal medical history and making up stuff. Then, to top it off, you imply that there's something wrong with my dad's procedure."

"But there is."

I snorted. "Let me guess, neurobiology happens to be a hobby of yours. In your spare time you like bowling, learning French, and critiquing the work of a bunch of PhD scientists."

"No. I know because it killed my brother." His voice was calm and even.

That took the wind out of my sails. How do you argue with someone once they bring up a dead brother?

"Listen, I'm sorry about your brother," I said softly. I held up a hand before he could say anything else. "But I don't believe the Memtex procedure had anything to do with it."

"Give me five minutes? Let me say what I came to tell you, and then if you want to ignore it, you can."

"I'm not *ignoring* what you say. I don't agree with you." I hated how it made me sound like my head was in the sand.

"Okay, feel free to not agree with me, but you'll listen?"

I chewed on the inside of my lip. "Yes, I'll listen, but we can't stay here." It was just a matter of time before one of my neighbors wondered what was going on and told my parents who they'd seen me talking to. That would bring up questions I didn't want to answer, including *What were you thinking?* "And you're not coming to the house." The idea of him in my house screamed *bad idea*.

"No problem," Neil said. "We can go to my place. I live in the Edgemont apartment complex. Do you know it? The one near the university."

My mind flashed to a run-down apartment complex by the highway. It was the kind of place where someone would have a sheet duct-taped up inside the window instead of curtains. That seemed an even worse idea. "We need someplace neutral," I said.

Neil nodded. "How about Café Rica? I can drive."

Taking rides from strangers was how people ended up in a trunk, before they were driven to a remote location where someone could dispose of their body in private after making a skin suit out of it. "I know where it is. I'll drive myself. I'll meet you there."

Neil stepped toward his car and stopped. "Hey, this isn't a ploy to get rid of me, is it?"

"Would it work, or would you show back up here again?"

"Look at that—we're getting to know each other already." He smiled and gave me a small salute.

Café Rica was long and narrow, like a hallway with tables squeezed on one side. The only windows were in the front and usually fogged over by steam, so by the time you got to the back, it was dark. It was the perfect place to hole up if you wanted to sit for hours with a cup of coffee and veg out, or if you were meeting someone on the sly.

Neil was clearly not aware that this was a clandestine meeting. He stood and waved when I walked in. I grabbed a latte and sat at the small table. Our knees bumped. I noticed he was drinking plain black coffee. Now I felt like my double shot, honey-no-sugar soy latte with the fancy leaf pattern in the foam was too fussy. I had snobby coffee. I stirred it so the pattern would disappear.

"It's great you're here. I appreciate you meeting with me," Neil said.

I sipped my latte. "Why were you watching me at the mall? Have you been following me?"

"No. I'm not great at the spy thing; it was just luck. I was at the mall to pick up something for my grandma when I saw you in that giant Carmen Miranda tin can hat." His eyes glinted. "I figured seeing what you were up to was worth sticking around for."

"It was a community service project." As soon as the words were out of my mouth, I wanted to take them back. It felt like I'd said that just to prove that I was the kind of person who volunteered. Like I was trying to show him that he wasn't the only person who had a cause. I put my coffee down on the rickety table and then picked it up again, wanting to have something to do with my hands. "I said I'd give you five minutes." I looked at my wrist as if I had a watch on.

Neil traced circles on the table with his cup. "I'm not real sure how to start. Guess I should have made a plan for this conversation."

"Start with your brother."

He nodded. "Marcus. He was seven years older than me. I was the accident kid, the one no one planned on. I have an older sister, too. She's nine years older." He ran his hands through his hair. "Marcus was a total overachiever. Great grades, in the school band, played on sport teams, that kind of thing. If you'd met him, you'd know he was going places."

"And you?"

"I wasn't feral or anything, but by the time my parents got to me as the third kid, they were more laid-back. Marcus and my sister had already done everything. I would always be the kid who did it last, so there was less pressure. Things in our family were good—and then they weren't.

"Marcus was in a car accident. It wasn't his fault, but his best friend was killed. Marcus was trapped in the car with him when he died. They were waiting for an ambulance, but it took too long." Neil didn't meet my eyes and instead stared down at his coffee.

I sucked in my breath, trying to imagine it. Stuck in a car with a cacophonous silence. Alone, but not alone. "He went for Memtex to get over it," I said.

"Yep. He was in this competitive grad program and he couldn't focus. At first it seemed to do the trick. He was back to being Marcus. Then he started having trouble. He wasn't sleeping right. Memory problems, visual things too—where he couldn't judge distance right. He'd bump into stuff or drop things. Then there were the mood changes. He was cranky all the time, almost paranoid."

"He'd been through a lot; it's not surprising he was having trouble." I took a sip of my coffee, the heat burning my tongue. I pushed down a wave of unease.

"But the Memtex should have helped, right? But it didn't. He went from depressed to confused. He was on edge. In the end he killed himself. Sleeping pills."

I let the breath I had been holding out in a rush. My planned arguments turned to damp ash in my mouth. "I'm sorry."

Neil pulled a wad of wrinkled papers out of his bag. "There are people who think Memtex could cause an early version of Alzheimer's. My brother had all the symptoms."

"But wouldn't his doctor have diagnosed that?"

"Who thinks a twenty-three-year-old would have Alzheimer's? No one. And it's not like a condition that shows up on a test; they can only diagnose it for sure by doing tests on the brain after death. My parents didn't do that because it never occurred to them it was an option. It makes sense, too, if you think about it: The treatment messes with the memory center, so maybe in some cases it goes too far."

The tight knot in my stomach released. It was a horrible

situation, but there were options, other reasons this might have happened. "Try to think of this a different way. Maybe your brother had issues. You said Marcus was an overachiever. He must have felt a lot of pressure. Then, even with the treatment, he'd still been through a horrible accident. The treatment doesn't promise to eliminate all problems, just dial them down. Maybe even with the guilt reduced, it was more than he could take. I'm not blaming your brother; I'm simply saying that it might not have been the treatment," I said.

"It's not just my brother. There are other people with similar situations." Neil nudged the stack of paper toward me. He'd printed off a zillion articles to make his point.

"Thousands of people have this procedure. Hundreds of thousands. If this was happening, it would be an epidemic." I had the urge to push the papers back to him, but I didn't want to touch them.

"Even if only five percent of people have this side effect, isn't that too many?" His eyes never broke contact with mine.

"The company tracks all sorts of data. They would know if this was a real concern."

"Unless they don't want to know. How much money does Neurotech make with this procedure? Millions? Billions? Do you think they're going to walk away from that because a small number of people have a bad reaction?"

I fought the urge to shove the papers onto the floor. "Yes, they would walk. They're doctors; they do this to help people, not hurt them. You're talking about my *dad*. You don't know him. If my dad suspected something was wrong, he would do something."

Neil stared at me across the table. "If you're so sure, then why not read the articles? Unless you don't want to know."

I grabbed the papers and shoved them into my bag in a giant wad. "Fine, I'll read them."

Neil didn't break eye contact. "This isn't just about me. I was outside the clinic that day. I was one of the protestors. I saw you go in."

I flushed. So much for my sunglasses master disguise and theory no one would notice. "How do you know it was me?"

"You're not the kind of girl someone forgets."

My heart skipped a beat. "I was visiting my dad. I do it all the time."

My heart beat faster. I was glad for the hum of conversation and jazz music playing in the background. It seemed like without the other sounds he would be able to hear the pounding in my chest, even though I knew that was absurd. I reminded myself he hadn't been inside the clinic. He had no idea what I did in there.

"For almost three hours?"

"What's your point?" I took another sip of my latte, but it was cold and bitter.

"You stumbled at the mall. Are you having vision problems?"

It took a beat, but then I realized what he was hinting at. I swallowed and it went down the wrong way and I coughed. "What?"

Neil leaned forward. "Are you having memory problems? Trouble sleeping?"

"Now you think I'm developing Alzheimer's? Well, that's just great. I suppose, on the upside, I might forget this meeting ever happened." I sat back, wanting to put some space between us.

"Are you having any odd symptoms? I'm being serious." He leaned even closer.

"So am I. Thank you for your concern." My mind flashed to the sound of the woman I'd heard in the mall, and I pushed away the thought. I looked down at the time on my phone. "I gave you more than your five minutes. I listened to what you had to say, and I still disagree." I shoved back from the table. I wanted to bolt out of the café.

"Wait!" Neil scribbled something down on a piece of paper and tucked it into my open bag. "It's my name and phone number. In case you change your mind. Or if you need anything."

I walked out of the cafe without saying anything.

chapter ten

Our house had a media room. That wasn't unusual, at least not in our neighborhood, but nothing my dad did was halfway. Our media room could have belonged to a Hollywood movie mogul. It had three rows of red leather theater seats, giant La-Z-Boy chairs that fully reclined, with armrests that flipped open to reveal cup holders. There were vintage movie posters on the walls. Originals. My mom had used a decorator to hunt them down. Heaven forbid anyone discover that we had a mere reproduction of the *Maltese Falcon* poster hanging on our wall.

There was even one of those rolling metal popcorn carts parked at the back of the room. I couldn't remember us ever using it. We weren't big popcorn-cooked-in-a-vat-of-oil people. We weren't big movie people either, but having a media room was one more thing my dad could have that demonstrated his success. It wasn't always clear to me what was more important to my dad: that he do well, or that everyone know just how well he was doing. My mom said it had to do with him having grown up poor. It wasn't that I didn't like having nice things, but I wished we didn't have to tell everyone exactly how much each of our nice things cost. Once, we were at dinner and the waitress told my dad she liked his watch. "Can you believe it cost over twenty thousand bucks?" he asked her, rolling up his sleeve so she could see it better. I wanted to crawl under the table. It was likely more than she earned in a year. Couldn't the guy just have said thanks?

I sat in the dark in the media room staring at the screen. I didn't have the sound on. I'd seen this movie hundreds of times. I didn't need the soundtrack to be able to quote entire sections. I let the black-and-white images wash over me. I kept pushing away the thoughts of the discussion I'd had with Neil, but the thoughts were like some kind of annoying poltergeist. They kept popping up, surprising me. What if something was really wrong with me?

"Can't sleep?"

I jumped. My dad stood in the doorway. He had on the old sweats he slept in and one of his *Star Trek* T-shirts. He chuckled. "It would be a shame if you developed my insomnia."

My dad had weird sleep habits. He would sometimes be up for a couple of days in a row and then the next day he would sleep for an entire day until dinner. The concept of day and night was more fluid in his world. He raised a good point; maybe my sleep problems didn't mean something was wrong with me the way Neil implied. My poor sleep could be nothing more than a bad roll of the genetic dice—sort of like my huge flipper feet, which also came from my dad's side.

"Woke up and then couldn't get back to sleep," I explained. I didn't mention the part where I was now worried there was something fundamentally wrong with my brain.

"This movie should help put you to sleep."

"Ha-ha." The movie was an old one, *To Kill a Mockingbird*. When I was little, I came home crying one day because someone had made fun of my name. My dad told me that I'd been named after Harper Lee. She wrote the book the movie was based on, and my mom had been reading it when she was pregnant with me. She didn't love the book, but she liked the name. I liked the book and I loved the movie, even if it was in black and white. I knew it had been made way before I was even born, but it still felt special, like it was something just for me.

"This movie would be better with aliens. Or if they blew something up. Heck, a good sword battle would do the trick too," Dad suggested. This was his criteria for any good movie. Mayhem with a touch of gore.

"I'm sure if they ever do a remake they'll consider some zombies."

We sat in the dark watching the screen "I was talking to your mom," he said.

"Uh-oh," I said.

"Nah, it's good stuff. We decided you should go ahead and get a new horse. Your mom called Laura; she'll help you sort out which is the best one."

My mouth fell open. "Really?"

"Yeah. We were going to wait to tell you for graduation, but you know how I am with keeping secrets."

I squealed and jumped up to give him a hug. "Thank you so much."

He patted my back. "You know I want you to be happy. Why you like the darn things is a mystery to me. They're like big giant stinky dogs, only they don't even fetch."

My mind raced, thinking through my options. "I'd love to get another Hanoverian, but Friesians are great too."

"Keep in mind, there will be a budget. We had insurance on Harry, but you still can't buy some Kentucky Derby winner."

I shook my head. He never bothered to get it. "Dad, how many times do I have to tell you? Horses that make great racers don't make great jumpers." It was a miracle he'd gotten me Harry in the first place. Most kids get a pony, not an elite jumper horse to start.

"Please, don't give me another lecture on horses. I'll buy you two, if you promise not to bore me with one of those." He hugged me again. "I'm glad to see you smiling. I told you that you didn't need the treatment."

I felt another stab of guilt.

"You always were my ray of sunshine. Don't tell anyone, but you're my favorite kid."

I rolled my eyes at this old joke. "I'm your only kid."

"That makes it easier to choose. Less competition."

I set a new world record for losing popularity points. I went from my dad's favorite child to his least favorite person on the entire planet in less than twenty-four hours. After school I went directly to the barn to talk to Laura. She'd already bookmarked some pages with horses for sale for my consideration. We spent a couple of hours talking about different options, and I started to get excited about having a horse of my own again. Laura was happy to let me use her horse, Dallas, but it wasn't the same. I missed Harry, but I wanted to ride again. I felt more like myself when I rode. It sometimes felt that if I could only find the trail that led back to my life before Harry died, then everything would work out.

I walked in the house for dinner with a bunch of printouts about the different horses, but as soon as I saw my parents, I knew showing them would be a bad plan. My mom stood in a corner of the kitchen, twisting a towel in her hand, and my dad paced back and forth in front of the granite island. I could see the vein in his forehead throbbing. He had that look that screamed, *Now is not the time to ask me to buy you an expensive horse.* I started to turn around to head up to my room when he spotted me.

"Where do you think you're going?"

I didn't get in trouble often. Growing up I wasn't prone to meltdowns, and I didn't push other kids down on the playground. I didn't sneak out of the house or steal money from my mom's purse. I'm not saying I'm perfect; there was the time Win and I drank my parents' Malibu rum when we were supposed to be babysitting her younger brother. That didn't end well for a whole number of reasons, not the least being that the smell of coconut now made me want to throw up. I couldn't even use most suntan lotions. I'd never be able to live in Hawaii. Based on my parents' expressions, this was going to make the Malibu rum incident look good.

"Anything you want to tell me?" Dad tapped his foot on the floor. "Or should I call you Emily Ludka?"

Uh-oh. It felt as if my body had suddenly fallen through the ice into a frozen lake, cold and painful. "I can explain."

"Really? I can't wait to hear this." Before I could open my mouth to give it a shot, he cut me off. "Do you realize what you did is insurance fraud? If I hadn't been the one in the billing office when the question came in, if I hadn't been the one to check with Josh about what happened, we could have taken this to the cops to investigate. How would you like to be having this discussion at the police station?" My dad's nostrils flared in and out, and his entire face was turning red.

I felt like kicking myself for being stupid. I should have realized that there would be a claim. Emily Ludka's family must have prearranged payment through her insurance company.

When she didn't show up, but I still had the procedure, the bill went through.

"How did you know it was me?" I asked.

"When we realized there was fraud, the security guard pulled video from the clinic. If he hadn't shown it to me first, it would have gone to the police." My dad's jaw thrust forward. He looked like he wanted to throw a punch.

"Harper, separate from the insurance, the point is that you had a medical procedure without our consent," Mom said.

"I know." My voice came out small and squeaky.

"Can you imagine if this had come out publicly? You made a liar out of me, too. I told the insurance company that it was a billing error to cover up what you did. They'll now be reviewing the past three months of invoices to make sure that was the only one. You've caused a lot of headaches for a lot of people, young lady." Dad put his hands on his hips.

"I'll pay for the procedure," I offered. "And I'll volunteer in the office if you want. I can make copies, or do data entry, or help with the billing." I scrambled to think of some way I could make it up to my dad.

"I think you've done plenty to ruin my company without messing around with the billing department." He noticed the papers in my hand. "Oh, and in case it wasn't clear, you can forget about getting a horse. And you're grounded." He searched for something else he could do to me. "And you'll be spending your weekend cleaning the bathrooms. *And* the garage."

I took a deep breath. "I know what I did was wrong. And I'm not arguing about my punishment—"

"I should hope not," Dad barked. His hand slapped down on the stainless steel Viking range, making me flinch.

"I'm trying to explain why I did it. I tried telling you how I felt after Harry died."

"You did this over a stupid horse?"

My dad's words felt like a slap. I stood up straighter. "Yes. I did it because of Harry. I loved him."

My dad opened his mouth to say something else, but my mom put her hand on his shoulder, and his teeth slammed shut with a click.

"I understand why you did this, but that doesn't make it okay." Mom's voice was even. She had a tendency to get calmer the more upset my dad got. "There's the issue that you disobeyed our express wishes. You knew we were against this. There's the fact that by going forward with the procedure, you caused trouble for your dad's business, but that's not all. You asked Josh to help you. You made him a part of your lie."

"He can kiss his internship good-bye," Dad added.

My stomach went into a free fall. Dad being mad at me was bad, but Josh losing his internship was a whole new level of bad. Even though I didn't like that Josh worked there, he needed that job. If he lost it, he wouldn't be able to pay for college. "Dad, you can't do that. It's not Josh's fault. It's mine. I asked him to do it for me." It might have originally been his idea, but I was the one who pushed him. I couldn't let my dad ruin his life.

"I don't care whose idea this was; the point is what he did wasn't right."

"I know, but he believes so much in the procedure, in everything you guys do at Neurotech. He only did this because he knew it would make me better. He really thought he was helping."

The idea of Josh being a fan of Neurotech seemed to calm my dad down a notch.

"The internship is everything for Josh. Please don't take it away from him." I could hear the pleading in my voice.

Dad shrugged, giving nothing away.

"I will do anything you want to make this up to you," I vowed.

Dad sighed. "You'll start by going to the doctor tomorrow. I want a full medical workup done on you to make sure everything's okay."

"Are you feeling all right?" Mom's face was wrinkled up in concern.

"I'm fine," I lied. Now wasn't the time to tell them I was having problems.

It wasn't until I went upstairs to my room that I realized both of my parents were worried about me having side effects. The side effects that they'd told me didn't exist.

chapter eleven

There weren't many places in a Catholic school where you could be alone with your boyfriend. They were afraid you'd start making out like mad. I suspected public schools weren't keen on public displays of affection either, but Saint Francis saw it as nearly a hanging offense if they caught you holding hands with a guy. Ms. O'Neil, our gym teacher, was always talking about how our bodies were temples of the Holy Spirit and that we should leave room for Jesus between whomever we were dating and ourselves. Win once said she thought it was creepy that Jesus wanted to watch. She got detention for that. Our school wasn't real "turn the other cheek" about snide comments about the Lord. Even from nonbelievers who paid the full rate for tuition.

Our school's ban on ever being alone with the opposite sex

was why Josh and I were hiding out in the library. If you went to the far back corner, there was a resource section, just in case the Internet ever died and people needed to consult a 1990s version of the encyclopedia in order to survive. We were sitting on the floor with our backs against the wall. The school might have been worried that we'd make out, but I never felt less like kissing someone than I did at that moment. I could also tell that despite the fact that he didn't want to be, Josh was ticked at me.

"I feel so bad," I said for the millionth time that day. It had become my own personal mantra.

"Don't. It's my own fault. You didn't make me do anything I didn't want to. It was my idea in the first place." He squeezed my hand. He didn't even mention how he'd tried to talk me out of the plan, but that fact hung between the two of us. It was another thing that tied me to him. He'd risked everything for me.

"My dad won't cancel your internship." I wasn't sure if I was trying to convince him or myself.

"I don't think he will either, but if he did, I'd deserve it. I didn't even think about how what we were doing could damage Neurotech." Josh shook his head like he couldn't believe how stupid he'd been. "I could kick myself. I didn't even think of the insurance claim."

"I guess neither of us has a life of crime ahead of us. We're not great planners."

"Guess not." Josh picked at his jeans.

"I can talk to my dad again," I offered.

"No. It'll be better if I do it. He'll respect it more if I talk to him directly; if he thinks I'm hiding behind you, he'll be even more disappointed in me. I'm meeting with him after school today. I plan to throw myself on his mercy and plead being momentarily stupid."

"It's okay if you're mad at me. You don't always have to understand. You only did it because I wanted you to." I leaned my head back against one of the shelves. I was vaguely exasperated. I knew Josh wanted me to apologize, but he wouldn't just come out and say he was ticked. He had to play this game where he acted like he was fine and I still ended up begging for him to forgive me. I had the sense my dad was going to forgive Josh easier than he would forgive me.

"If your point is that I wasn't planning to sneak other people in for the treatment, then you're right, but that doesn't change anything. I did it because I thought it would help. And it did help—you're feeling better, right?" Josh said.

I paused. Josh pulled back so he could see my face.

"You are feeling better?"

"Yes. Mostly." I pulled on the hem of my uniform skirt. Considering that the school didn't want us to be sexually active, you'd think they would know better than to dress us up like a bunch of naughty schoolgirls. "I feel better about Harry. I can think about him now without falling to pieces."

Josh pushed the hair out of his eyes. "It's fine if you're still a bit sad. The procedure doesn't wipe the memories out. Some people still find they have these residual feelings; that's perfectly normal."

I hated how he sounded. Just because he worked at Neurotech, he acted like he knew more than me about the procedure. "It's not that. I've just had a couple strange symptoms." I forced a laugh, trying to make it seem like no big deal. "I'm not even sure they're related to the treatment; I'm pretty strange on my own."

"Symptoms?" The worry in his voice came through loud and clear.

"Maybe 'symptom' is the wrong word. There's some stuff that's odd," I said.

"Tell me."

I leaned back. The truth was I was relieved to talk about it with someone. "Right after the procedure I felt really great, but then I started having more trouble sleeping. I'm waking up. Like jolting up, how you do when you're having a nightmare. The thing is, I've been having trouble sleeping since Harry died, so it isn't new so much as worse."

"What are your dreams about?"

"That's the thing. I don't really remember anything, or what I remember is just this sliver. As soon as I start to focus on it, it gets even harder to recall," I said.

"What do you remember?"

I tilted my head back against the wall and closed my eyes.

"There's a woman. It's like she's my mom, but she's not my mom. Does that make sense?"

"Dreams are like that all the time—you're in a house that you know is home, except it's not home. Stuff like that." Josh waved his hand for me to continue.

"It's weird because nothing really happens in the dream. It's boring stuff, but then I hear her scream and I feel this huge sense of dread." I shifted, feeling uncomfortable even saying it aloud. "It's not always a dream."

Josh's forehead crinkled in concern. "You hear it when you're awake?"

I almost didn't want to tell him. Even thinking about it made me antsy. "Yes. The time at the mall—I heard it then. Like, it's not a dream, more like something I'm remembering."

Josh let out a slow breath. "You should have told me sooner."

"Then there is one other weird thing. I smell things." I could see his eyebrow go up. "I smell barn smells. Hay, leather, stuff like that, but not when I'm at the barn. It happens at random times. Sometimes it smells like burning meat." I took a deep breath and was happy that the only thing I could smell now was the comfortable musty smell of books and a hint of the mint gum Josh was chewing.

Josh rubbed his chin while he thought. "The barn stuff could be connected to Harry. We know memories are coded in different parts of the brain and different things can bring about recall. How you might smell cookies baking and suddenly think about your grandmother. Maybe your brain is still struggling to remember Harry and it's triggering the smell center."

"Fair enough, but meat burning? Or hearing a woman scream?"

He shrugged. "That doesn't make sense. My best guess is that they're false memories. Sort of like a short circuit in your head. Your brain is connecting different things, and that mashup is popping up like a memory. It might be the procedure, or it could be because you've been upset. You said your trouble with sleep started before the procedure."

"A fake memory? You think I wouldn't remember what really happened to me?"

"The brain does all sorts of weird things. Having a fake memory isn't that unusual. It's nothing to worry about."

Easy for him to say. His brain wasn't the one short-circuiting. "You remember those protestors here at school?" I asked. "One of them came to my house. The guy who tried to help me up when I fell."

"What?" Josh's voice was loud. He lowered it as soon as he remembered we were in the library. "What was the guy doing at your house?"

"He saw me at the clinic and then when I passed out at the mall. He guessed that I had the treatment."

"Did you tell him anything?"

"No."

"Why is he stalking you and following you around town?" Josh's face was scrunched up in concern.

"I don't think he's stalking me. He said I'm the kind of girl people notice; he just happened to see me."

Josh snorted like the idea was absurd. My teeth clenched. I stared at the shelf of reference books across from me because if I looked at Josh I might snap. I needed to stay calm and rational. I didn't want him to dismiss what I was saying because I was too emotional.

"He brought me all this information on possible side effects from Memtex. Some people say it causes early Alzheimer's."

Josh laughed it off. "There are people who say it's responsible for everything from warts to seizures. People can say whatever they want, but there's no data to back it up. Memtex is one of the most researched products out there."

"Then what's causing my symptoms?" I felt slightly better that he was so sure it wasn't any big deal. Josh was obsessed with Neurotech; if there were anything to the rumors, he'd be all over it.

Josh shrugged. "Stress, maybe?"

"I wasn't stressed until all of this started happening," I pointed out.

"Not exactly. You were stressed when Harry died. You already admitted that you were having sleep problems before you ever had the procedure."

I hated that he used the word "admitted" like I'd confessed to a crime. "It's worse now," I said.

"Maybe we should talk to your dad. I'm not sure you should have canceled your doctor's appointment."

"No way." I turned his head so he was looking into my eyes. "I'm serious. I'm fine. I don't need to see anyone. Do not tell my dad."

Josh rolled his eyes. "At least tell him about the stalker."

"Neil's not a stalker," I huffed. Was it that hard to believe that some other guy had noticed me?

Josh cocked his head. "Neil? You're on a first-name basis with this guy? Don't you see? This is the kind of thing people like him do. They suck up to people. Act like they're doing you a favor, or that they like you. You can't trust this guy."

I felt a flash of annoyance. I had one overprotective dad. I didn't need another one in the form of my boyfriend. "I wasn't planning on having the guy move into my house. I met him, in a public place, so he could give me some information."

"I bet he has some angle," Josh said.

I was annoyed with how smug he was. "How's this for an angle? His brother died after taking Memtex."

Josh rolled his eyes again. "It makes for a good story."

"You think he made up a dead brother?" My voice came out clipped, but I felt a ripple of unease. I hadn't double-checked Neil's story. But could he make up something that detailed?

"I don't want to have a fight. I'm just pointing out that he could have told you anything he thought would get you to listen to him." He held up a hand to stop me from saying anything else. "Maybe he's telling the truth; there's no way for you to know. And it doesn't matter. What matters is what is going on for you. One thing I'm sure of is that you don't have early Alzheimer's." He took my hand and squeezed it. "I promise. My best guess is that everything you've experienced is some residual memory combined with stress because you were hiding it from your parents. I bet in a couple of weeks it clears up."

"Probably." I didn't feel nearly as certain as he did. My mind churned over what was going on.

"Trust me. Everything will work out." Josh winked. He stood and pulled me up, dismissing my concerns like they were nothing. "The bell's going to go off. I'll walk you to class."

I let him guide me down the hall. He talked about his exam in math, but I was only half listening. I'd been with Josh for so long that I often knew what he was going to say before he even said it. It wasn't that what he said was boring, just predictable. Sometimes I wanted him to say something that would surprise me, but I supposed the benefit of dating someone for a long time was that there weren't surprises.

We passed under the statue of Saint Jude, patron saint of lost things. I wondered if I should say a prayer to him to help me find my sanity. There was something I hadn't told anyone, something I was finding hard to put into words. Some of the things in my dreams, the fake memories as Josh called them—I didn't want them to go away.

chapter twelve

You know someone is a good friend if they are willing to help you shovel horse shit.

Win tossed a rake full of dirty straw and shavings into a wheelbarrow and then stopped to brush her hair out of her eyes. "I have no idea what doing stuff like this is supposed to teach a person. Parents talk a big game about how they're teaching us a lesson, but what the hell is the lesson supposed to be? That life is unfair? Most of us know that already."

I dumped another load into the wheelbarrow. My arms were already aching. "I have no idea." My parents had told me that being grounded wasn't punishment enough. In fairness, having to hang around our giant house—which had every electronic device known to man, spa bathrooms, a media room, and a sauna—wasn't exactly a real hardship. My dad wanted me to clean the bathrooms, but we already had a maid who came twice a week and did them. Wiping down already-clean counters wasn't rough. They called Laura and arranged for me to go to the barn and muck out the stalls. I think they thought that was an appropriate amount of shit for me to be dealing with. Win came with me, which was cutting the work in half and giving us a chance to hang out, since I was only allowed to go to school and the barn.

"It's a good thing I like your company," Win said. "The things I do to spend time with you."

I tossed her my water bottle. "I owe you one."

"One?" Win's perfectly tweezed eyebrow arched. "Oh, I think when we get into ruining-manicure territory, we're talking about more than one. We're talking a big favor here. If I need an organ, I expect you to cough up a kidney no questions asked."

"Any organ I'm not using is all yours."

"And I want a chance to ride your new horse when you get it." Win hefted a bag of shavings over her shoulder and started to spread them around.

"*If* I ever get another horse," I said.

"Your dad will back down. He loves telling people about his future Olympian. If he can't brag, how will everyone know how fabulous he is?"

"He's not like that." He was exactly like that, but it bothered me when other people noticed.

Win paused to wipe her brow. "You don't have to defend him all the time."

"I don't."

"Parents are supposed to be annoying. It's their job." She waved off whatever I was about to say. "You think about what kind of horse you might get? Vanners are nice."

"And cost about twenty thousand."

Win shrugged like it wasn't a big deal. "Insurance should cover some of it. How much did your dad have on Harry?"

"I don't know." I pushed the wheelbarrow out to the back of the barn and dumped the dirty hay and came back in to hang up my rake. "I'm guessing now isn't the best time to ask him either. I'm doing my best to fly under the radar until all of this blows over."

"Laura would have a copy of any insurance policies in her office," Win said.

A flutter of excitement rippled through my stomach. "Think she would let us see them?"

Win cocked her hip. "Never ask permission when there's a chance they'll say no. Much easier to apologize later." She headed over to Laura's office.

I trailed after her, my rubber Wellington boots squeaking on the floor. "I'm not sure this is a good idea. Adding breaking and entering to my crimes isn't going to get me off my parents' shit list anytime soon."

Win turned the knob. The door clicked open. "Look! No

breaking required. It's unlocked." She paused in the doorway. "Honestly, would Laura care we were in her office? If you were coming in here to use the phone or grab a bridle, would you even think about it?"

"No," I hedged.

"There you go." Win slipped inside.

I looked around to make sure none of the grooms were near and followed her. Laura's office might have been in a barn, but it looked like it could have been a fancy library in a British estate. The back wall was floor-to-ceiling bookcases stuffed with everything from books about various horse breeds to the mystery novels she liked to read. Her desk was an antique rolltop, one of those ones with all the little cubbyholes for papers. Next to the desk were two modern metal file cabinets that looked out of place.

Win was already kneeling by the desk and sliding open one of the file cabinet drawers.

"I'm not sure we should go through her stuff." I hovered near the door.

"I'm not planning to read her diary. It's not like she's going to keep a list of her sexual history out here. All of this is stuff related to the stable. Besides, we're looking for paperwork on your horse. Technically, they're your records."

I had a sinking feeling that if Laura came around the corner and saw us elbow deep in her things, she wasn't going to see it that way. Win shut one drawer and moved on to the other cabinet. Her fingers ran quickly over the tabs, her bright red nails flashing. She pulled out a folder and held it aloft.

"Bingo." She plopped the file on the desk and I stood next to her. The folder had Harry's official name, Hermes of Caelum, on it. Win flipped past copies of the invoices for his boarding and farrier bills. There was a copy of his original registration papers, and in the back of the stack was the insurance sheet.

Win whistled. "Girl, you can get yourself a fine horse."

I saw the insurance amount, but something else caught my eye. I pointed at it. "Hey, check that out."

Win shrugged. "So?"

"It's the date that we took ownership, but that's the year before I was born."

Win shot me a look. "I thought you got the horse for your sixth birthday."

"I did." I stared at the page as if I expected the numbers on it to change. It didn't make sense. I remembered getting Harry. I remembered every bit of it. Neither of my parents were interested in horses; why would they have bought one for themselves? Why would they have kept a horse hidden until my sixth birthday? I was all for a birthday surprise, but planning one before someone was even born seemed a bit excessive.

"We should go," Win said, suddenly sounding nervous. She went to sweep the papers back in the folder.

"Hang on." I whipped out my phone and took a couple

of photos of the page before sliding it into the folder and then shutting the file cabinet with a click.

Win stuck her head out to make sure the coast was clear. We left, pulling Laura's office door closed behind us. We went up to the empty lounge that overlooked the indoor arena, and Win fired up the cappuccino machine. "Well, that was weird," Win said, summarizing my feelings. "What are you going to do with the pictures? Very spy thriller to think of taking them, by the way. You know I love it when you're all sneaky."

"I don't know. I wanted a copy." I didn't tell her the first thought that had come into my head: If something happened later and the file disappeared, I wanted proof. I sounded paranoid. I leaned back on the leather sofa and tried to relax. The lounge at Hampton Mews was better than most people had in their home. Money can't buy everything, but it can make a barn into a palace. An image of the date kept flashing in my head. "It doesn't make sense, does it?"

Win watched out the window to the arena below. A group of young kids were practicing cantering in a circle. "Not really. Could be one of those things where once you know the answer it will make perfect sense. Might be a simple typo or something."

"Maybe." I watched the horses run around in the paddock below. Win didn't like conflict. If she could believe in an easy answer, she would. "Lately it feels like a lot of stuff's not making sense in my life."

"The false memory thing?" Win asked. I'd told her Josh's theory about what I was experiencing. I'd even looked it up. He wasn't wrong about the brain screwing with a person. Memory was pretty fluid. I read one study that talked about the weakness with eyewitness testimony. If people saw a robbery and then were asked to pick who they saw out of a lineup later, their minds would replace the image of who they saw with the person in the lineup. Even if later they saw the real criminal, they wouldn't recognize him. The other story that freaked me out had to do with how other people could mess with your memory. They'd done this study where they had people tell a family member a totally made-up memory: *Remember when you got lost at the mall and fell into the fountain?* The person would at first say they didn't remember it. Then the family member would add more details: *You must remember. You were wearing that red coat. The one with the buttons shaped like little boats.* The subject would then start remembering the situation, even though it had never happened. Even after they were told it was a fake memory, most of them would argue, saying that it couldn't be fake—they remembered it too clearly. What I'd learned from my research so far was that the brain was a weird thing and not to be trusted.

Of course, if you can't trust your own memory, you're sort of screwed. That pretty much summed up my life at the moment.

"This would be when I should admit you were right; I

shouldn't have had the procedure," I said to Win. "All I wanted was to stop feeling so lousy about Harry, and now everything is a million times worse."

Win sighed. "I think it started with Harry, but that wasn't all," she said. "Don't get me wrong; I got why you were upset. Harry was an awesome horse." Her voice trailed off.

"But," I said.

"But you seemed over-the-top upset. There was something not right about it. Off."

"I had Harry since I was a little girl." I felt the need to justify how I had acted, even though I was uncomfortable with it myself.

"Apparently, you had him since before you were born. And even if what you remember is right, isn't that weird? To get a Hanoverian for a six-year-old? They're huge. It's not exactly a starter horse. I always thought that was strange."

I felt the fight ooze out of me. I didn't know what to think anymore. I could try to debate it or try to understand it. "What do you mean about me acting off?"

"Like I said, I expected you to be sad—it was an awful thing, and I know you really loved him—but I still thought you would act like you."

I rubbed my head. "What do you mean, I should have acted like me?"

"Positive. Trying to find something good out of the situation."

I sighed. "God, I must be annoying." I flashed on an image of one of those Disney princesses singing a fa-la-la-la song to a bunch of chipmunks, completely oblivious to the fact that someone is trying to slip her a poisoned apple.

Win smiled. "Sure, you're irritating sometimes, but on the whole I like you that way. You do things. You don't sit back. You're always looking for a way to turn a situation around, to make something positive out of something shitty. I thought you'd use what happened to Harry as motivation to raise money for the SPCA in his memory or become a vet so you could find a cure for colic. That's more your typical MO."

Her words felt like a blow. As soon as she said them, I knew she was right. It was almost as if I could step outside myself and see an alternate path. One where I responded to Harry's death by making it matter instead of sitting back and doing nothing. Donating money to a camp that helped disabled kids learn to ride, or to stop animal abuse. "Something's wrong with me."

Win was quiet for a second. "I think you might be right. The question is, what's next?"

I jumped off the stool. "I figure this out and find a way to make it better. After all, that's what I do."

chapter thirteen

They say there's no place like home, but anyone who says that has clearly not seen my hometown. I was born in a small town. It's close to Washington State University in the southeast part of the state. My dad went to school there, and for the first few years after graduation he worked in their research labs. Our family moved to Seattle not long after he founded Neurotech, just before I turned ten. I couldn't remember us ever going back to visit. We didn't have any family in the area, and now that I was driving into town, I realized why we didn't stop by just for the heck of it. The place looked boring with a capital *B*. I could have checked most things on the Internet or by calling around, but I'd hoped that if I went there in person, I would have some flash of insight, shake something free in my brain.

My only insight so far was that this town was clearly where run-down strip malls went to die. On each side of the road there were clusters of stores: payday loans, dollar stores, shoe outlets, and every fast-food emporium known to man. The kind of place where the hair salons have those annoying names like the Kwick Klip and Wild Hair. Everything looked washed out. The snow had melted a few weeks ago and mud was everywhere. Not much looked familiar, although when I passed the Dairy Queen I had a memory flash of going there as a kid for ice cream cones dipped in the waxy chocolate.

I turned off the main road. I really hoped this five-hour drive wasn't going to be a huge waste of time. I didn't mind the long drive—I was used to going a long way for a horse shows—but I didn't want this to be pointless. As far as my parents knew, I was staying at Win's for the night, while in reality I was driving back and forth across the state. I'd just been taken off my official grounded status. Technically I was still on parole, and I was already lying again.

I glanced down at the passenger seat and the handwritten directions. Win had loaned me her SUV, and for the life of me I couldn't figure out her GPS. Her car had more gadgets than seemed possible. If a rocket launcher had popped up from the roof, it wouldn't have surprised me at all. I couldn't even figure out the radio. It kept randomly skipping stations. I didn't like driving Win's SUV. It felt too much like trying to control a school bus.

I didn't have my own car. I'd been promised one for graduation, but until then my parents felt I could use theirs. It wasn't like there weren't enough to choose from. My dad had three cars. There was a restored two-seater 1960s Aston Martin sports car that he only took out on sunny days. Most of the time it sat in our garage, where he could go out and buff it with a soft cloth. It was his "I'm James Bond" fantasy car. He had a BMW sedan that he drove most days, and a big SUV that he drove when the weather was bad. He said we needed the SUV in case we ever needed to move or haul things. My mom didn't even bring up the fact that we weren't the type to move or haul things ourselves. If we bought something large, we would pay to have it delivered. She just smiled and rolled her eyes when he brought it home. The thing drank gas like it was its own mini environment-destroying machine. My mom had a Lexus, which I drove most of the time if I needed a car. The problem was there was no way she wouldn't notice me putting a spare six hundred miles on it. Thus I was stuck trying to maneuver Win's giant luxury SUV on this road trip.

I cruised past a church, and another memory clicked into place. We used to go there. I could remember shifting in the pew, my butt growing numb from sitting on the hard wood, and how I wanted to go home where I could watch cartoons on TV. We didn't really attend church much anymore. Sometimes at Christmas we'd go, but that was it. I couldn't remember when we'd stopped going on a regular basis.

I coasted to a stop in front of the elementary school. I got out and walked around the squat one-story building. There was no one around on a Saturday. I cupped my hand to the glass and peered in the windows of a classroom. Around the tops of the walls the teacher had hung brightly colored letters and numbers. They'd cut out tulips from construction paper and taped them along the rail to the whiteboard. There weren't any desks, just large tables with itsy-bitsy chairs pulled up around them. It seemed impossible that I'd ever been that small. I strolled around to the side of the building. The playground was covered in a thick carpet of wet pine needles from the giant trees that ringed the outside. There was a row of swing sets and a climbing gym shaped like a pirate ship.

I sat on the swing and pushed off and tried to remember what I could. The school was familiar. I had a flash of walking down the hall to the cafeteria, jumping between the black and white checked tiles. My second-grade teacher was Ms. Klee. Someone in my class had spilled water on my art project, and when I cried, Ms. Klee let me be the leader of the line for the whole week. I'd broken my arm in this playground. I'd been standing on the swing, and when I jumped off, my pants got snagged in the chain, and I fell face-first and broke the fall by sticking my arm out. My memories felt almost like photographs, short images, some bright and clear, others distant and fuzzy. Some disappeared entirely the moment I tried to focus on them. There were also big black holes. I could remember breaking my arm, but when I tried to remember Mom taking me to the hospital, there was nothing. I remembered Ms. Klee being nice to me, but I couldn't even remember who my teacher was in fourth grade.

Win described her memories like a bread-crumb trail. One memory would jog another and that would lead to another until they started to string together into a longer story. My memories were more solo. If they had ever been connected, the string that held them together had dissolved long ago. Win also seemed to remember more about when she was young. We couldn't decide if that was because she had a better memory, because she'd had a more interesting childhood, or if there was something off about me.

I walked back to the car. Seeing the school hadn't knocked anything useful free; maybe my childhood home would. Our house wasn't far from the school. I drove there without having to look at the map; there was some memory at least. I parked across the street and stared at our old home. Clearly, things in our lives had changed a lot since my dad started his own company. The house was even smaller than I remembered. We could fit it three or four times over into our current place. It was a small brick bungalow that looked like it must have been built a long time ago. The whole neighborhood was full of old houses. There was a bike lying on its side in the driveway. A group of kids a few houses down were running around in the front yard playing some version of football, or possibly trying to kill one another. It looked like a regular neighborhood, one that screamed "average America" and got used in political commercials during election years.

I stared at the house, waiting for something to happen. Nothing. There were a few more snapshot memories. We used to have the Christmas tree right in the front window. My bedroom had pink curtains, and I didn't like them; they were too girly. I wanted something more grown-up. In the kitchen there was a built-in alcove with benches for the table. I could picture the layout of the rooms and how at Halloween we kept a giant wooden bowl filled with the candy on a small marble table by the front door. I could remember a birthday party with clown cones from Baskin-Robbins. My best friend had been a girl named Nicole. She'd convinced me we could camp out in the backyard during the summer, but we'd gotten scared and run inside before midnight. I remembered the house was a collection of odds and ends. Not like now, where my mom bought furniture by the roomload, designed to go together. Back then our idea of design was just having things that were mostly clean.

I'd really hoped that seeing my hometown would make a difference, but I had no more information than I'd had before I came. I had one last stop before I was going to need to turn around and head back to Win's place. It was my last chance to figure something out. I had no memory of where we'd stabled Harry when I was little. There was only one large stable that advertised it was available for boarding, but in this area there would be a lot of farms that would have taken in private boarders. If we hadn't kept Harry at the big stable, I had no idea how I'd find out what private barn we'd used. I crossed fingers I'd get lucky.

Rolling Meadows was at the end of a long road. A road that had last been repaved some time around the Revolutionary War, based on the giant potholes that were large enough to nearly eat Win's SUV. The front paddock had a group lesson going on, with four young riders trotting in a circle around the instructor. I watched them for a few minutes before going inside.

An older woman polishing a saddle looked up. "Can I help you?"

"I think I used to used to board my horse here, and I wondered if you might have the old records," I said.

She stood up and brushed her hands off on her jeans. "How long ago?"

"I'm not sure when we started." I didn't add that the whole reason I wanted to see the records was to check the dates. "We moved the horse eight years ago."

She shook her head. "'Fraid you're outta luck then. We shred records after seven years."

"Maybe you remember him? His name was Hermes of Caelum, but we called him Harry."

"Sorry. I've only been here a few years."

My hopes fell to the floor in a limp heap. I'd been sure that if I saw things from my childhood again, memories would fall into place, or there would be a big "aha!" moment, but the trip had been for nothing. "Okay, thanks."

She snapped her fingers. "Hey, you should check with Juan. He's been here forever. He might remember."

A jolt of adrenaline hit my system. "Where do I find him?" If she told me he was on vacation, I was going to start screaming. My emotions couldn't handle much more of the roller coaster.

She jerked her head toward the door. "He's out back working with one of the colts."

I spotted him right away as soon as I stepped outside. He had a young horse on a lunge lead. The horse would start to rear, and then Juan would lean forward and make a soft clucking noise in the horse's face. He might have been in his fifties, or he could have been a hundred and ten. His skin was as worn as an old saddle left outside for a few summers.

He saw me standing there and nodded to let me know he'd be with me when he could. I watched, impressed. He had the touch. A regular horse whisperer. You could see the horse responding to his slightest movement. He circled the horse a few more times before he slipped the bridle off and stroked its nose. Juan whacked the horse on the side and let it run loose.

"Pretty horse," I said, leaning over the fence.

"They're all pretty. Just sometimes it's easier to see." He smiled, his teeth flashing white in contrast to his dark skin.

"Some wear it on the outside, some on the inside. The really blessed have it both in and out."

"I'm looking for information about a horse that might have been boarded here years ago. Hermes of—"

"Harry." He kicked a clot of dirt with his boot.

My heart lurched. "You remember him?"

"Hard to forget him. He's a beauty."

My eyes filled with tears, surprising me. I'd thought the feelings were gone. "He died."

Juan pulled off his gloves and wiped the sweat off his face. "Sorry."

I liked that he didn't say anything else. He just let me be sad. I quickly rubbed my eyes to clear them. "I was hoping to fill in some blanks about when he was young. Do you happen to know how long he boarded here?"

He shrugged. "Jeez, hard to say. I'm not much for keeping a calendar. It was a long time ago."

"What do you remember about him?"

Juan paused. I appreciated that he was thinking about it. He wasn't giving me a flip answer. "Spirited. Loved to jump, that horse. You can train just about any horse to show, but some of 'em, some of 'em love it. You can see it."

I smiled. Harry had loved it.

"You're the little girl, ain't ya?"

I jerked and he laughed.

"Not that hard to figure out. You got the same smile. I

remember you on that horse even when you was a wee bitty thing."

"Do you recall when I got the horse? Was it for my sixth birthday?" I held my breath, waiting for him to answer. I wasn't sure which way I wanted him to answer—confirming what I'd always known or opening up a whole new option that was starting to seem more and more real.

He burst out with a laugh. "Sixth birthday? Where'd you get that idea? Child, you were riding that horse when you were still in your mama. I used to tease her that she was going to push you out into the world while in the saddle."

"My mom?" I was confused. She hated horses.

"One of the best horsewomen I ever met. When you was a baby, she would put you in one of those baby slings around her chest and trot around the ring with you on the horse. We joked that you were going to ride before you walked, and that was pretty much true."

I strained to make sense of it. My mom had zero interest in horses. I couldn't remember her ever riding. She didn't even like to be around the barn when I was there, let alone on a horse. She'd always maintained she was scared of them, and she sure acted afraid. She backed away quickly when Harry got too close, like she thought he was going to chase after her. And why did I remember getting Harry for my birthday if he'd been around since before I was born?

"You okay?"

I looked up, almost surprised to see Juan still there. "Yeah. I'm okay." It was a lie, but there wasn't anything else I could say.

"Wish I could be more help. Anything else I can tell you?" He rested his boot on the fence rail, but I could see him glance quickly at the colt. He had work to do.

I shook my head no and thanked him for his time. There's no right way to ask someone what's wrong with you. And even if I did ask, he wasn't going to have any answers, but I had a hunch who might.

chapter fourteen

I drove back across the state as fast as I could without risking a ticket. I didn't even stop for dinner and instead wolfed down a chicken sandwich from a fast food joint while driving. I stopped outside town and did a quick search on my phone to get the exact address. I drummed my fingers on the steering wheel. This was a bad idea. I should wait until morning, but I didn't want to. I texted Win to let her know what I was doing and that I would be later getting back to her place than planned. I ignored her return text telling me that what I was about to do was stupid and to call her first. I turned the phone off so I didn't have to listen to it buzz.

The address I found online led me to the apartment building Neil had mentioned. It used to be a hotel. One of those cheap motels where you park in front of your room and at the end of the hall there's a vending machine with stale candy bars and cold soda. It had been redone to offer low-cost housing a few years ago. I knew a lot of college students and arty types lived there. I spotted Neil's beat-up car in front of one of the units and knocked on the door before I could lose my nerve.

"'Bout time you got here." The door flung open. Neil stared at me in surprise.

"I didn't know I was late," I said.

He blinked, staring silently at me for a second. "Sorry. I thought you were one of my friends. He's supposed to bring back subs." He looked past me as if he thought someone behind me might be sneaking up with sandwiches. "How did you find me?"

"That day you came by my house. You told me you lived here." He stared at me as if he was somewhat shocked I'd remembered. Music was blaring inside the apartment. "I should have called first. I wasn't even sure you'd be home." I hadn't called on purpose. I was afraid he might not want to see me, or that he would put me off. I had to see him now before I lost my nerve. "I wanted to ask you a few things."

"Sure, c'mon in. Welcome to my castle." He turned off the music. "Castle" might have been overstating things. It was highly unlikely Neil's apartment was going to show up in a design magazine, unless it was as a "before" picture. He crossed in front of me and swept a pile of stuff off the sofa and dumped it in the open door of the bedroom. The apartment was small, and the carpet felt almost spongy under my feet. There wasn't even a separate kitchen. The living room had a counter along the back with a small fridge and a two-burner stove. He wasn't going to be making Thanksgiving dinner in this place.

"Can I get you something to drink?" Neil opened the fridge. "I've got water and orange juice." He pulled the carton of juice out and sniffed it. His face recoiled, and he dumped it in the sink. "Scratch the juice option. I can make coffee."

"Water's fine."

Neil grabbed a glass off the shelf and looked it over. It must not have met inspection, because he grabbed another one. He filled it up and passed it to me and motioned for me to have a seat on the sofa.

I sat down and nearly spilled the water as I sank to the floor. I was willing to bet this sofa had been a "free for the taking" find on a corner. I wasn't even sure it had any functioning springs left. Neil sat on the only other seat in the room, his desk chair.

"I hope I'm not busting up your Saturday night plans." Now that I was here, I wasn't sure how to start the conversation.

"Nah. I'm just writing letters. If my friend ever shows up, we're going to watch a movie."

"You're writing letters?" My voice must have echoed my disbelief, because he held up a sheet of paper on the desk as proof.

"Letter, you know, retro communication. It's to my sister."

"Doesn't she have a computer? Or a phone?"

Neil laughed. "You should see your face. It's like I told

120

you there was no bathroom here and we use an outhouse."

"Please tell me there's a bathroom," I said.

"Yes, there's a bathroom, and yes, my sister has both a computer and a phone." Neil leaned back against the desk. "The thing with letters is that they take effort. You can fire off an e-mail in a minute and a text in less than that. You don't even have to think about it. I want my sister to know I spent some time. Besides, who doesn't like getting something in the mail?"

I tried to remember the last time anyone had written me a letter and drew a blank.

"I also don't like to have all my communication tracked," he added. "That's why I ask people to memorize my number versus putting it in their phones."

My eyebrows went up.

"You know the government scans e-mail and phone traffic, right? Not to mention how your computer is tracking everything, from what sites you surf to what you buy online. They have huge profiles and data files on everyone."

"So?"

Neil looked like the top of his head was about to lift off. "So? Are you comfortable with companies tracking all of that stuff? They know where you are. They can predict things about you. Did you hear about the case with Target?"

I shook my head no.

"Along with most stores, they track everything you buy. They use those purchases to make predictions about what you might want to buy next and then send you coupons." He paused to make sure I was following him. "So they send this one fifteen-year-old girl coupons for baby stuff. They realize that her buying patterns match those of someone who is expecting. Her dad flips his lid. How dare the company make this assumption? Then it comes out that his daughter is pregnant. She hadn't told her parents yet. Target figured it out before they did." He leaned back in his chair. "Tell me you think that's creepy."

"Sure, it's weird, but that's part of life now."

"Speak for yourself. That's why I don't have an e-mail account except at school, no cell phone, and I pay cash whenever I can. I'm off grid as much as possible."

His approach seemed a bit over-the-top conspiracy theory to me, but you can't show up at someone's house and insult him. Especially if you're planning to ask him to do you a favor. It was sort of neat that he was so passionate about something. I could tell it mattered to him. "The whole low-tech thing makes you very hipster. Trendsetting," I said.

He dropped the serious expression. "Fine. You come by just to mock me, or is this turnabout because I showed up at your house?"

The smile on my face disappeared. It was like I'd almost forgotten why I'd come, but it came rushing back. "I wanted to ask you about what you know about Neurotech."

Neil cocked his head. "Don't get me wrong, I'm happy you stopped by, but I would think if you wanted info on Neurotech, your dad would be the go-to person."

I ignored his comment and pressed forward. "You've done a lot of research about the company and the side effects. Has anyone reported having new memories?"

"New memories?"

I shifted on the sofa. "Not really new. Recovered. Things they had forgotten that were sort of shaken free."

Neil stared at me. "Why are you asking?"

"I'm just curious." I shoved my hair behind my ears and hoped I looked casual. Times like this I wish I had longer hair I could hide behind.

"What memories are you having?" He leaned forward, his elbows on his knees.

"I'm not having any memories." My jaw clenched. "I shouldn't have come. I knew you'd try to twist this around."

Neil pulled his chair closer to the sofa. "Easy. You're not the one having memories. My mistake. Go on. Tell me about this other person's problem. Your friend of a friend."

I pulled on my hair. I know he didn't believe me, but it made me feel better that he was willing to play along. "Have you heard of it happening to anyone?"

"No. You checked the official side effects of the treatment before you had it, right?"

I hadn't looked at anything. There were forms that detailed the side effects that I'd initialed before I went in, but I hadn't read them. No one read those things. It was like when you went onto a website—who read the user agreement? No one. "Maybe you could remind me," I suggested.

Neil sighed. "Okay, as I'm sure you recall, the most common side effects of the treatment that Neurotech admits to are headaches, dizziness, and difficulty with sleeping. There are also a statistically significant number of people who find the treatment doesn't have the impact they wanted. They're still having an emotional reaction to whatever they went in to have blasted out."

"That doesn't happen to that many people," I said, interrupting him.

"Not many," he admitted. "But it happens enough that there are research numbers behind it. The big unknown is people having a really bad side effect. Early Alzheimer's."

"I looked at the research you gave me," I said. "We're talking about a small number of people who are reporting that as a possible side effect. Really small. And even with that group, they don't know that some of them even have Alzheimer's for sure."

Neil leaned back in his chair and put his feet up on the sofa next to me. "True, but if the treatment causes this in only less than one percent, don't people still have a right to know that? That they're risking losing it all? Sure, if they're trying to block something huge, war memories or having been attacked, something really bad, they might still do it, but if they're trying to get over a breakup? Maybe not."

I chewed my lip. I wanted to disagree with him, but I couldn't. He was being too reasonable.

"To get back to your original question, I haven't heard of anyone reporting having recovered memories, but it doesn't mean it hasn't happened. The brain is a weird thing; there's a lot science doesn't understand about how it works. Then you factor in that Neurotech spends a lot of money to make sure that people reporting negative side effects are hushed up."

"That isn't fair. It took a lot of money to bring the procedure to market; you can't blame the company for protecting their investment." My voice came out clipped and short.

Neil stared at me. "Is there a reason you're pissed at me for answering your question?"

"I'm not pissed." I went to stand, but the sofa had me sucked to the floor like it was a worn corduroy black hole, so I swam around before I could get to my feet. I shouldn't have come here for help. I'd thought because he'd researched the company he might know something or have a fresh outlook on things, but this was a mistake. Neil reached to help me, but moved back when I shot him a look.

"Just for clarity, assuming we spend more time around each other, if this isn't you being pissed, what would you call it?" He smiled, and I felt irritated that he could joke about it.

"We're not spending time together. I have a boyfriend, Josh." I felt flustered, which annoyed me even more. "I came over to ask a question, not hang out."

"Would that be the question that didn't make you pissed when I answered it?" He held up a hand before I said anything else. "Sorry, I couldn't resist. You're cute when you get riled up and bust loose. It's like I get to see the real you."

I flushed. "There isn't a fake me."

Neil cocked his head to the side as if he were trying to get a different perspective. "I get the feeling there's a lot more to you than people would think. You're not some society, popular, empty-headed Barbie doll."

I grabbed my bag off the floor. "Wow. Am I supposed to thank you for that?" I shoved away the feeling that there was a part of me that was pleased with what he said. If I considered someone telling me I wasn't empty-headed to be a compliment, I needed to up my game.

Neil stood. "Hey, I'm sorry. I didn't mean to tick you off. I was just teasing. I'm bad at the whole communication thing, so I joke around. Total defense reaction. I don't care why you came over; I'm glad you did."

"Why? No one else around for you to make fun of?"

"No, that's not what I meant." Neil's feet shuffled on the threadbare carpet.

"Well, sorry to disappoint you, but hanging around to be your joke isn't my idea of a good time." I stuck my chin in the air.

His face was serious. "You're not a joke. Not to me. You might be the most interesting thing to happen to me in a long time." Neil took a step closer. My heart thundered in my chest. Part of my brain was screaming for me to back away, but another part wanted to see what would happen next. He started to lean forward, when suddenly there was a pounding at the door. It sounded like a SWAT team trying to break it down.

The door flew open, and a lanky Asian guy practically fell into the room, holding a bag from Subway above his head like the sword Excalibur. "I have brought sustenance!"

Neil and I took a quick step apart. The Asian guy's eyes widened. "Whoa. Sorry about that. Didn't think anyone else was here. I mean, what are the odds he'd have a girl over? Didn't mean to interrupt anything."

"You weren't interrupting anything. I was just leaving." I moved toward the door.

"Trey, meet Harper. Harper, this is my friend Trey. You can usually recognize him by his love for fantasy novels and his complete lack of personal boundary space and inability to wait to be let in someplace."

Trey held out his hand. "Greetings, fair maiden."

I stared at him, at a loss for what to say. Was he about to start quoting from a *Lord of the Rings* movie or something?

"Sorry, channeling my inner geek. Nice to meet you." He smiled and gave a short bow.

I pushed myself to smile back. "You too. I have to go."

"Don't leave on my account," Trey said. "I'd even share my sub with you. Unlike this guy, I don't get those nasty pickled pepper things on mine."

"Pickled peppers elevate the sub to something more than fast food," Neil said.

Trey made a face at me. "I grew up eating chicken feet on Sunday at my grandmother's, and even I know pickled peppers are disgusting on a ham-and-cheese sub."

I giggled. Trey looked proud of himself for getting a laugh out of me.

"We're going to watch a movie. Stay," Trey said.

"I can't. I need to go." Part of me wanted him to convince me to hang out, and another part of me wanted to escape.

"Come by again. Anytime. Not just if you have a question about Neurotech," Neil said.

Trey's eyebrows shot up and he glanced at me, and then back at Neil. "Is she . . . ?" Neil's look froze him midsentence.

I stared at Neil and Trey, but neither of them said anything. I could feel my face getting red. "Well, thanks for seeing me," I said.

"Now that you know where I live, don't be a stranger," Neil said.

I smiled stiffly, hoping that my expression communicated that I didn't have any plans to show up here ever again. I'd come because he was the only one I could think of who might have the answers I needed. I was glad he hadn't tried to kiss me. I shut the door behind me. I told myself that I didn't care what Trey had meant by the "Is she . . ." comment. I didn't care if Neil had been talking about me to his friend. It didn't matter what he said.

I didn't care. Much.

chapter fifteen

Win's mom opened the door. She looked like she could
have been walking down Fifth Avenue in New York
instead of having a Saturday night at home. She was wearing
fitted black pants and a white blouse that looked so crisp it
seemed you could grate cheese on the pressed seams. If I'd been
wearing that shirt, it would have been all rumpled from the
day and most likely would have had something spilled down
the front.

"Winifred, Harper's here." I loved Win's mom's accent.
When she said my name, it sounded like "Hopper." It was like
having the Queen of England announce you.

Win stood at the top of their giant staircase and waved me up.

"Hey, Bryne. Good to see you." Win's dad came out of the
kitchen holding a bottle of beer, which looked impossibly small

in his grasp. His hands were the size of baseball catchers' mitts. He called everyone by their last name. Win said it was a sports thing. It was your last name or some weird nickname.

"You girls want to watch some baseball?" Win's dad had a giant projection-screen TV and a cable package that ensured he never missed a single sporting event anywhere in the world. Including things like darts and lawn bowling that no one else watched.

Win's mom gave a dismissive sniff and walked past him. He followed her out of the room without waiting to see if we were interested in the game or not.

"What's up with that?" I asked Win at the top of the stairs as I followed her back to her room.

"They're fighting again. My dad found a suspicious e-mail from some guy that goes to my mom's gym." Win tried to sound bored and disinterested, but I could sense the tension.

"Do you think the e-mail means she's cheating?" I asked. I really hoped her mom wouldn't be that stupid, but it wouldn't have been the first time.

Win shrugged. "Why they fight about it anymore is a mystery to me. He had to know it would happen again. It's apparently impossible for her to hang around a guy unless he's chasing her. She lives for attention. Why bother being mad about it if you're not willing to do anything? I'm sick of them having the same fight. You'd think they'd be tired of it too. I wish someone would tell them that I'm the one who is supposed to have all the drama in my life. They're supposed to be the boring parents."

I sprawled across Win's bed. Her room was bigger than Neil's entire apartment. She sat at her desk, her legs folded under her and her braids tied up in a silk scarf. I told her about my trip and my talk with Neil. One of the things I liked best about Win was that when it was important, she really listened. She didn't listen with only one ear while planning what she'd say next. She gave the other person her full focus. As soon as I stopped talking, she turned to face her computer.

"The guy wasn't joking about being off grid." Win clicked through several screens. "He's not on any social media sites, no blog, and has zero Google presence. It's like he's in the witness protection program or something. The only thing I can find on him is a picture on his college's website. His name is listed in a photograph of the school's social justice program." She squinted at the screen. "He's kinda cute in a naughty rebel way. I didn't notice when he was outside the school."

I blushed. "I don't care that he's cute."

Win rolled her eyes. "Sure."

"I don't," I protested, although I was happy Win thought he was good-looking.

"Fine. You're above all of that. I, on the other hand, am a shallow bitch and can't help but notice that he's easy on the eyes." She pursed her lips in a kissing motion at the screen. "I love me a naughty boy."

"Hold your hormones back for a moment and focus. What do you think about what he said?"

Win spun her desk chair so she was facing me and propped her feet up on the mahogany hope chest. "Which part?"

"Do you think people are tracking everything we do online?"

"Sure. Our phones have GPS. Your parents can download an app that will tell them wherever you, and your phone, happen to be. Companies are tracking all sorts of things. I mean, tell me you don't think it's random that when you go online you get ads for shoes and horse equipment instead of bladder control devices and support hose? They track what you click on. They probably know more about you than I do. The real question is if it matters."

I sighed. "Does it bug you? The idea that people are spying on you? Manipulating what they know to sell stuff?"

"Sure, but it doesn't bother me as much as not having access to my phone." She shrugged. "Part of life."

"I don't like it," I said.

"How do you feel about the part where there's something dodgy about Harry?" Win asked. "Either the groom you met up with is lying or delusional, or your memory is seriously screwed up."

"I don't think the groom is delusional. He knew Harry; he's not confused."

"Is it possible your parents had Harry for years and you were wrong about getting him for your birthday?"

I rolled over so I could face her. "But I do remember it. I can picture it in my head perfectly."

"Do you? Or is it a story that everyone's told you so often it feels like a memory? My parents have told the story a thousand times about how when I was just three I stripped naked at my grandmother's garden party in front of Princess Anne, who was there. I've heard that story so often it's almost like I can remember it. That it was hot, that I didn't like the itchy dress, stuff like that, but I don't know if I really remember it or not. Maybe someone told you that story and eventually it felt like it was real."

I tossed one of her throw pillows in the air and caught it while I thought it over. "Could be. Of course, there's still a problem—either I have a totally false memory in my head or someone told me a story enough times to make me think it's a memory. Either way it's pretty messed up."

"Not a random someone. Your parents would have to have been involved; otherwise they would have told you that never happened." Win's face was serious. "Do you want to fool around with this? Do you really want to know?"

I sat up. "You think I should ignore it? Just pretend everything's fine?"

"Almost everything *is* fine. We're talking about stuff that happened when you were a kid. And not really important stuff. Does it matter if your parents had Harry before you were born or got him when you were six?"

My mouth opened to protest and then shut with a click.

Did it matter? The fact that I had a false memory seemed like it should be a big deal, but maybe I should ignore the whole thing. "Why would they lie about it?"

Win scoffed. "Who knows why parents do half the shit they do? They may have a good reason, or something they thought was a good reason at the time."

I thought about what she said. "What if this isn't the only thing they lied about?"

Win crossed the room and flopped down next to me on the bed. "Don't take this the wrong way, okay?"

It's been my experience that no good conversation has ever started that with that line. It's what people say right before they insult you, but you have to take it because you already promised not to get mad. I waved for her to continue.

"Life has all sorts of nasty bits. Things we don't want to think about. Things we wish didn't exist."

"I know that," I huffed.

"You know it, but you don't *know* it. Look, you get that there is still racism, but you've never been followed around in a store just because you're black. You can say it's a horrible thing, but you can forget about it sometimes."

I opened my mouth to argue.

"It happens to me. Even if I want to ignore it, I can't. It doesn't matter how I dress, or talk, or the fact I've got my dad's platinum card in my purse. To those people I'm just some black girl in their store. There are people who hate other people because they're gay. They don't know them. Don't want to know them. They prefer not to, because if they took the time to get to know those people, they might have to confront the fact that they're bigoted assbags. You and I can think it's horrible, but somebody like Andrew Shield? He has to know it. He has to think before he goes out that if he looks too flaming, he runs the risk of someone beating him up."

I swallowed down a wave of nausea. Andrew was one of the few people in our school who was openly out. He'd transferred to our school because he'd been beaten up in the bathroom at his old school. The first few weeks he'd had a black eye and stitches in his lip. No one said anything about it. We acted like we didn't notice, because it seemed like the most polite thing to do.

"Andrew knows there's hate. He has to factor that knowledge into everything he does. He can't just hold hands with his boyfriend without wondering what kind of trouble that might cause. That's different from you and me being aware that it happens. Personal knowledge is different. It changes how you do things. How you see the world. There's all kind of ugly in this world, but when you see it up close, once it happens to you— you have to deal with it. You can't ignore it even if you want to."

Her words were sharp and pointed. I wanted to cover my ears or bury my head under her pillows to hide from them. "I know," I said in a small voice.

"The thing is, if you unearth something nasty about your parents, you can't go back. You can't *un-know* it." Win looked concerned, maybe even a bit scared for me. "How bad do you want to know the truth? You need to think before you do anything else."

"But—"

"Seriously, do you know what I would give to not know the details of what's happened between my parents? I wish I hadn't snooped to figure out what was going on with them and could tell myself that it was a fight about something stupid like the water heater. Now I know my mom's a cheater and my dad puts up with it. Think about it before you dig further. If you go digging around, you might just find out something you wished you never knew."

"Would you do it? Would you want to know?" I picked at my thumbnail.

Win closed her eyes. "Maybe." She opened her eyes and looked at me. "Don't go thinking that means I think it's a good idea. I just don't learn from my mistakes. All I'm saying is that you've lived this long without knowing what was going on; if you sit on this for a few days while you think it over, it won't matter."

"I'll think about it," I said.

We sat silently for a moment. "I don't know about you, but I think better with ice cream." Win winked.

I smiled. "Me too."

She grabbed my hand and we ran downstairs.

chapter sixteen

Ice cream has a lot of benefits in addition to calories. Alas, it doesn't solve all problems. I kept replaying my conversation with Win on a loop in my head, trying to figure out what I wanted to do. A huge part of me wanted to go back in time to before any of this had happened. When my biggest problem was trying to figure out if I was in love with Josh or with the idea of being in love with him and if I had the guts to end it or if I would just ride it out until we went off to college. I got the idea that maybe if I could sort out that first problem, other things would start to fall into place. Whatever I felt for Neil was confused with everything else that had happened. I wanted to get back to how I used to feel for Josh, when things made more sense.

I flung the door open and kissed Josh.

He took a step back. "Wow. Do you greet everyone at the door like that?"

"Of course. Why do you think the UPS guys fight over who gets to deliver here?" I'd taken extra time and made sure my hair and makeup were perfect. Maybe the distance I'd felt with Josh lately was about the fact that we were too used to each other. I needed to make an effort.

"It's the muscles they get from carrying heavy packages, isn't it?" Josh winked.

I leaned in so I could whisper. "Honestly, it's that I'm crazy about those brown shorts."

"I've missed you," Josh said.

"I've been around."

"Around, but busy."

"Well, you've got my full attention now." I slipped out of his hug and headed down the hall to the kitchen to grab my bag. I hadn't told him about my trip across state. Part of it was that he'd be mad that I hadn't taken him with me. Then there was the fact that I'd seen Neil again, and I knew how he'd feel about that. That was one of the problems with dating Josh. We'd gone out for so long that I knew what he thought of things before we even had the discussion. If I actually told him, it would be like I'd have to go through the whole thing twice, and once in my head was enough. Win was right. I needed to give myself some time. If I decided to do any more digging, I'd talk to Josh, but until then there wasn't a point.

"I checked out some movie times," I said. I tossed my shades in my bag on the off chance that the sun bothered to come out.

Josh went into our fridge and pulled out a carton of juice. He held it up to see if I wanted any. I shook my head, and he reached into the cupboard to get himself a glass.

"It comes down to if you're in a thriller mood or more comedy." I smiled. "After, I thought we could grab some food and maybe take a drive or something." I went to wink at him so he'd know what I meant by the "or something," but he was busy looking in our pantry for a snack. Seduction is hard when they're more interested in a jar of mixed nuts. I was getting a sinking feeling my fancy bra wasn't going to get a chance to show off.

"I talked to your dad; he mentioned the idea of all of us going to Maker Faire down at the science center today."

I deflated. "Your idea of us going out on a date was to double with my mom and dad?"

He looked over and noticed my outfit for the first time. "I didn't know it was a date date."

"Well, you've been saying how we haven't been hanging out much, so I thought that was the point. Not doing something with Win and Kyle. Just us. I wasn't thinking we'd spend time with my parents instead."

"But it's Maker Faire."

I stared at him blankly.

"You know. People show up who make stuff. Last year there were the guys who did the robots and the other guy who made that laser light thing." He could see in my expression I wasn't impressed. "Remember, you liked the people who were doing the metal forging."

"I remember it."

"C'mon. Admit it. It was fun last year," Josh said.

It had been fun. Not like WOW-I-can't-believe-how-much-fun-I'm-having fun. It was more seeing how excited he and my dad were. They loved things like that. Anything that looked like it could earn its own Discovery Channel special was right up their alley, and Maker Faire was full of that stuff. Smart people making weird things in their basements and garages. "All right, I wasn't going to say anything, and leave you thinking there was only a thriller or a comedy to choose from, but there's even a science fiction movie option," I said, trying to tempt him.

Josh laughed. "Holding out on me, huh?"

"Consider it more me trying to broaden your horizons." I held my breath. Josh loved science fiction flicks. I wasn't crazy about them, but I was crazy for the idea of having time alone with him. How was I supposed to find the spark in our relationship? Parents and romance didn't go together.

"The thing is, I pretty much already told your dad we'd go with him and your mom."

I froze in place. "I wish you'd talked to me before you made plans with my dad."

Josh kissed my cheek. "I didn't set out to make plans. We were talking about work stuff and it just came up."

I nodded and suddenly pretended to have a huge interest in the matching salt and pepper shakers my mom had on the counter. "Of course, your very important job."

Josh took a step back at my tone. "I get that it isn't glorious, but it beats making fries at a fast food joint. You might not find this stuff interesting, but it's what I want to do."

The *and I'm lucky to be doing it after what you did* hung in the air. I didn't know if he intended it to sound like an accusation, that it was my fault he'd almost lost the internship, but that was how it felt.

I sighed. "Sorry. I'm being cranky. I know the job is a big deal. I wanted to spend the afternoon with you. Just us. Things have been . . ." My brain searched for the right word to describe how I'd been feeling. Ever since Harry died, it was as if the entire world was out of gear. It wasn't that my feelings for Josh had changed so much as it felt like our relationship was stuck in neutral. Not moving forward, but not moving backward, either. It had been coming for a while, but now it seemed glaringly obvious. It wasn't that I didn't like him, but I worried that I should like him more than I did. It seemed like we'd already drifted apart. We were almost more friends than anything else. That couldn't continue. We had to fix things or walk away. "Things have been off," I said.

"You've been through a lot lately. Everything's going to be fine." Josh put his arm around me and pulled me close. I let my head rest against his shoulder and breathed in his smell—a combination of Zest soap and the woodsy cologne he always wore.

"Road trip!"

Josh and I sprang apart as my dad barreled into the kitchen.

"Hope I'm interrupting something," Dad joked. He punched Josh playfully in the arm and Josh laughed. I didn't.

"You guys ready to go?" Dad rubbed his hands together. "I made a reservation at Travolata for later. They're doing a roast pig tonight."

"I don't really feel like pork," I said.

"You love their communal Sunday feasts." Dad didn't even look at me when he said it. Instead he grabbed a small bottle of Pellegrino out of the fridge for the car.

"I don't want a big heavy dinner."

"It's not the restaurant," Josh clarified. "Harper was hoping to do something else this afternoon."

Dad's eyebrows drew together. "You don't want to go to Maker Faire?"

I felt a layer of enamel grind down as I clenched my teeth together. It wasn't that Josh was wrong, but he didn't have to point out that it had been my idea not to go. Would it have been impossible for him to say that *he'd* changed his mind and decided he wanted to do something else?

"I was in the mood to go to a movie. We could do Maker Faire some other time," I suggested.

My dad's shoulders dropped. "It's only on for the weekend.

It's over after today." He looked like an eight-year-old who'd just discovered there was no Santa Claus.

Josh shot me a glance. Even without him saying anything, I could hear him in my head. *Are you sure you don't want to go? Look how bad your dad wants us to.* My resolve was faltering. It was clear what Josh wanted to do. Maybe the two of them should go together and just leave me at home.

"This doesn't have anything to do with how you've been feeling, does it?" Dad looked into my eyes. "You're not having trouble with being in crowds?"

"How I'm feeling?" My glance slid over to Josh, who was suddenly very interested in his shoes.

"Now, don't be mad at him. He was just worried about you."

What part of *I don't want to tell my dad* had been confusing for Josh? He still wasn't looking at me.

"I'm feeling fine," I said.

"I've still gone ahead and made another appointment for you to come back in. No arguing this time. I let you back out of the earlier appointment, but now we're going to be sure. I want to have everything checked over by my team."

"I'm fine," I repeated. My throat felt tight, as if I was about to cry.

"Maybe, but I don't think either of us wants to take a chance with our favorite girl," Dad said. Josh nodded and smiled next to him.

"Now, with that cleared up, are you guys in for Maker Faire

or not?" Dad smiled. "They've got robots," he said in a singsong voice.

I forced myself to press my mouth into a smile. "Sure."

Dad high-fived Josh. "Now we're talking. I'll get the car and scare up her mom. We'll hit the road in ten."

As soon as he walked out of the room, I whirled around and faced Josh. "Are you kidding me?"

He held up a hand as if he thought I was going to rush him. "I was worried. I didn't plan to say anything to him about our conversation; it sort of came out."

"How do you say something like that by accident?" I shot a look over my shoulder to make sure my dad wasn't sneaking back up on me.

"I asked him about side effects from the procedure. If he knew of any people having trouble with what felt like new memories. As soon as I said that, he guessed I was asking about you. He's not mad."

I put a hand on my hip. Josh hadn't spent the past week mucking out stalls.

"Okay, he was ticked when he first heard. And he had every reason to be; what we did could have caused a huge amount of trouble. But more than being ticked, he was worried."

"I don't want to go back to the clinic. I'm fine," I said.

Josh hugged me. "Then there's no reason not to go back. You have to trust us." He smiled and took my hand, leading me out to join my parents.

chapter seventeen

I always wanted a dog. My dad liked the concept of a dog, but the actual hair, poop, and drool were less appealing to him. That was how I ended up with no less than twenty stuffed dogs. Bribery. There's no doubt stuffed dogs have some advantages, but if you want a guard dog, a stuffed dog isn't going to cut it. They're cute. They're cuddly. But let's be honest, they have fluff for brains.

I paused outside my dad's home office door and listened again. The house was quiet. If we'd had an actual dog, I could have relied on him to bark a warning when my parents came back. It would also have helped if we'd lived in a house that wasn't so freaking large that my parents could park in the garage, come into the house, dance a rumba up the stairs, and I still wouldn't hear them until they discovered me snooping.

My parents were at a charity event, a fund-raiser for building schools in third-world countries. My mom loved these things. Not the building-schools part—the party aspect. She liked an excuse to get really dressed up. My dad hated them. He wasn't great in big social situations. He did well with a small group of friends, but in large groups he'd get more and more reclusive. He'd sit at the table and play with his phone. If he did talk to anyone, it was like he forgot that conversations were supposed to go both ways and ended up lecturing someone about whatever topic was his current passion. They rarely stayed at these things for long, but it was one of the few events where I could count on both of them being out of the house at the same time.

I turned the doorknob and then froze when I heard a sound. An instant later I realized it was just the furnace kicking on. I forced myself to take a deep breath. Either I needed to do this or I needed to forget about it, but I couldn't keep dithering over it. I'd already wasted too much time thinking about it. The advice from Win stuck in my head. I'd tried to convince myself I didn't want to know anything. I got along well with my parents. I had a good life. There was nothing to be gained from snooping around. The problem was that now that I knew there was a secret, I couldn't stop thinking about it. It was like having a sore tooth. You would tell yourself to leave it alone, but then you'd find your tongue poking at it. I kept wondering why they would have lied to me about Harry. No matter which way I approached the idea, I couldn't come up with an answer that made any sense. I used to accept everything at face value, but I couldn't do that forever. If I did, I'd still be living at home believing in Santa. It was time to grow up. They'd lied to me, and I needed to know why. I flung the door open and walked into the room.

My dad's desk took up a huge amount of space in his office. It was a mammoth antique thing. It had belonged to some guy who had been an officer in the Confederate army. I was no lumberjack, so I had no idea what kind of wood it was carved out of, but it was big, heavy, and meant to impress. The walls were lined with bookcases that a cabinetmaker had custom designed for the room. It would have looked like a formal library except for the fact that nearly every shelf was covered with action figures. Whatever happens, don't call them dolls. My dad was really sensitive about that. He'd been collecting them for years. He had something like four different kinds of Batman figures and a bunch of other superheroes I didn't even recognize. Some on the top shelf he'd had since before I was born.

I stood behind his desk and slid the top drawer open. If there were ever a worldwide paper clip shortage, I would know who was responsible for hoarding them. There were piles of them in the drawer. My fingers ran over the dried-out pens, Post-it notes, and loose change. Nothing interesting. His computer sat on top of the desk. I nudged the mouse to see if it was turned off or merely in hibernation mode. It lit straight up, but the cursor blinked where the password needed to be entered. It wouldn't take high-level deduction skills to sort this out; on the pad of paper next to the phone there was a list of what I was pretty sure were his passwords. My dad didn't keep work documents on his home computer, so he didn't worry too much about security. My hands hovered over the keyboard. If I logged on, there would be a record. Most likely my dad would never check. The only reason he kept a password on the computer was on the off chance that someone broke in and stole it.

On the other hand he might check. If he did, he'd want to know what I'd been doing in his office. There wasn't a house rule that I wasn't allowed in his office, but it was implied. I had my own computer. There was another desktop off the kitchen that I could use if I wanted. There was absolutely no reason for me to use his. Other than snooping.

I went through the rest of the file drawers. There were papers related to the house, bank statements, and a bunch of warranties for stuff we didn't even own anymore. There was nothing about Neurotech. He must have kept everything at work.

I tapped my fingers on the desktop. Even if he had stacks of paperwork from Neurotech, most likely I wouldn't have been able to make any sense of them. And he wasn't the type who would keep a diary where he listed various lies he and my mom had told me. What was I even looking for? Did I think there was going to be a file in his desk labeled SECRET STUFF I'VE BEEN HIDING FROM HARPER—NO PEEKING!?

I slammed the desk drawer shut in frustration, and the desk shuddered from the impact and bumped the bookshelf.

My heart froze. One of the Batman figurines on the top shelf teetered back and forth and then pitched off the shelf, falling in slow motion. The figure hit the polished hardwood floor with a disturbing crack.

I dropped to my knees and picked up the doll. His right hand was snapped off at the wrist. My eyes searched the floor and I spotted the plastic hand; it had fallen under the desk. I grabbed it and held it against his arm in the hope that it would either snap right back on or somehow magically heal itself, but he appeared to be lacking in that superpower. A clammy sweat broke out all over my body. I was screwed. They were all collectibles. He would notice it had been ruined. My hands were shaking.

I leaned back and took a few deep breaths so I could think of a solution. Superglue! I grabbed the doll and flew down the stairs to the kitchen. My mom had a desk against one wall where she did the bills and some of her craft projects. I yanked open the drawer. Tape, staples, scissors, more paper clips. My heart was slamming in my chest. I could picture them walking in the door while I stood there with a broken Batman in hand. I kept rummaging, and then my fingers found the tube of glue and pulled it out.

I sat down at her desk and tried to calm down. I was shaking so badly I was going to end up with a glob of glue on him or end up gluing my fingers to the doll. That would round this experience off perfectly. The sharp chemical smell of the glue filled my nose, and I carefully put a small dab on the doll and then held the hand in place, making sure it was facing the right direction. With the way my luck was going, I would glue it on backward. I blew on the hand, praying for it to dry quickly. Every nerve on my body was on high alert, listening for the sound of their car pulling into the garage.

I bolted back upstairs and dragged a chair over to the bookcase. I gave Batman a once-over. You couldn't see the crack unless you were really looking. It wasn't like my dad took these things down to play with; they just sat on the shelf. I couldn't imagine him ever wanting to sell them where a collector would notice. It was unlikely he'd ever know it had been damaged. With luck by the time he did find out, I'd be in my forties and well beyond being grounded.

I climbed up on the chair and slid Batman back into place. I couldn't remember if he'd been facing straight out or on an angle, but I was going to have to choose. He had been close to the edge, which was why he'd fallen off in the first place. As I slid him onto the shelf, I noticed a piece of paper that must have been underneath the action figure. I slid it off so I could get a look. It wasn't a paper; it was an old photograph. I turned it over, and the image made me hold my breath. I gripped the bookshelf with my other hand.

It was a picture of a woman. She was wearing a lab coat and

smiling at whoever was taking the picture. There was nothing about the picture or the woman that stuck out, but I couldn't stop staring. I knew this woman. She was the one from my dreams. My breath was coming short and shallow. The hair on my arms was standing up as if she were a ghost instead of a photo. What was the picture even doing here? Had it been stuck up here and forgotten, or was it supposed to be hidden? My hand scrambled along the shelf, feeling for anything else, but there was nothing.

I heard the distant sound of the garage door rumbling to life downstairs. Shit. They were home. I checked Batman to make sure he was on the shelf. I hesitated. I should put the picture back where it belonged, but I couldn't shake the feeling that it belonged with me. I shoved it inside my sweater and jumped off the chair. I slid the chair back into place and ducked out the door, pulling it shut behind me as I heard my parents come into the kitchen.

I took a few steps away from the office door and met my parents as they came up the stairs.

"What made you think he was interested in talking about video games, and even if he was, what made you think he wanted a blow-by-blow of your strategy?" My mom laughed. "You should have seen his face. He looked panicked. I thought he was going to chew his arm off to escape."

"He asked!" Dad protested. "If you're boring someone, they should say something, not just sit there." He saw me at the top of the stairs. "Next time your mom wants to drag me to one of these things, remind me how much I hate them."

"Next time I go, I'm taking her," Mom shot back.

I forced myself to smile. I was certain my dad would somehow be able to see the photo under my sweater or that it would fall out and drift down to the floor like an autumn leaf.

"You have a good night?" Mom asked. She held her high heels in one hand. "Get up to anything good?"

"Nope." It wasn't even a lie. Whatever I'd done, I was pretty sure it wasn't good.

chapter eighteen

I shouldn't have ordered a latte. I didn't need any caffeine. I was already practically humming with energy. I fidgeted in the chair and tried to be patient while Neil looked at the picture. My foot bounced up and down. If we were going to have any more clandestine meetings, we were going to have to meet at a yoga studio or something. My anxiety level couldn't take any more coffee.

"I don't know if there's a way to figure out who she is," Neil said.

My heart sank to the floor. I reached for the picture. "Okay. It was a long shot."

Neil pulled the picture toward him. "Don't give up that easy. I'm not sure how to do it, but I'll try. I can ask a couple of people."

"You can't tell them where you got the picture." My words came out in a rush.

"I won't." Neil turned the photo over and looked at the blank side and then back at the woman in the shot. "You have no idea who she might be? Or when the picture was taken? Any information would help."

"No." My fingers picked at the rim of my paper cup. "It might be no one important, but I can't shake the feeling that I know her. I had a few dreams, and I'm not certain, but I'm pretty sure I saw her in them." This was an understatement. I was practically obsessed with the picture. Stalkers had a more casual relationship with their victims than I did with that photograph. I'd pulled it out a thousand times a day since I found it. When I went to school, I took it with me, tucked inside my phone case. I'd shown it to Win, but she had no idea who it was either. I checked our family photo albums, searching in the background to see if she was in any of the group shots, but I didn't see her. I'd searched my brain for anyone else I could ask, but couldn't think of a single person. I could have asked my parents, but that would have meant admitting I'd found the picture. I was pretty sure I knew how it had gotten there. Several years ago my dad had had the hardwood flooring replaced in his office. They'd moved out all the furniture. He'd put stacks of paper that had been in desk on his shelves so the desk would be light enough to move. The photo could have easily been left up there by accident. Even if my dad had put it up there on purpose, it was because he didn't want me to find it. If they'd been hiding it from me, they wouldn't tell me the truth anyway.

Neil pulled out his backpack and put the picture inside his history textbook. I felt twitchy letting it out of my sight.

"What will you do?" I asked.

"I know some people who do work with facial recognition software. A lot of police departments are using it to track protestors. They want to identify who they think might be trouble-makers; then if something happens, they have a list of possible suspects. A bunch of social media sites use it too, so you can identify and tag people in pictures. I'll have my friends run this photo through to see if they can find matches anywhere online or something."

I drummed my fingers on the table. "I don't think she's a protestor."

"I don't either, but the software works the same way. It's worth a shot." Neil leaned on the table. "By the way, what does a protestor look like?"

I flushed. "You know what I mean. She doesn't look like she's . . ." My brain searched for the right word. "Edgy."

A smile spread across his face. "Edgy. Cool. I always wanted to be edgy." He made a dramatic face as if he were a character in an adventure novel. "Neil O'Malley. Edgy. Righter of wrongs. Savior of damsels in distress."

I tossed a wadded napkin at his face. "I'm not a damsel, or in distress."

He placed his hand over his heart as if he'd been mortally wounded. "I will have you know there are many damsels who seek out my assistance. I wasn't necessarily talking about you."

I blushed. There was no reason for that statement to annoy me. Neil didn't owe me anything. I had a boyfriend, for crying out loud. There was no good reason for me to feel a rush of excitement when he flirted. He was likely just being nice. "I'm certain the damsels line up outside for a chance to buff your shining armor."

He wagged his eyebrows. "Buff my armor? That's a term I haven't heard before."

I flushed even hotter. "That's not what I meant."

"Well, lucky for you, my damsel line is presently short and I have time to help you out."

"I do appreciate it." I picked up my coffee cup, but it was empty already. "I can pay you for your time."

Neil looked hurt for a moment, like I'd insulted him. "Nah. This one is on the house. I owe you for showing up at your school. I knew your dad was going to be there, but the protestors never should have chased after you." Neil's face turned serious. "I want you to know, I feel bad about that. Protesting is important to me, but I don't think that gives us the right to go around hassling innocent people."

"My dad's innocent," I said, then wished I hadn't said a word. Sticking up for him was second nature.

Neil's jaw hardened. "It's not that I think your dad is a bad guy. I don't even know him. I think what his company does is wrong. He owns the company. I think he has a responsibility to pay attention to what his company does. I'm happy to help you out, but I'm not willing to let Neurotech off the hook until I'm convinced nothing is going on there."

"You protest a lot of things, don't you? I mean, it's not just Neurotech."

"You don't get to be edgy if you're a one-protest kind of guy." He waited for me to smile. "Everybody has to have a hobby. Some guys collect stamps or they bowl; I protest. I started getting involved with Neurotech when my brother died, but I've branched out. Women's rights, gay marriage, environmental stuff, genetically modified foods." He waved his hand to show there was a long list. "I cover pretty much the whole spectrum."

There were a lot of kids at school who cared about different issues. A few times a year there were signs to either join or sponsor someone who was doing a run or bike ride for everything from breast cancer research to literacy programs. I couldn't think of anyone who actively protested anything. None of us seemed passionate enough. I'd never noticed before, but now it felt like we were missing out. "Why do you do it?" Neil looked up as if he was surprised by my question. "Why do you protest all this stuff?" I clarified.

He opened his mouth and then shut it, giving himself time to think. "I don't know. Shouldn't we do stuff that makes a difference? Life can't be all video games and watching TV, can it? It feels as if my life matters if I do something that makes an impact."

I found myself nodding. I knew exactly what he meant.

He laughed. "Whoa, I'm getting deep." He picked up his cup. It was empty too. "Let's get out of here."

"What?"

"Let's go for a drive. I want to spend more time with you, but I don't want any more coffee." He stood and held out his hand to help me. "C'mon, I won't force you to walk around with a sign or anything."

There were a thousand reasons I could think of to say no, but I got up and followed him out to his car.

Neil drove into downtown Seattle, and we walked onto the ferry for Bainbridge Island. He seemed to know without my saying anything that I wanted to go someplace where there would be no chance anyone would recognize me. Not that I was doing anything wrong by hanging out with him, but I didn't want to have to explain it. We walked along the main street in Bainbridge, poking in the various stores and art galleries. I found it interesting that he had an opinion on everything. At the end of the road there was a gas station that rented bikes. Neil's eyes grew big like a kid on Christmas.

I shook my head. "No way. I haven't been on a bike since I was little."

"Days like this are made for bike riding." He spun in a

slow circle. The sun was out, a minor miracle in the Pacific Northwest.

"I'm really slow on a bike," I hedged. My legs were strong from horseback riding, but my cardio was kinda lousy. "You'll be miles ahead of me. I'd be by myself. I'll probably be eaten by a bear. Then you'll have to protest bears."

"Trust me. The view will be worth it, and the bears owe me one since I picketed to protect their habitat." Neil went inside and came back out with the owner. The guy unlocked a tandem bike.

Neil bowed low. "Presto. No way you can fall behind, *and* I'll take on any possible bears who aren't appropriately grateful."

We got on the bike, and after a few abortive tries we managed to get going without swaying out into traffic. We took a road that followed the shore. Between the trees I could see views of the ocean. Since I was in the back, I didn't have to worry about steering, so I could take in the scenery. The air smelled clean and fresh, and for the first time in weeks I felt lighter. The wind blew through my hair. It wasn't the same as horseback riding, but it was close.

"Hey, are you pedaling back there?" Neil called over his shoulder. "It feels like I'm doing all the work."

I laughed. "I told you I was slow."

"There's slow and then there's not pedaling at all. Now kick it into gear—we've got a hill coming up."

We pedaled up the hill, my quads burning with the effort. I hadn't been riding as much as usual. It felt good to use my legs. I had my head down, and when we crested the top, I looked up, shocked. The trees had been cleared, and you could see all the way back to the city.

"Whoa."

Neil stopped. "Told you, great view. Now will you admit I was right?"

I rolled my eyes. "You were right about the view. I'm not giving you a blanket right about everything."

"I didn't think you were the type to let anyone get away with anything easy." Neil got off the bike and motioned for me to join him on the bench. There was a plaque on it. The brass was worn down, but I could still make out the engraving. MARCUS O'MALLEY—NOW HE CAN SEE FOREVER.

My finger touched the brass lightly. "Your brother?"

"My grandparents have a place over here. We used to come all the time as kids. My parents both work, so in the summer we used to stay with my grandparents. This was one of Marcus's favorite places. My parents had the bench put up after he was gone. The park service has a program."

I sat; the wood slats of the bench were warm from the sun. Neil sat next to me, his face tilted up. It was perfectly quiet. Just the whisper of the wind through the trees. "This is nearly perfect," I said.

"Nearly?"

"We should have brought water or something."

Neil sat up and pulled his backpack over. He unzipped the top and took out two sweating bottles of water. He tossed one to me and then reached in and pulled out a bag of cookies. He tore it open and passed it over. "Picked them up at the gas station when I rented the bikes. Now will you admit I'm right more often than just once?"

"Maybe."

"You're a hard one to please." He held up one hand before I could disagree. "Don't get me wrong. I think that's a good trait."

I kicked at the layer of pine needles on the ground. "You know, the thing is, I used to be happy pretty much all the time. Until all this happened. My friend Win warned me against even looking into it. She said you can't un-know something. The ignorance-is-bliss theory."

"She's got a point, but that's not how I see it. I'd rather know. If I know, then maybe I can do something. Change it. If you don't admit there's a problem, then you can't change it. If you don't have some ugly stuff in your life, how do you recognize the really good stuff?"

We sat silently on the bench.

"I'm afraid," I whispered. "What if I find out something . . ." I couldn't put it into words. It sounded too awful, even with only Neil to hear it. I wanted to trust him, to take him at face value, but I didn't know him that well. "What if I find out something I can't forgive?" What if something really bad had happened to me as kid? What if I'd done something and my parents didn't want me to know about it? What if everything I believed was based on some kind of lie? And if it was a lie, then the truth had to be really ugly, didn't it? I bit down on my tongue to keep from spilling my every fear. Even though he'd been great to me, he didn't hide the fact that he was no fan of my dad. I couldn't tell him, even if I wanted to.

Neil reached over and squeezed my hand for reassurance. I held his hand an instant longer than I needed to before I let go. "You lured me up here with the sunshine, fresh air, and cookies just to get me to spill my guts. Now you're going to have to tell me a secret so we're even," I said, trying to lighten the moment. I needed to change the topic before I said too much.

"Processed chocolate chip cookies have a way of making people talk." He looked out over the water. "I'll tell you a secret. You asked earlier why I protest so many things."

"Stuff matters to you," I said.

He rubbed his nose. "It does, but that's not all of it. I do it because *I* want to matter." He sighed. "When my brother died, it gutted my parents. He was the golden child in our family. You don't have any brothers or sisters, do you?"

"No." In my head I heard my dad always telling me I was his favorite.

"If you grow up with a bunch of siblings, you sometimes find yourself jockeying for position. From the moment I was born, I officially took on the role of the screwup. The pressure was off. My parents had already staked out which of us was the smart one, who was the athlete, and who was musical. Whatever I was going to do, either my brother or sister did it already and most likely better."

"I don't know about that," I offered.

Neil laughed. "Trust me, you don't know the two of them—they define type A. The thing is, I didn't mind that much. It meant no one expected too much of me. I sort of floated along. Then Marcus died."

"It must have been hard."

"You know that whole theory about the different stages of grief?" He waited for me to nod. "I got stuck in anger for a while. I was pissed about everything. Pissed at the doctors for not helping. Pissed at Neurotech for not disclosing the side effects. Pissed that my parents didn't do something before my brother was too far gone. Pissed at my brother. Pissed at my sister for moving on with her life and focusing her grief on doing something. I turned into one of those guys always looking for a fight. Huge chip on my shoulder. I got suspended for getting into scuffles the beginning of my senior year."

"Fights?" I tried to picture him taking a swing at someone. It seemed as odd as if he'd told me he could fly.

He nodded. "Not my finest hour. I'd find an excuse to get mad. It felt like a release—suddenly it was okay to start whaling on someone. I was so mad that everything Marcus was, everything he would have brought to the world, was just gone." He snapped his fingers. "Just like that."

"What happened?"

"My football coach. He pulled me into his office. I was sure he was going to yell at me for getting suspended because it meant I couldn't play for a week."

"You were on the football team?" I don't know why I was surprised. He was built like an athlete.

Neil flexed his arm. "Running back. We were almost state champions when I was a senior."

"Really?" I was impressed. I never hung out with the jock crowd. They were a foreign species to me. I liked that he had these unexpected sides, that there were things about him that I didn't know.

"No. Well, unless you count being third from the bottom in our division, nearly state champions."

I punched him lightly in the shoulder. "No, it doesn't count."

"My coach was used to having a team that was underfunded. He told us it wasn't important if we won; what was important was that we tried our best to win. That stuck with me. He knew we weren't ever going to be the champs, but he kept after it. Anyway, he pulled me into his office and told me I had a choice to make. I could run around being a dick and waste my life, but that didn't do me any good and it didn't do my brother any good. He said I had an obligation to do something with my life. I had to do the work of two to make up for the loss of my brother." Neil sighed. "That's when I got into all the social justice stuff. I decided I had to do something that really mattered."

I felt tears in my eyes. I let my leg press against his so he would know I was there. "I think your brother would be really proud of you, but you don't have to do twice the work. That's not fair."

"Hate to be the one to bust your bubble, but life isn't fair." He smiled at me. Our eyes locked. I couldn't look away. It felt as if every nerve on my skin was hyperaware of him. I could feel where we touched. Our hands. Our thighs side by side on the bench. Our shoulders. The heat between us soldered us together. His breath was on my face. My heart skipped in my chest. He leaned forward and I leaned to meet him, our lips millimeters apart.

What was I doing? I pulled back, yanking my hand out of his. I closed my eyes. It was as if his gaze had some type of magical property that was intoxicating. I was dating Josh. I'd dated Josh forever. What I felt for Neil was something else. Maybe it was the excitement of someone new or the fact that he was helping me, but I had to get control. I had questions about if I wanted to be with Josh, but that didn't mean I could go around kissing other guys. Right?

"I'm sorry," Neil said. "I shouldn't have—"

"No. I'm sorry." The last thing I wanted was to talk about it.

"Must be all this sun. Messes with the brain." Neil got up and put some distance between us. The air felt cool on my skin where we had touched. He fumbled with his backpack. I realized I was staring at his hands, the long fingers and how they looked capable and strong. Like he could build things. I forced my gaze away.

"I should get back," I said. "I've got a double date tonight."

"Sure." Neil looked at his watch. "If we hurry, we can catch the next ferry."

We got on the bike and pedaled back toward town. I told myself that Neil was right. It was just the combination of fresh air, sunshine, and the conversation, but I couldn't even convince myself. I wanted things with Josh to be sorted out. For someone to wave a magic wand and either make things between Josh and me right again or magically get me on the other side of the breakup so I could miss all the ugly parts.

chapter nineteen

The movie theater smelled like scorched popcorn. I took that as a bad omen. It wasn't as if I'd expected it to be a fine dining restaurant, but when the menu only requires them to make hot dogs, nachos where the cheese comes out of a pump, and popcorn, you sort of expect them to get that much right.

Kyle and Josh walked over to where Win and I had saved seats. "I got you plain M&M's," Josh said, handing me the bag.

I looked down at the bag, disappointed.

Josh raised an eyebrow. "What? You always get M&M's."

He was right. I always did. He didn't even have to ask. So why did I suddenly want something else? Hot Tamales, or a Kit Kat bar. Anything.

"Still full from dinner," I mumbled.

Kyle handed Win a tub of popcorn. "Extra butter, two shakes of salt."

"Did you make sure they put the real butter on, not the butter-flavored oil?" Win inspected the bucket with a wary eye.

"Would I let my girl eat oiled popcorn?"

Win flushed. She moved her purse so Kyle could take the seat next to her and the two of them started talking. Josh flopped down and pulled out a bag of gummy bears. He always got gummy bears. Sometimes they would stick in his teeth with bits of orange or red goo wedged in there.

"Want one?" He held the open bag to me. "Normally I don't share, but I don't want Kyle to show me up." He cocked his head toward Win and Kyle. Kyle was holding a giant paper cup so Win could have a sip. She giggled and took a drink. "Seems like things must be going well for those two," he whispered to me. He didn't need to whisper. Even though they were right next to us, they were only paying attention to each other.

"If it wasn't, he'd have that straw shoved up his nose so fast he wouldn't know what hit him."

Josh snickered. "Remember when that guy on the debate team at Central High grabbed Win's ass last year?"

I snorted. We'd been at a tournament. Win was a brilliant debater. She could be a future lawyer if she wanted. The guy from Central had come up behind her and made some comment about how he loved a woman with such a great mouth and then whacked her on the ass.

Win had turned around slowly. People in the room could practically feel the temperature in the hall drop by a few degrees. Some people from our school took a step back as if they expected Win to blow him up right where he stood using only the power of her mind.

"Funny. I like a man with a good mouth and one who knows what to do with his hands. 'Course, those who don't know must be reduced to randomly groping strangers and hoping for the best." She froze him with a look. "Let me be clear. Touch me again and I'll use this mouth to scream assault so fast it will make your head spin."

His friends laughed at him. "Bitch," he spat at Win.

She laughed. "Bitch? That's the best you can do? No wonder you're ranked so low in debate." She leaned forward into his face. "Honey, was that supposed to upset me? You know who never gets called a bitch? The quiet girl in the corner who doesn't say peep and lets the whole world walk over her. Some of the women I admire most in the world get called bitch, so I'm going to take what you said as a compliment." She waved him off with a waggle of her fingers, her bright red nails winking in the light, and then walked off as the crowd of students around her applauded.

"Kyle is a brave man for taking her on," I said to Josh.

"Brave or madly in love. Maybe a bit of both." Josh popped a few more gummy bears in his mouth. I told myself that the sound of his chewing was not annoying me despite the wet smacking noise he was making. "He's going to ask her to prom," Josh said.

I spun in my seat to face him and lowered my voice to make sure they couldn't hear me. "Really? Already? Prom isn't for another two months."

"I think he wants to nail down the deal before someone else asks her."

I glanced over at the two of them. They were already slouched down in their seats, their hands in the popcorn bucket.

"We should check into a limo rental. See if we can get one other couple to go in with us. There would be room, and it will keep costs down. If Michael and Molly can manage to keep from breaking up every two weeks, they would be an option."

"For prom?" I asked.

Josh gave me a look. "It seems a bit much to take a limo just to go to McDonald's. Yes, prom."

"I guess I didn't know we were going," I said. Josh's face showed his disbelief. "I mean, we hadn't talked about it."

"I didn't think I needed to formally ask you." Josh sat up straighter in his chair. "Are you considering other offers?"

"No." I could hear the annoyance in my voice. "But it wouldn't kill you to not assume that you don't even have to ask."

"Don't worry. Lately I don't assume a thing." He looked away.

I felt like pointing out that he'd assumed I'd want M&M's,

but that seemed so petty I couldn't even say it. "What's that supposed to mean?"

"It means I don't know what's going on with you. You're always busy. You never want to hang out."

"Never? Don't you think that's a bit extreme? Let me think . . . it was so long ago that we last hung out. It was, gosh, yesterday." When I'd gotten home from the stable yesterday, I'd come in the house to find Josh and my dad splitting a pint of ice cream in my kitchen. Just two guys releasing the stress of a busy day at work. My dad had gone upstairs to his office and Josh and I had done our homework together.

"You know what I mean," he said.

"No. I don't." I pushed away the image of bike riding with Neil. Why had that felt so different? When had what I felt for Josh turned into this mess? I was more interested in hearing from Neil about going for coffee than I was about the idea of going to prom with Josh.

I hadn't heard from Neil since the day we went to the island except for a two-line e-mail from his school account saying he was following up on our project and would let me know when he found anything. Not that I'd expected him to write me some kind of love letter. I'd pretty much leaped in the opposite direction when he tried to kiss me. He must have thought that I hated him. "We saw each other yesterday and again tonight," I said.

"You blew off your appointment at the clinic the other day," Josh pointed out.

I clenched my teeth. It wasn't enough I had to hear it from my parents? My dad had made another appointment for me to get checked out by one of his doctors. I'd ended up getting stuck late at school working on a group project for my government class. It wasn't my fault. Was I supposed to be blamed for bringing down everyone's grade to make an appointment I didn't even want?

"I had to do the Student Senate project," I said. "It went way later than expected. Holly Garandy's in my group. She's incapable of doing anything quickly; you know that. She's a walking example of OCD. She checked everything we did six times."

"You shouldn't take advantage just because it's your dad. There are people on wait lists to get those appointments."

I felt my face tighten, my expression freezing into place. "Excuse me? He's my dad. Who are you to say I'm taking advantage of him?" My voice came out clipped and sharp.

Win kicked me. I realized the people around us were listening in. Kyle was staring at the screen as if he were fascinated by the advertisements that were scrolling by.

"Sorry," I said softly to Josh.

"This is what I meant earlier. Everything I say is the wrong thing."

I suddenly felt like crying. "It's not that it's wrong. I'm on edge, a bit cranky, that's all." But it was the wrong thing. Our relationship was falling apart, but neither of us knew how to end it.

"But that's why your dad wants you to see someone. It's not like you to be this—" His voice broke off. I could tell he'd been about to say "bitchy" but had thought better of it. "You're not usually this on edge. He's worried about you. I'm worried about you. You're not your usual happy-go-lucky self."

"Maybe sometimes you have to be in a bad mood to really appreciate the good moods," I said.

Josh put his arm around me. "I don't believe that."

I pushed down the urge to tell him that of course if he didn't believe it, it must not be true.

"Sorry for ticking you off. I didn't mean to hassle you about your dad."

"I know. I'm sorry about getting pissy."

"Best part of fighting is the makeup nookie," Win said, and both Kyle and Josh laughed and I tried to join in, but it sounded weak.

Win squeezed my arm. "You okay?" she whispered.

I didn't even know how to answer.

Josh pulled me closer as the previews flickered to life on the screen, the Dolby sound booming over the theater, making the seats vibrate. "You know I love you, right?"

I didn't answer. I was sure I would start crying if I did. Instead I nodded. I leaned my head on his shoulder and let the movie images wash over me and wondered what was wrong with me that it didn't seem like enough anymore.

chapter twenty

Our school trustee board must have been entirely made up of hoarders. I'd never seen any of their houses, but I was willing to bet they were the kind of places where you had to squeeze through pathways in the junk, where thousands of takeout containers had been saved, there was no running water anymore, and there was the very real possibility that at the bottom of a pile of junk there would be a squished, mummified cat.

I based this theory on the appearance of our school storage room.

"I think they have every copy of the school paper," Win said. She peered at the stack in the corner. "There are bins filled with them. I bet they date back to the eighteen hundreds. Who keeps that kind of thing?"

"It's possible that nothing has ever been thrown away in the entire history of this school," I said. "There's a shelf in the back with canned goods on it. The mystery of why hot lunch is so bad has at last been answered. The food is from the Eisenhower administration."

Win kicked a box. "How the hell are we supposed to find a bunch of dance decorations in all of this?" She sneezed. "There's most likely some kind of deadly mold spores in here."

"Is there a reason we can't get new decorations?" I pushed past a rack of dusty choir robes.

"My exact question to the school board, but I ended up getting a lecture on the importance of not wasting school resources. Apparently, before they'll approve any money for the prom committee, we have to make a list of what existing stuff we can use."

I had zero interest in being on the prom committee. Win had volunteered me. I couldn't tell if she was punishing me for something, or if she'd thought I'd actually want to do it. We had to pick a theme and location by the end of the week. People were walking up to me in the halls and giving me their deep thoughts on which theme was the best choice, Silver Fantasy (what the heck did that even mean, anyway?) or Southern Nights. Both sounded stupid to me, but despite my being on prom committee, no one was asking my opinion.

"Found 'em," Win called out. I joined her across the room. She pulled out a few Rubbermaid containers labeled

DANCE DECORATIONS. She popped the top off one and rolled up her sleeves. "There's a bunch of stars in here." She held one up. "They're silver. If we go with that theme, we could stick them everywhere, maybe dig some white Christmas lights out and wrap them all over everything. There are some tea lights in here; those would work with either option." She shifted through the contents of the box. "Whoa, check this out." She pulled out giant bright red plastic lips that were molded into a kissing position. "You have to wonder what sort of theme that was for."

"Porn Prom," I suggested. Win giggled. "Maybe they have some other body parts or one of those inflatable dolls buried at the bottom."

"Only if we get lucky," Win said.

I opened up the next container and started to pick through for anything that might be useful, wasn't already completely trashed, or hadn't been eaten by vermin. If anything scuttled out of one of these boxes, I was going to run first and ask questions later. I sighed. The whole thing seemed like a waste of time.

Win stopped picking through her box of decorations and stared at me. "Don't get me wrong, I'm not ranking this as a highlight of my high school career or anything, but you're acting like this is some kind of painful dental procedure. Aren't you excited about the dance at all? It's prom. These are the misty watercolor memories you'll look back at fondly when you're old and peeing in your own pants."

"You always know how to make anything sound good." I dropped a starfish-and-seashell streamer (Undersea Adventure theme?) back into the box. "I don't know. I guess with everything going on lately, it's hard to get too worked up about prom."

"Prom, or going with Josh?" Win asked. She made a face when she saw my shocked expression. "You don't think he's the only one who's noticed, do you? That junior girl, the one who is in all the advanced chem classes? She's practically praying a novena you two break up in time for Josh to both get over you and then fall madly in love with her before the dance."

My brain scrambled to think of who she was talking about. "The girl with the sort of hipster glasses and dark hair?" Win nodded. "Why does she think we're breaking up?"

"Because it's crystal clear things are off with you two. You used to be hooked at the hip. Now you practically recoil when Josh gets close to you."

"I do not."

Win put her hands on her hips. "Good relationships don't come along all that often, you know. Look at my parents."

"Josh and I are not turning into your parents." I tossed a few decorations out of the box.

Win glanced at me out of the corner of her eye. "It's your relationship. I'm just trying to figure what you're up to."

"I'm not up to anything." I couldn't even talk to Win about things without her rushing to defend Josh. It would be one thing if I'd believed it was because she really thought we belonged together, but the truth was she'd made Josh and me into her proof that true love existed. It wasn't fair.

Win shrugged and went back to the box of decorations. She pulled out a silk top hat and put it on. "This is grand. I might keep it. I doubt they'd notice it was missing." She tipped the rim up. "You can say you're not avoiding him, but you're acting weird around him. I might go a bit more global and say you're acting weird in general, but around him it's more noticeable."

"I know you want me to be with Josh forever, but I can't promise that's going to happen. We're going to different schools next fall, and it feels like we're already heading in different directions. I think we have been for a while. I'm not saying we will break up, but I'm going through a lot now."

"Does 'a lot' happen to be a freshman at the local community college and go by the name Neil?"

My mouth fell open. "What?"

"Don't look at me like I've gone barmy. Look, if things with you and Josh can't be worked out, I think that sucks, but if you want to have any kind of ongoing friendship with him, you can't cheat on him. That's my problem. You're better than that. You need to respect what you guys had even if you don't want it going forward."

I threw my arms up in the air. "I'm not cheating on Josh." My heart winced. I hadn't technically done anything that counted as cheating, but I'd have been lying to myself if I'd said I didn't feel anything for Neil.

"You talk about this Neil guy all the time."

"I do not," I insisted.

Win rolled her eyes. "We can play this game all day if you want, but if you ask me, you should see someone about your denial issues."

"I'm not in denial. If I talk about Neil a lot, and that's *if*, then it's because he's been helping me out with all the research." I could feel this lie piling on top of the others.

"And the reason you asked him versus, say . . . oh, I don't know, let me think." Win tapped her foot as if she were trying to chase down her train of thought. "Oh yes, why not ask the guy you've been dating for two years? Who, more than that, has been your friend. Wouldn't he be the one most likely to want to help you out?"

I sighed. "Of course I think Josh would want to help me, but he's not exactly coming to the situation unbiased. He thinks my dad is the best thing since sliced bread, and he's not going to do anything to blow that internship. It's his ticket to college. I can't expect him to approach the problem with fresh eyes."

"So you figure that the guy who believes his brother died because of Neurotech is unbiased?" She crossed her arms. "I don't know him, but you should be careful. You don't know what his angle is. He could be using you to get information or something."

"Neil would never do that." My voice came out hard.

"Don't get your knickers in a knot with me; I'm stating the obvious. And the reason you're mad is because you know I'm right. You don't know him that well. He might be a nice guy and he might not. As your mate, it's my job to make sure someone's looking out for you. Even if you don't seem to want my help." She looked at my face and then took a step closer. "You don't know him that well, do you?" She took a step to the left to make sure she was still directly in front of me when I tried to turn away. "Just how much time are you spending with this guy?"

I'd wanted to avoid telling Win about how often I'd seen Neil for just this reason. "Easy, Sherlock Holmes. No need to get out the waterboard and resort to torture. When I met him about the picture, we went over to Bainbridge Island for a few hours." I shrugged to show it was no big deal. Win didn't break her stare. "And I saw him a few other times for coffee so he could give me updates on what he's been doing."

"Pretty cozy."

"It's not like that." I shifted uncomfortably. "Okay, he kinda made a move, but I shut it down. He's fine with being friends."

"Kinda? Do you hear yourself?" She pulled a roll of silver streamers out of the box. "If you like him, that's your business, but don't fool yourself. There's something going on between the two of you. You need to figure out if it's that you like him, or if he's a distraction from everything going on, or if you're looking for an excuse to break up with Josh. But you shouldn't lie to Josh while you sort it out. Be with him or don't, but don't play games."

I pushed away the box. "I don't *know* what I want with Josh. I am doing my best to sort it out. It's possible that two people could simply grow apart without it being some big drama or betrayal." I wanted to tell her not everyone was her mom, but I knew that wouldn't go over well.

"Maybe that's the problem. There's no reason to break up with him, so you're looking for a way to make him do it. You're going to have to work a lot harder if you want it to happen. He's crazy about you. He's not going to give up without a fight."

I sat down on the Rubbermaid container, suddenly exhausted. "I know. I don't want him to give up." I rubbed my forehead. "Maybe I do. I don't know."

Win sat down next to me. "What's bugging you? Is the whole thing where he's in love with your dad driving you nuts?"

"Yes. But that's not new. He's a great friend, but I don't know if what I feel for him is enough. But at the same time I don't want to lose him in my life; he's one of my best friends. I don't want to let go, and I don't want to hang on. Then everything he does seems to drive me crazy lately. I should like that he and my dad get along, right?"

"It beats him and your dad hating each other." Win sighed. "I don't know what you want me to say."

"Ever since I had that treatment, everything feels screwed

up. It's the dreams, and the feeling that there's something my parents aren't telling me, but it's more than that. It's like my old life suddenly doesn't fit. I'm uncomfortable in my own skin. Maybe that's why I like hanging out with Neil. He's not part of the past, so I don't have to worry about how he fits in with the old."

"Fair enough, but you can't string things along. Or Josh, for that matter. You could turn around one of these days and discover that you don't have to worry about fitting things into the past because the past has picked up and done a runner."

"I'm not stringing Josh along."

Win got up and brushed off her uniform skirt. "Whatever."

I watched her rifle through the boxes. She flipped her braids over her shoulder. "Now you're mad at me?" I asked her in disbelief. She didn't turn around. She continued to pull the silver stars out of the box. "I can't believe you're annoyed about this. When did you become Josh's mom?" I knew she was right that I was out of line, but it was her job to support me, not judge me.

Win spun around. "This isn't just about Josh. This is about you. You're cutting him out altogether because he's so biased." She made finger quotes in the air when she said "biased." "I'm not sure what excuse you've found for not including me in things."

"I include you," I protested.

"And that's why you told me all about Neil."

I gave an exasperated sigh. "Don't make this into something it's not. You've been busy with Kyle."

Win's nose twitched. "Are you saying this is my problem?"

"I wasn't the one who said we had a problem to start with."

"Fine. Then tell me why you're blowing off prom."

"I'm not blowing it off. I'm in this stupid storage room looking for decorations, aren't I? Despite the fact I didn't volunteer; you did that for me." I kicked the box closest to me. "What am I supposed to do, spin in circles, skip through fields of flowers?" I clasped my hands under my chin. "Golly, I'm so excited."

Win's eyes narrowed. "I thought you would want to be involved. It's the biggest dance of high school. Our last big blowout before graduation. Even if you didn't go with Josh, we'd still go together. Now I know you've got much more important things to do, like saving the free world along with your Rebel with a Cause."

"Biggest dance of high school? Do you hear yourself? I'm glad you're falling for Kyle, but don't tell me you're going to turn from cynical into a Hallmark card. Excuse me if I don't get all lathered up about a stupid high school dance," I said.

Win crossed her arms over her chest. "It's a big deal to me. It'll be the first time I've ever gone to a dance with someone I love."

Her words hit me like a shot, shutting me up for a split second. "You're in love with Kyle?"

She shook her head like she couldn't believe how slow I was on the uptake. "Yes. You don't have to look so shocked. He told me he's in love with me, too."

"You didn't say anything," I said.

"I tried. Every time I talk about him, or anything else, you mumble something and stare off. You're not interested. The only thing that matters is what's going on with you." She bent over and gathered up the pile of decorations she'd pulled out of the boxes. "I'll let the rest of the prom committee know you've quit."

A wave of guilt washed over me. "I'm not quit—"

Win waved off what I was going to say. "Don't do us any favors. It's obvious you don't want to be bothered. You've made it clear you think the dance is stupid, so don't bother wasting your time on doing anything for it."

I stood and picked up a cardboard star that had fallen to the floor. "Win, I don't want to fight with you."

Win snatched the star out of my hand. "Fine, we're not fighting. Whatever you want." Her voice was distant and cold.

"I want to be on the prom committee. I really do." I couldn't believe the words coming out of my mouth. Five minutes ago the dance had seemed irrelevant, but now I didn't want to lose a chance to be involved. I could see Win's expression wavering. "C'mon, give me one of those stars."

Win started to smile, but then stepped on some loose sequins that had spilled from one of the boxes. Her foot slid out from under her and she began to fall backward. Her mouth pursed into a perfect small Lifesaver O as she went down.

Suddenly it felt like someone hit me in the back of the head with a two-by-four. My field of vision went black, and I had a flash. I was at the top of a stairwell above a foyer, a gray slate stone floor just in view down below. A bookshelf off to the side was stuffed with books, almost every free inch covered, with an old school globe on the very top. The woman from the picture was about to fall. She reached out to steady herself. The bookcase stopped her for a moment, but then her hand slipped off and she tumbled down the stairs with a gasp. The globe teetered at the top of the bookcase for a moment, then came crashing down after her. It broke into pieces when it slammed into the floor below.

"I swear this school is trying to kill me," Win said.

My attention snapped back to her. I blinked blankly. Win had fallen onto one of the cardboard boxes. Her butt was jammed down in the box, which was filled with tablecloths. Other than her dignity, nothing else seemed to be hurt.

Win stood and straightened her skirt. "If you're sure about wanting to be involved—"

"I just had another memory," I said, cutting her off. "There was some kind of accident. A fall. I saw it. I think it's another piece of the puzzle." I stopped talking when I saw Win's face.

"Oh my God. I can't believe we're talking about it again. You can't give it up." She shook her head in disbelief.

"No, you don't understand."

"I understand fine. When you're ready to be a part of this world instead of the one in your head, let me know." Win stormed out the door. It swung closed behind her, the hydraulics keeping it from slamming shut. Instead it closed with a soft whoosh, leaving me alone in the storage room.

The room, which had felt claustrophobic when I'd first entered, now made me feel safe. Maybe no one would find me in there, hidden among the boxes and stacks of stuff.

I sank back onto a Rubbermaid container. Hot tears filled my eyes and ran down my cheeks. The woman in my memory was the same as the woman in the picture I'd given to Neil. I had no vision of her after the fall, but I was suddenly quite sure that she'd never gotten back up again. Neil wasn't going to find her anywhere.

chapter twenty-one

I'd never been the most popular girl at Saint Francis. No one followed me around and copied what I wore or how I did my hair. However, I was part of the inner circle. Now I was getting a glimpse at how people who were bullied felt as they navigated the school day. The day after the fight with Win, I was doing my best to avoid her in the halls. If I heard her voice, I ducked into the bathroom or a classroom. I could feel my Spidey senses on high alert. Anytime I heard someone giggle, I whipped around, convinced they were talking about me. The halls felt like a war zone.

I was walking toward the cafeteria when it hit me: I had no idea where to sit. It wasn't like there were assigned seats, but everyone tended to congregate at the same tables day after day. I could picture Win getting up and leaving the table if I joined our usual crowd, and the idea of sitting by myself felt scary. Everyone would stare as if there were a spotlight directed at me. They'd all wonder what was going on and start speculating. I stood outside the cafeteria and peered in.

"You okay?" Josh said behind me. I jumped, startled by his voice.

"Win and I had a fight," I admitted.

"Yeah, she told me this morning in history."

"What did she say about it?" I asked, trying to figure out how much he knew. I didn't think she'd tell him about Neil, not that there was anything to really say. I'd been clear with Neil I wasn't wanting to make things romantic. I pushed away the thought that I hadn't been quite as transparent with Josh and that I was sending mixed messages to both of them. I'd stewed on the fight with Win all of last night. I felt bad I'd been so preoccupied that I hadn't realized how serious she and Kyle were getting, but she hadn't exactly been pounding down my door to tell me all about it. She was mad because I wasn't psychic, that I hadn't picked up on her signals. It wasn't fair. Yesterday I'd been too crazed to apologize, but now I felt like she owed me an apology too.

"She wouldn't say why you guys were fighting."

I shifted, my shoes squeaking on the tile floor. "It's complicated."

Josh sighed. "Everything is complicated these days." He

cupped my elbow. "Come on, let's go have lunch. You guys will get over it. You've been friends forever."

I pulled my arm back. I knew he didn't mean it that way, but it felt as if he were implying we were being silly, overemotional girls. "I don't want to have lunch and pretend everything's fine."

"So what are you going to do? Eat your lunch in the parking lot?"

Saint Francis didn't exactly have a great outdoor space. There was one battered picnic table in front of the school by the flagpole. It was worn and weathered and was likely to give you a rash of splinters if you were brave enough to sit there.

"Maybe. The weather's nice," I said.

Josh stared at me as if trying to figure out if I was serious. "Okay then, let's go."

"You're coming with me?" I looked back toward the cafeteria. "I thought you'd want to have lunch with everyone else."

"I want to be with you." Josh put his sack lunch down on the floor and turned me so we were face-to-face. "I know you're going through a lot right now, but it's important to me that you know I'm there for you."

My lower lip started to quiver. "I know," I whispered so quietly that I wasn't even sure if he heard me.

The rest of the day felt like a near-out-of-body experience. I went through the motions. Attended every class and shuffled through the halls smiling blankly at people. All I wanted to do was leave, but

A) My situation wasn't going to be any better by skipping class and getting in trouble for that, and

B) I had absolutely no idea where I would go if I did skip. It wasn't as if I could go home—my mom would wonder what I was doing there—and I'd never needed a secret hideout before.

I bolted out the door after the final bell and headed home in my mom's car. Close to our neighborhood I passed a beat-up Toyota on the side of the road. I turned around. It looked like Neil's car. It pulled out into traffic behind me. I slowed down slightly and I saw the car flash its lights in my rearview mirror. It was Neil. I drove into the gas station on the next corner. He drove slowly past my car.

"Don't park here; there are security cameras," he called outside his window. "Meet me by the strip mall on the next block." He drove away without waiting for me to answer. I peered up and noticed the black security cameras on each of the pumps. I fought the urge to slump down in my seat. It was all turning very CIA. Was he being serious, or was this just part of his weird off-grid paranoia?

I sat in the car, my hands on the steering wheel. There was no doubt in my mind that Neil had something important to tell me. He'd been waiting for me to drive by. I took a deep breath and drove after him. Now I had to figure out if I was ready to hear it.

As soon as I pulled into the strip mall lot, I saw him. He was outside his car, pacing back and forth. He looked relieved when he saw me. Maybe he'd thought that in the two blocks I'd decided to take off.

"Do you really think someone is tracking us on security cameras?" I asked as I got out of the car.

"I don't think so, but I didn't want to take a chance." He kicked a piece of gravel across the parking lot. "Better safe than sorry."

I didn't like how he was looking at me. He had dark circles under his eyes like he hadn't slept, and his hands kept fidgeting. "What?"

"I have some answers about the woman in the picture." He passed the photo back to me.

"She's dead," I guessed. His eyes widened and he nodded. "I had a hunch that would be what you would discover," I said. I didn't tell him about the flash of memory I'd had in the storage room. As much as I wanted to tell him everything, Win was right. I needed to be careful. I chewed on the inside of my cheek. "What else did you find out?"

He jammed his hands in his pockets and stared down at an empty McDonald's cup on the pavement as if it held the answers to the mystery of the universe. "I'm not sure how to tell you. I'm not even sure if I should tell you."

"You can't keep something like that a secret. I'm the one who asked you to find this information out." My stomach clenched.

"Easy. I'm not saying you don't have a right to know what I found; what I meant is that I'm not sure if I'm the best person for you to hear the news from. I thought it might be better if your heard it from a counselor or something," Neil said.

"Just tell me."

"Her name was Robyn Bryne."

"She had the same last name as me?" My stomach tightened another notch. It felt like my body was being squeezed in a vise.

Neil nodded. "She was married to your dad." He pulled out a sheet of paper. "They got married their last year of college."

His words didn't make sense. No matter how my brain tried to put it together, it didn't fit. "That's not possible. My mom and dad got married around that same time. My dad would have said something if he'd been married before." I reached for the paper but stopped short of taking it from his hand.

Neil looked scared, which made me even more frightened. "She was married to your dad until you were nine."

"How is that possible?" The idea of my dad having a whole other family was unreal. It felt like a huge gaping hole had just opened up in front of me. What if he was one of those guys who showed up on talk shows because they had two families at the same time who never knew about each other? Maybe I met her when I was young and that's why she seemed so familiar. Did my mom know about her? "My mom is going to freak out when she hears this."

"I'm not convinced she's your mom."

I stood blinking at him. There was a faint buzzing sound in my ears.

"Robyn Bryne died, and three months later your dad married the woman you know as your mom. You would have been nine when they married. Marriage licenses are matters of public record. You don't have to believe me. In fact, you should check it out yourself."

"I was nine?" I swallowed. I felt like I might throw up. Most of my baby pictures and photos from before we moved were gone. My parents had told me they were lost in the move. We had some, but now I couldn't remember if there was a picture of all of us together as a family when I was really young.

Neil nodded.

"That's when we moved here," I said. My voice sounded strange in my ears.

"Have you ever seen your birth certificate?" Neil asked.

I blinked. "My birth certificate?" I repeated. "I don't know. I don't think so." Wait. Did he think this Robyn was my mom?

"It could be faked, but that would be something to check."

I felt light-headed. I might have started swaying, because Neil took a step forward and grabbed me by the elbow.

"Here, sit down." He looked around. The parking lot wasn't chock-full of benches. My knees were weak. It was as if whatever muscles were responsible for holding me up had decided to take a break. I sank down onto one of the cement bars that were at the front of each parking space. Neil guided me down, making sure it was more of a sitting versus a falling.

"I triple-checked everything." He sounded as if he wanted to apologize.

"You remember stuff from when you were nine, right? I mean, sure, maybe people don't remember stuff from when they were toddlers or even five or six, but people remember stuff at nine, right?" My voice sounded high and tight even to my own ears. "Even if someone has a crappy memory, they'd remember having a different mother, wouldn't they? How can I remember details like how my dad brought those Baskin-Robbins ice cream cone clowns to my first-grade birthday party at school, and not remember that I used to have a totally different mom? This isn't possible." My breath was coming hard and fast, and I felt a smear of oily sweat popping up on my forehead and underarms.

"Here, let me get you some water." Neil dove into his car and pulled out a metal water bottle. He unscrewed the top for me, but when I reached for it, my hand was shaking so hard he ended up guiding it to my mouth so I could take a drink. The water was warm, and I had to remind my body to swallow. It was like it had forgotten what to do.

"The clown cones had purple icing hair. I remember that. I specifically asked for purple. I didn't want pink. I hate pink." My vision was filling in with black stars, and there was a loud rushing sound in my ears.

"Shit. I knew I should have gotten someone else to tell you. I might be wrong about all of this, but I can't come up with any other answer. Are you going into shock? Don't take this the wrong way, but you look really bad." Neil stared down at me.

I dropped my head between my knees. I had a vague memory from tenth-grade health class that that was what you were supposed to do when you thought you might pass out. Neil sat next to me and rubbed my back. When the black dots in front of my eyes cleared, I looked up. "How is it possible that I don't remember her?"

Neil wiped his hands on his jeans. "I've been thinking about it. Is it possible you've had the procedure before?"

"The procedure softens your memories. It doesn't wipe them out."

"But it could, couldn't it? If someone, I don't know, cranked up the machine, it could wipe those memories, couldn't it?"

Neil didn't say who he meant when he said "someone," but it was obvious, wasn't it? It would have to have been my dad. Who else could have done it? My stomach acid started to eat a sour hole in my guts.

"I started dreaming about her before the procedure. It started when my horse died." I bit down hard on my lip, trying to ground myself with the pain.

"I thought about that," Neil said. "Losing your horse was really emotional, right? Maybe that shook something free."

I flashed to what the groom had said and to the date on

Harry's papers. "I think the horse used to belong to her, to Robyn."

Neil rubbed his chin. "I don't know enough about how the brain works, but maybe if your memories had been buried, losing Harry was enough to make them start to come back."

"Do you think people know you were checking into her history? Is that why you didn't want to be near any cameras?" I wanted to look around to see if there was anyone watching us, but I didn't want to give in to the paranoia.

"I didn't want to take any chances. There's been some weird stuff going on—people following me, or at least I think I'm being followed. I couldn't tell you in an e-mail or on the phone. I didn't want to take the chance that anyone else would know. Just in case."

"She fell, didn't she? That's how Robyn died," I said. The flash I'd had when I'd been with Win ran through my head. She'd fallen down the stairs and I'd been there. I'd seen the whole thing. I'd seen it and then somehow blocked it out of my memory. Or someone else had. Things were falling into place. When the groom had talked about how my mom had loved to ride, he hadn't meant the mom I always knew; he'd meant this other woman. Robyn. The black dots started to fill my vision again, and I forced myself to take a deep breath.

"I don't know. The information I found simply says there was an accident. What makes you think she fell?" Neil looked freaked out. If he was shocked, I was willing to bet I looked worse.

"I'm starting to remember more things." I took another deep breath. I could smell exhaust from the road out front; it clung to the back of my throat in a greasy film. "Do you think when I went in for the procedure it could have sped up the memory recovery? If losing Harry started it, did having the procedure speed it all up?"

"I don't know," Neil admitted. "My major is social justice. We're way out of my league in terms of science and medical knowledge, but I'm guessing it did."

I liked that he didn't try to pretend like he had the answers. "My dad was really against me getting the procedure. Maybe he knew it was a risk. He wants me to go back in to see his doctor. He's set up an appointment for next week." I pressed my hands to my legs to stop them from shaking.

Neil gripped his knees. I could feel the tension in his body where our shoulders and knees touched. "You can't go."

"I know." I didn't tell him that I'd already missed two appointments. It was going to get harder and harder to come up with excuses to avoid going to the clinic. "I know this looks bad, but I'm not ready to assume the worst. You said yourself there could be other reasons." I refused to believe it could be as bad as it felt right now. There had to be some other explanation. I had to be careful not to jump to some worst-case scenario.

Neil made a noncommittal noise.

"There's no reason for someone to wipe my memory," I

pointed out. "Even if I had a different mom, why would that have to be a secret? If she died in an accident, that's tragic and sad, but it's not the kind of thing you don't tell a kid. Maybe it was so traumatic that I blocked it out myself and my dad just went along with it." My voice had an edge. Maybe I'd freaked out. Had I coped so badly that my dad thought I was better off not remembering her at all?

"I'm sorry," Neil said.

His words surprised me. "Why are you sorry? I asked you to figure out who she was. It's not your fault what the answer looks like." I tried to make my voice light to lessen the tension. "Besides, you're not a huge fan of Neurotech. This news pretty much confirms every rotten thing you suspected."

"I'd be lying if I said I had a lot of love for your dad's company, but I swear to God, I didn't want you to get hurt in this whole process."

We sat silently in the parking lot side by side.

"What do I do now?" I finally asked.

"I don't know, but I believe you'll figure it out."

I laughed. "Your faith might be misplaced."

Neil squeezed my hand. "There's a lot of stuff I don't know. But believing in you is something I'm sure of."

I wasn't sure he was right, but it made me feel better to know he believed it.

chapter twenty-two

I'd only gotten high once, and I wasn't even sure it should count since I hadn't done the actual smoking. Even if I ran for political office someday, I was pretty sure it couldn't be used against me. It had happened the summer after sophomore year and was a contact high from hanging out in the kitchen at a party. The people around me had been smoking up a storm, and suddenly two thoughts came instantly to my mind:

1) I was stoned

2) I could no longer feel my own lips.

I didn't like the sensation of being high. Instead of feeling either invincible or giggly, I felt paranoid. It occurred to me that at some point someone was going to pop up and declare that my entire life was just a prank others were playing on me. When the effect wore off, I swore I'd never do it again.

Now I had the same out-of-body, disconnected feeling all over again, only this time no weed was being consumed.

"Pass the kale," my dad said.

Mom handed it to him and went on talking about her dissatisfaction with our yard service. They'd apparently done a hatchet job on the Japanese maple in the back. She'd tried to stop them, but the guys didn't speak English very well.

I pushed my chicken around on the plate and counted the number of times I chewed to avoid screaming and running in circles around the table. The food felt like thick tasteless paste in my mouth. I found it almost impossible to swallow. I'd tried to skip the family dinner, saying that I had to study, but my mom hadn't gone for it.

Of course, she wasn't really my mom anyway, so what did it matter?

My brain started to shut down. I kept counting the number of times I chewed as a way to focus. I glanced down and saw that my hand was gripping my fork with white-knuckled intensity. It took me several seconds to get my hand to listen to the command in my head to loosen the hold. I wanted to stand up and hurl the silverware at my parents, scream that I knew they were liars, but I didn't. I just sat there quietly while the music provided a surreal backdrop.

Mom had made a rule about no TV at dinnertime, so now she would play some kind of classical music on the Bose sound system while we ate. I didn't think either of my parents knew much about classical music, or even liked it, but they wanted to be the kind of people who ate to Mozart. There were a lot of things in our lives that were just about how it looked. Our whole family was a lie. A facade.

I wanted to ask them what was going on, but I didn't have any idea how to even start the conversation. I'd opened my mouth a thousand times since I'd heard the news from Neil, but then I'd end up walking away. I knew I'd only have one chance to speak to them about it for the first time. It seemed important that when I did bring it up, I did it right. Now I just needed to figure out what "right" looked like.

I also couldn't bring it up when I didn't even know how I felt about it. I swung between feeling crushed and wanting to cry and feeling the sharp sting of betrayal. One minute I was choking on rage and the next I wanted them to pat me on the back and tell me everything was going to be fine. I wasn't sure what going crazy felt like, but I was pretty sure this was close.

The whole situation didn't seem possible. My parents sat across the table from me eating dinner like nothing was different. My dad had a piece of kale stuck in his teeth and was wearing one of his science T-shirts that said COME TO THE NERD SIDE—WE HAVE PI. Mom was still blathering on about the yard service. She was more than happy to give people an opportunity, but was it asking too much that they either knew what they were doing or could at least understand directions in English? My parents didn't seem like the type of people who would be capable of pulling off some type of elaborate ruse to wipe out my past. It was like discovering that your sixth-grade teacher, who liked to make crafts with Popsicle sticks and wore Birkenstocks, was in fact an ex–CIA agent who used to be responsible for taking out foreign operatives.

It was unreal. My life had turned into an episode of *The Twilight Zone*. I half expected my dad to stand up, peel off his face to reveal a lizardlike alien, and admit he was from outer space. My dad was nothing if not logical. If anything he was rational to a fault. Wiping out my memory didn't make sense. There was no reason not to tell me the truth. If I'd had a different mom, why not tell me about her? What else were they hiding?

"Earth to Harper."

I jumped in the chair when I heard my name.

"Someone's a million miles away," Mom said. "Your dad asked you if you wanted to go grab some ice cream after dinner."

"I've got homework," I said aloud. Inside my head I was screaming, *How can you talk about ice cream when everything in my life is a lie?*

"You sure you can't knock off for a night?" Mom smiled. "Not even for mint chocolate chip?"

Dad tossed his crumpled napkin at my mom. "Are you crazy? We should be encouraging that kind of focus on studying; we'll be paying for college next year." He winked at me. "Keep up that dedication and you could major in science. Take over the company someday."

I pressed my mouth into a smile and hoped he couldn't tell I felt like throwing up. Was this conversation actually happening? We were talking about ice cream instead of this huge lie?

"I want you to make that appointment at the clinic."

My heart froze. "I don't need to go. I'm feeling fine."

"And we want to make sure you stay fine," my mom said, waving her fork in my direction with a smile.

"Okay, sure." I wasn't sure how I was going to get out of it, but I'd worry about that later. There was no way I would go back. I wasn't sure, but there might be a way the doctors could tell that I remembered everything. Right now the only advantage I had was that they didn't know that I knew. Until I had a plan, I intended to keep it that way. "Can I be excused? I really do have a bunch of homework."

"Go get 'em, tiger. We'll bring some ice cream back for you," dad said.

I slipped out of the dining room. Could a guy who called me tiger really hide another mother from me? If I went to an appointment, would they find a way to block my new memories all over again? I was almost at the stairs when I had a thought. I flipped the light on in our den. One wall had floor-to-ceiling bookcases. Unlike my dad's office, which was stuffed with action figures, this room had been completely done by my mom. It looked like a page out of a Restoration Hardware catalog.

I could hear my dad joking with my mom while she did the dishes. My fingers ran over the shelves. They smelled like the lemon polish the maids used every week. Finally I saw the book and pulled it off the shelf. A hardcover version of *To Kill a Mockingbird*. I tucked it under my shirt like I was starring in a spy movie and smuggled it into my room.

I shut the door behind me and leaned against it. I wasn't cut out for all this sneaking around. My heart was slamming into my ribs at what felt like a thousand beats per second. I hadn't picked a major yet for college, but it was safe to say that anything spy-related was going to be out.

I crawled into bed with the book. I'd always known I was named after Harper Lee. I'd thought it was a bit weird that my mom would name me after an author when she didn't even like to read that much. Who names their kid after an author unless they truly love that writer? Was this additional proof that she wasn't my mom, and that the mysterious Robyn was? Or was it that my mom was actually my mom, but my dad had been married to Robyn and was having an affair with my mom? Then after Robyn died he'd married my mom and never let me know about his earlier life?

I'd read the novel at least a half dozen times. I flipped through the pages. Maybe I thought the answers to what was going on would somehow jump out at me like pages in a pop-up book. Nothing. I rubbed the pages. Maybe, like a genie, the answers would appear. Nothing.

Wait.

I rubbed the inside page again. It felt thick. Thicker than

the other pages. The paper felt different too. I ran my thumb-nail against the edge. There were two pages glued together. I sat straight up and clicked on the bedside lamp for better light. I tried to peel the pages apart, but they were stuck firmly together.

I dashed into my bathroom and cranked the hot water in the tub all the way on. I tapped my foot on the tile floor, wait-ing for some steam to build up. I held the book open over the steam and counted to one hundred. The pages were soft and damp, but the glue showed no signs of giving up. I wanted to throw the book against the wall, but I knew that wasn't going to accomplish anything.

I ran back into my room and held the page up in front of my light. I could just make out something. I pulled the shade off the lamp so there was nothing to diffuse the light from the bulb.

Dear Harper—
Always follow in your heart what you know to be true.
Love, Mom

There was a date below. The date of my first birthday. I traced the words with my finger. I'd seen my mom's hand-writing thousands of times. On notes for school, grocery lists, Christmas cards, checks, permission slips, and recipe cards. The handwriting in the book wasn't hers. There was no denying it anymore. My mom wasn't my mom. Now the only thing I had to figure out was why everyone was lying to me.

chapter twenty-three

I drummed my fingers on the steering wheel. If I was ever in the market for a new best friend, being timely was going to be on the list of necessary traits. I waited in the stable parking lot for Win. I'd checked the schedule in the barn, so I knew she had a lesson. Talking to her at school wasn't going to work. I needed a place where we could be alone. It was drizzling, and the clouds felt like they were pressing down from the dirty, silver-colored sky. I checked the clock in my car for the thousandth time. Her lesson started in two minutes. Win's SUV swung into the parking lot with a spray of gravel, and she jumped out, juggling her huge Coach bag, her riding helmet, and a giant Starbucks latte. She was like a high-fashion Sherpa.

"Hey," I called out as I scrambled from my mom's car.

Win paused and then looked at the stable. I could tell she

was shocked to see me. "I can't talk; I'm late for a lesson." She motioned to the barn.

"I know. I've been here for almost thirty minutes." I motioned to her coffee mug. "I bought you a coffee, but I think the one I got you is cold."

She tossed her hair. "Not my fault. I didn't know we were meeting."

So much for my caffeine olive branch breaking down the barrier.

"I needed to talk to you," I said. "I thought I could catch you before your lesson, but I can wait and talk to you when you're done."

"I have to go home right after." She juggled the items in her hands. "Don't make that face—I really do. My grandmother is in town from England. Required family time with Nan. Forced fun, that kind of thing."

"Any chance you could be a bit late?"

She hefted her bag up on her shoulder. "This is so vital it can't wait?"

"Kinda." I swallowed. "It's important, Win."

She stared out at the road for a beat. "Okay."

Win went into Laura's office and declared that there was a prom committee crisis so she was going to have to cancel her lesson with no notice. She made the crisis sound on par with a possible nuclear reactor meltdown, with the survival of all humanity, or at the very least our prom, on the line. I wasn't convinced

Laura bought the lie. She looked back and forth between the two of us. She must have had a sense that whatever we needed to talk was more than just wanting to chat about boys. Laura took riding seriously. Anyone who blew off lessons disrespected her time and didn't give the horses their best. I wasn't sure what annoyed her more, us letting her down or the horses.

"All right. This time I'll give you a pass. There's no one in the lounge if you need a place to talk." Laura froze Win in place with her stare. "I expect you'll put in some extra practice this week, and next week I want to see the outcome of that extra work. Is that clear?" Laura waited for Win to nod before looking away.

Once excused, we fled upstairs to the lounge. Win dumped her bag and helmet on the table. "I lied about prom and now I have to do extra practice this week when I don't have time for it. That's earning me bad karma right now. Somewhere the universe is planning to kick me in the ass, so this better be good."

"I hate that we're fighting," I said. That didn't even begin to cover how bad I felt about it. My stomach was boiling over with acid.

"The fact we had a fight isn't my fault," she said. "Don't put this on me."

"I didn't; that's not what I meant."

Win wouldn't meet my eyes. It made me think the whole thing was bothering her more than her tough-girl act was letting on. This had been the longest we'd ever been mad at each other. We'd never lasted more than a couple hours before.

"I found something out last night, about what's been going on with me, and I needed to talk to someone."

Win rolled her eyes. "That's what this is about? A quick apology so you can launch into the next thing happening in your life? For this I bailed on my lesson?"

"What I need to talk about with you is important."

"And my life isn't?"

I took a deep breath. "I know I haven't been spending as much time with you, or paying attention to everything going on for you, but what's going on for me right now is huge." I was frustrated she couldn't see my point.

"I call bullshit on your theory. Because your stuff is more important, then what's happening to me shouldn't matter? How about the fact that there are kids starving to death in Africa? That's more important than your stuff. There are wars going on; that's more important too. If I have a headache, it doesn't hurt any less because someone else has cancer. I still have a headache. What's happening with me is a big deal to me. The fact that it's a big deal should matter to you, and it hasn't."

I sat down in the chair. Now I was getting a headache. "I need help, Win. I don't know what to do. I know I haven't been a great friend, and I deserve every bit of anger you feel. I should be asking about Kyle, and I will, but right now I need you. I know it's not good enough, but I'm honestly doing the best I can."

She sighed and sat down on the leather sofa. "Go ahead."

I spilled everything. The found photograph, Neil finding

Robyn's identity, and the pages pasted together in the book. When I stopped talking, Win was quiet.

"That is seriously fecked," she said at last.

"Indeed."

Win took a long, deep breath like she was trying to organize her thoughts. "I might have been wrong. Your stuff is more messed up than the African kids. Okay, so you're sure this Robyn woman is your real mom?"

"Not a hundred percent—I'm open to another suggestion—but unless someone's got a great idea, I think I have to face up to the idea that she's my real mom. Otherwise the timeline makes no sense."

"Why the hell wouldn't your dad tell you? Not telling someone that they had a different mom is just . . ." Her voice trailed off as she searched for the right word. "Bonkers."

"I have no idea. I spent all of last night trying to figure it out. My best guess is that after she died, he wanted me to move on without being sad."

"What are you going to do?"

I shrugged. "My big plan was to talk to you."

Win raised an eyebrow. "You're supposed to be the smart one in this duo. I'm the good-looking one with the snappy comebacks."

"I was thinking we could branch out. High school's almost over. Time to try new things. I was going to give you a chance to be the ideas person."

Win rolled her eyes. "I suppose the good news is that there's really a limited number of options to consider. You can either confront your parents directly—"

I opened my mouth to protest, but she waved me off.

"Let me finish before you start tearing down my ideas. You can confront your parents directly. Or you can tell someone else, some adult who might be able to do something."

"Who? Mr. Ross?" Mr. Ross was Saint Francis's guidance counselor. He was a nice enough guy, but overly perky. He smiled too much. He was like a character on a little kids' TV show, the kind who talks too loud and asks obvious questions.

"I said someone who could do something, not someone who looks like he survived a lobotomy." Win was not a huge fan of Mr. Ross. He'd once told her to "stand proud" because "brown is beautiful." It was his attempt to be all urban and racially sensitive. If looks could have killed, she would have taken his testicles out through his nose with a mere glance. No one needed to tell Win brown was beautiful. If you didn't think it was, then that was your problem, as far as she was concerned. "You could go talk to the police," she said.

I shook my head. I knew how that would go. "They would nod and smile at me, then drive me home to my parents. Or have me locked up in a mental ward. What if I talked to your parents?"

"Mine?" Win shook her head. "Don't get me wrong, my dad is great if you need someone to explain what a touchback does versus a wide receiver, and in a pinch he can cover stuff like fixing a flat tire, but this is way out of his league. My mom . . ." Win sniffed dismissively. "She's not the type to be a big fan of causing a fuss. No way she's getting involved between you and your parents. That reeks of an emotionally messy situation, and she doesn't even do those in our own family."

I wanted to kick myself. I should have known her parents would be a bad plan. My brain rolled through the list of adults I knew. I liked Laura, but technically my dad paid her to be my trainer. I couldn't be sure she was impartial. I imagined myself knocking on the door of Mrs. Custler, who lived across the street. She was in her sixties and divorced. She used to say all the time that marrying well had been her full-time job, but she could afford to retire now. She always brought her margarita machine to the neighborhood Fourth of July party. She was the only one I could think of who wouldn't automatically assume I was making up stuff about my parents, but I couldn't imagine what she would do to help me. "I don't know."

"You still have another choice." Win counted the options off on her fingers. "Ask your parents, get another adult to help, or ignore the whole thing until graduation."

"Ignore it?" My voice was full of disbelief.

"We've got less than two months until graduation," Win pointed out.

"And then what?"

"Then you've got more options. Maybe when you're at

UDub you'll figure something out. Maybe you'll find out more information, or if you do confront your parents, at least you aren't stuck at home, or, who knows, maybe there's some caped crusader there who can tell you what to do. The point is, you're eighteen, you'll be out of high school, and that changes everything."

"I'm not sure I can wait that long." I picked at my thumbnail. "My dad's scheduled me to go to meet with his doctor."

"Can he do some kind of test to figure out what you remember?"

"Maybe. I don't know. I'm not sure I want to risk it. What if the doctor does something and I don't remember all of this?" Win and I stared at each other across the small table.

"Have you talked to Josh?"

I sighed. "No."

"Are you afraid he's going to choose your dad over you?"

"No," I said quickly. She'd put her finger right on the issue. It wasn't that I didn't think Josh liked me, but I was pretty sure he liked my dad better.

"It's not that I don't appreciate your faith in me, but let's be honest, out of our merry band of friends, who is the one with a fancy scholarship to Stanford?"

"Josh."

"Who's almost certain to be our class valedictorian?"

"Josh," I answered again.

"So, given that the guy does math equations for fun, I think we can agree he's the smart one in the crowd. He'll know what to do. You guys have your issues, but he's been your friend a long time." She dug her cell phone out of her bag. "Call him."

I pulled on a loose thread on the edge of my shirt.

Win ducked her head so that she caught my eyes. "Serious. No fecking about—what's going on with you two?"

"Josh is great." My voice sounded flat in my own ears.

"You trying to convince me or yourself?" She tossed her hair back. "Nothing against your skinny smart boy, but I've found my own man candy."

I laughed. "Man candy?"

"Have you seen Kyle without his shirt? The boy is ripped. He makes David Beckham look washed up."

"You do have it bad for him."

Win flopped back on the leather sofa. "You have no idea. I see him in the hall and my stomach does a full Olympic gymnastics routine. When he reaches for me, it feels like every nerve in my skin reaches back out to touch him. Everything he says I want to soak up and have him tell me more." She glanced over to me. "I'm pretty new at this love stuff, but I'm fairly sure that's how you're supposed to feel. When you think of Josh, is that what you feel?"

"I like Josh," I said.

Win chucked one of the throw pillows at my head. "Do you hear yourself? I really like when the cafeteria has those oatmeal chocolate chip cookies. I like the color gray. I like when a good song comes on the radio when I get in the car. I think when you're talking about the guy in your life, it should be more than 'like.'"

I started to cry. "I don't know what happened."

Win pulled me over to the sofa so I was next to her and patted my back while I cried.

"There's no reason for my feelings to change. He hasn't done a thing," I sobbed. "I used to love how he would take care of things, but now it feels like he's my second dad. It's like he's smothering me. I know you think we should stay together and that what I'm doing is wrong. I feel like the worst person in the world."

"Now, don't go getting all overly dramatic. That's my job," Win said. "It's not like you're clubbing seals, or bulldozing virgin forests, or chopping up people in your basement. You've got a long way to go if you want to be the worst person in the world." She held up a finger. "Not that I'm suggesting you try. And I guess I did want you and Josh to stay together. I liked you guys as a couple, but your relationship isn't supposed to be about me. If your feelings have changed, you have to tell Josh."

"I don't want to hurt him, and I don't want to lose him altogether."

Win shrugged. "Not sure there's a way around it." She tossed me her phone. "Call him. Have him meet you here. Talk to him about what's going on. With everything. Your memory and him."

chapter twenty-four

Josh was there in less than twenty minutes. He always looked out of place when he came to the barn. He wanted to like horses because he knew it was important to me, but you could tell he felt uncomfortable. To him they were like really large dogs that didn't sit and stay on command. It didn't help that Harry had bitten him once when he was feeding him a carrot. Josh was more a lab or living room kind of person.

He knocked on the lounge door and poked his head in. He seemed to sense the mood in the room and shifted nervously in the doorway. Win patted me on the knee as she got up.

"I'll leave you two so you can talk," Win said. She grabbed her stuff off the table.

"Why don't we all get some dinner?" Josh shoved in his hands into pants pockets. I could tell he wasn't interested in being alone with me. "We can talk over some Thai food," he suggested.

"No can do, I've got nonoptional family time planned. My nan in town means a command performance. She's not quite the royal family, but she likes to think she is. The queen must be obeyed." Win blew kisses at both of us. When Josh turned his head, she gave me a firm nod before walking out.

"What's going on?" Josh asked.

I blew out my breath in a slow stream. "I'm not really sure where to start."

"Looks like you and Win made up."

"I think so. I wasn't being a great friend to her." I swallowed. "I haven't been a great girlfriend to you, either."

Josh crossed the room and sat next to me. "It's okay. I know things aren't going well. Losing Harry. Feeling off since the procedure. I still feel really guilty about that."

I felt my heart tighten in guilt. "Don't apologize. It was what I wanted."

"All the more reason I should have stopped you. You were depressed." He squeezed my hand. "I know it's been rough, but things are going to get better. Your dad has you set up to see Dr. Delaney. The guy's a genius. If there's anything wrong, he'll sort it out."

"There's nothing wrong with me." I felt a ripple of annoyance. He was going into problem-solving mode again, like he was going to sort out all my silly little worries.

"Of course not. You're perfect." He smiled. "Just have him check it out, give you a clean bill of health."

I inched back so we weren't so close on the sofa. I was starting to feel claustrophobic. "You don't understand. What's happening to me isn't something wrong. They're memories. I'm recovering memories."

"Memories. Sure, it could be." Josh kept his voice calm and even. The way people talk to the elderly or really young. He was just playing along with me. "I'm sure it feels like that."

I pulled my hand back. "It doesn't feel like that; it *is* that." I got up and grabbed my bag off the table. I rummaged through and pulled out the picture. I passed it over to him. "This photo isn't a feeling. It's real."

Josh glanced down at the picture.

"It's a woman named Robyn."

"Okay."

"I'm pretty sure she's my mom."

Josh's eyebrows scrunched together. "What are you talking about?"

"She was married to my dad until I was nine years old. She's the woman that I've been seeing in my flashbacks."

"I don't understand." Josh stared down at the photo. He turned it over as if the answer might be written on the back.

"Join the club. My best guess at this point is that after she died, my dad wiped my memory."

Josh blinked rapidly, as if he were trying to clear something from his eyes. "He wouldn't do that; it would be too risky. Unethical."

I almost felt bad for him. He seemed more crushed than I'd been. The idea of my dad lying was foreign to him. It was like someone had told him for the first time that Santa wasn't real. "He must have done it. How else can you explain it?" I didn't want to be cruel, but I needed him to see it.

Josh stood and started pacing back and forth in front of the window that looked down on the practice ring. He'd pause as if he were about to say something and then start pacing again. I could practically see the wheels in his brain turning as he tried different theories and then rejected them. "How did you find this? Was it that guy?" he asked.

"His name is Neil."

Josh waved away my words. "Whatever. Was he the one who gave you the photo?"

"I know you don't trust him—" I started to say.

Josh cut me off. "The question is, why do you trust him? I checked him out, you know." He nodded when he saw my look of shock. "That's right. He has a criminal history."

"For what?"

"Does it matter for what? He has a record." Josh crossed his arms.

I refused to let him take me off track. Neil had told me he'd been in fights after he lost his brother, he might have been busted for that or for protesting, but none of that mattered.

Josh was focused on the wrong things. "Neil didn't give me the photo; I found it in my house. I also checked the information he gave me myself. The marriage license between Robyn and my dad is public record."

Josh spun away from me and started pacing again. "There has to be a reason for all of this. We must be missing something. It's like trying to put together a puzzle when you don't have all the pieces. When we have everything, it will make sense. We should talk to your dad."

I grabbed his arm and made him stop. "No."

"He's the one person who will know—"

"I said no. I'm not talking to my dad until I have more information. I'm also not seeing that doctor until I know what's going on. I'm only telling you to see if there's something that I'm missing."

Josh stared at me. "You can't think your dad would do something to you. He's crazy about you. You're his daughter."

I sat back down on the sofa and buried my head in my hands. "I don't know what I think anymore." Whatever I thought I knew about my dad, my family, my entire life, was now uncertain and shaky.

Josh crouched down in front of me. "We'll figure it out together. You know you can count on me, right?"

My throat felt tight. "Josh, that's something else we have to talk about."

"Don't." He took both of my hands. "Don't make any decisions when you're upset; you can't know what you want when you're like that."

The sad thing was I was now surer of what I wanted than I had been in a long time. "This isn't anything you've done; it's me." I hated that I was saying the most clichéd breakup line ever. "I know I'm not being a good girlfriend right now."

"That's okay." Josh swallowed hard, and I could see his Adam's apple bob in his throat. "Being a couple means understanding that there are ups and downs. I don't mind carrying a bit more of the load now while you focus on other stuff." He gave me a halfhearted smile. "I'm a guy, but I'm not so clueless that I think it's all about me all the time."

I hated this conversation. "You've never acted like it's all about you. That's not the issue."

"Then what is the issue?" There was a hint of sharpness in his voice. His jaw was tight. I could tell he wanted to ask if it was Neil, but he wouldn't say the words.

"I don't know who I am right now. Everything I thought I knew is upside down." I thrust the photo in his face. "I don't even know who my real mom is anymore. It's possible everything I knew before the age of nine is completely made up."

"What I feel for you isn't made up. It's real." Josh thumped his chest with his fist.

"I know. I don't doubt that you love me."

"You just doubt if you love me back." His eyes were filled with tears, but he didn't cry.

I longed to tell him exactly what he wanted to hear. I wanted to throw myself in his arms and tell him we'd be together forever, but I couldn't. "It's not black-and-white. I love you. You're one of my best friends. But somewhere along the way that's what we became. Friends. I don't think we should go—"

"Stop." Josh stood up. "Don't say it, okay? Don't say you'll always love me and hope we can be friends. I can't stand the thought of you saying that."

"The last thing I want is to hurt you," I mumbled.

"Then don't." He ran his hands through his hair. "Look, I get it. You're going through this awful thing and stuff is messed up. No wonder you don't know what you want. But you don't have to make a decision right now. You don't have to throw away what we have. It's been good, right?"

I nodded, not trusting myself to speak.

"Then, let's not break up. We can just . . . put things on hold. You need some space. I can give it to you. We'll take a step back." He took a large step back as if to show me what he meant. "Just don't break up with me unless you're sure. We've been together a long time. I'll give you space if you promise not to give up on us."

"Okay." My voice came out almost as a whisper. I knew I shouldn't back down. Things between us weren't going to change, but I didn't have the guts to insist.

Josh's face showed instant relief. He knelt down and hugged me. "I love you, and I'm here if you need me." He pulled back when he felt me stiffen. "Sorry. No problem, no more hugging for a while." He waved his hands to show how much space was between us. He stood up and started looking around the room. He grabbed a small notebook that sat on the counter by the phone. "Consider us officially romantically on hold. But just because we're on hold doesn't mean I can't help you." He started making a to-do list. Josh loved a good list. "I'll check at work to see if there are any records of you ever being in the clinic before and also if there are any records of anyone having bigger chunks of their memory wiped."

Josh tapped the pencil against his lower lip while he thought of other things he could do. Win was right; he would think of what I should do next. I knew I should feel relieved to have him on my side, but instead I just felt sad.

chapter twenty-five

The first time I kissed Josh, I cut his lip open. In fairness, I'd only kissed two other people before him, so I wasn't exactly well practiced. In fifth grade my best friend at the time double-dared me to chase Tyler Winters on the playground and kiss him. I wasn't the kind to back away from a dare. She held him down while I planted one on him. He acted like he was grossed out, but I was pretty sure he liked it. In eighth grade I kissed Brian Inversoll. I knew he liked it because he got an instant hard-on. It was difficult to say who found that more awkward, him or me.

I found out Josh liked me in a roundabout way. His friend Chris asked Win what I thought of him. Win cleverly dodged the question to give me some time to consider the idea. She and I sat on the radiator in the second-floor girls' bathroom and dissected Josh's positive and negative traits. The more we talked about him, the more attractive I found him. Even things I hadn't been too sure about, like the way he wore his khaki uniform pants a bit too high and baggy, seemed sort of endearing. It was only later that I found out that his mom bought his uniforms secondhand, so getting a great fit wasn't always an option.

We kissed for the first time at the fall dance in the hallway outside the gym. We'd already danced two slow songs together, and I knew when he offered to buy me a Diet Coke from the machine that it was less about refreshment and more about being alone. I was really nervous. I was afraid that all the dancing, combined with the packed gym, had made me sweaty. I tried to catch a whiff of my own pits as I followed him out into the hall. I was also mad at myself for not having taken a Tic Tac when Win offered one to me. Now that we were getting ready to kiss, I was afraid my breath smelled like monkey butt.

Josh took my hand and was mumbling something about how nice I looked. I could feel the thump of the bass from the music in the gym keeping pace with my heartbeat. I knew he was nervous too, and in an uncharacteristic burst of confidence I decided to go for it. I leaned in to kiss him at the exact second he closed his eyes and bent to plant one on me. Our mouths slammed together, and Josh cut his lip on his teeth.

We got better at the kissing thing. Although I'd kissed two other guys, I tended to think of Josh as my first. He was the one where I figured it out. Where kissing felt natural, versus having a hyperawareness that someone else's tongue was in my mouth. We were going to be at different colleges next year, and while we'd avoided talking about it in detail, we both understood it wasn't going to be easy. Even though the logical side of my brain grasped the odds, I'd never been able to imagine him not in my life.

I sat on my bed going through a shoe box I had of stuff we'd collected together. Movie tickets, Valentine's Day cards, notes passed in class, the ribbon from the corsage he'd given me last year at the spring dance. I picked up a framed photo, the two of us sitting on a log at a bonfire down on the beach. Josh had his arm thrown around me, and we both smiled up at the camera. There was no doubt I liked him, but did I love him? I knew deep down I didn't, at least not like I used to, but I couldn't say when I'd stopped. I didn't think that being in love meant every moment had to be head over heels, but it seemed that at least some of it should be.

My phone rang. I recognized Neil's number. He'd called earlier in the day and I hadn't called him back. I was sure if I spoke to him, the first words out of my mouth would be how Josh and I were on a break. That would leave both of us wondering:

A) What exactly did I mean by "taking a break," and

B) Why did I feel the need to tell him?

"Hey." I shoved the framed photo of Josh and me back

in the box as I answered the phone. I couldn't talk with him looking up at me.

"Can you meet up with me?" Neil asked.

My heart skipped a beat. "Now?"

"It's important. Remember where we had that big talk?"

"The parking lot by—"

"Don't say the place, but yes, there. Meet me inside that store." Neil hung up without saying anything else. I stared down at my phone. I wasn't sure if I was ready to see him and to face whatever he had to tell me now. I sat on the edge of the bed. I shouldn't go. I should call him back and tell him it was too late, or come up with another excuse. I needed time to sort out how I felt about Josh. Seeing Neil was going to confuse things, and the last thing I needed at this point in my life was any more confusion.

My foot beat out a fast pattern on the carpet. Why would I start doing the smart thing now? I grabbed my bag off the floor and left a note for my parents before running out the door.

I walked in the grocery store and looked around but didn't see Neil. I was standing at the entrance when suddenly a cart bumped me lightly from behind. When I spun around, I realized it was Neil wearing a sweatshirt and a baseball cap shoved down low. "Anyone follow you here?" he asked out of the side of his mouth.

"Um. I don't think so."

"Grab a cart and meet me in the produce section." Neil walked a few steps to the side and pretended to take an interest in a display from the floral department.

I hesitated for a minute and then went outside to get a cart. When I got back inside, I saw Neil in the produce section looking over some bananas. I parked my cart next to his.

"What's going—" I got out before Neil held up a finger indicating I should be silent.

"Look at the fruit, not at me," he said. I raised an eyebrow. "In case someone is watching."

"You think someone's following you?"

"Yes. Maybe you, too." He must have been able to see my disbelief on my face. "Someone was up at the college asking about me. Asking some of the people I go to school with if they'd seen us together."

"Who—"

Neil grabbed some bananas and wheeled away. "Dairy case in two minutes."

I stood there staring down at the fruit. A woman reached past me to grab a bunch of bananas and I peered over at her. Was she spying on us or just trying to make sure she got her five servings? The woman ignored me and moved on. She was either really good at acting casual or she had zero interest in us. I pushed my cart up and down the produce section for a minute and then stood over the different types of cheese on display.

Neil pulled his cart so that he was standing behind me, fac-

ing the other direction. "There's more. Someone from Neurotech complained to the police department that I vandalized their
building," he said.

My brain scrambled to catch up to what he was saying. "I
don't understand." I turned to face him, but when he shot me
a look, I spun back around and focused on the Brie cheese. He
pulled his cart around so he was standing next to me.

"They say I set a Dumpster on fire. The police were very clear:
I was very lucky that the company was not choosing to file charges,
but this was my final warning. If I'm caught on the grounds again,
if I'm found 'nosing about,' they will come after me." He caught
my eye. "I didn't do it. I didn't set anything on fire."

There wasn't a cell in my body that doubted him. "Neurotech is covered in security cameras. They can't claim something
that isn't there."

"Thought of that. Apparently, the footage was accidentally
erased, but a guard is willing to testify he saw my face." Neil
wiped his hands on his pants and looked around. "If it ever
went to court, who are they going to believe? Me? I've been
open about how I feel about the company. They'll bring up my
brother and say it's a long-term grudge. They'll point to my history of protests and say I finally went too far. No way anyone
would think they were setting me up."

"Why would they lie about you being there?"

"The police made it pretty clear. I'm not to get near Neurotech or you."

My mouth clicked shut in shock. "Me?" I squeaked.

"Yep. The officer mentioned you by name."

I gripped the handle of the cart. "A bunch of the security guards at Neurotech are former cops. They could have called in some favors. It might not have been an official police visit."

"Their guns and uniforms looked pretty official." Neil's eyes darted around. "Cereal aisle. Also, put something in your cart; it looks weird empty."

I walked along an aisle and dropped a few random things in the basket. I pulled out my phone and pretended to be checking a list. I could use the reflection on the screen to see if there was anyone behind me. No one seemed to be following me, but I didn't have a clue how I would tell unless they were holding a giant I AM FOLLOWING YOU sign.

Neil was waiting for me in the cereal aisle, pretending to compare the ingredients between two different boxes. He put them back on the shelf when he saw me. "I don't think anyone has followed us here, but I still think we should be careful. They're serious about not wanting us to be in touch. The cops that came by knew my school schedule and address. They'd done their homework. Someone should have told me that you were the kinda girl to get a guy in trouble. My mom warned me about your type. Wrong side of the tracks and all that."

I tried to match his lighter tone. "Here I thought you were the rebel bad boy."

Neil pressed his hand to his chest. "Me? Heck no, that's

just an act. I do it to get women. Chicks dig bad boys."

"Chicks, huh?" I raised an eyebrow. "Hordes of them, I imagine."

"Have to beat 'em off with a stick, but like I said, I'm just putting it on. You're the dangerous one." He poked me in the side with his elbow.

He was joking, but I could tell having the cops talk to him had thrown him. If they moved forward with pressing charges, he could be in real trouble. "I'm sorry I got you mixed up in this," I said.

Neil shrugged. "It's okay."

I stared at him. "Why?"

He wrinkled up his face in confusion. "Why is it okay? I dunno, I'm pretty mellow. Could be a knight-in-shining-armor thing. Liking to help out the damsel in distress."

"No. Why are you helping me?" I realized I was practically holding my breath and made myself exhale normally. "I think I'd be the kind of person you would hate." I tried to explain. "You know, my family. The fact that we have money. What my dad does. Why bother with me at all?"

"Remember the first time I saw you?" He smiled. "Your friends were trying to get you out of the school parking lot because there were all these protestors and the journalist chasing you down, and ninety-nine-point-nine percent of people would have been terrified, but when I dared to imply your dad wasn't a stand-up guy, you gave me a piece of your mind. I liked that you stuck up for your family. You had this core of steel."

"Turns out I might have put too much faith in my dad." I sighed. "I'm always doing that, assuming things will be fine."

"That was another thing."

"What, that I tend to be delusional?" I tossed a box of Frosted Flakes in my cart. "My friend Win says I'm terminally positive. Like having Mary Poppins around all the time."

"I like it." He stared down at his hands. "After my brother died, I decided that the world was shit. Why was my brother in the accident to start with? Then, how bad must things have been for him to want to die? Why did this have to happen to my parents? And it wasn't just our family. How come companies get away with polluting? Heck, not just polluting, but making massive profits while they do it. There are people who hurt kids or torture animals just for kicks. Most politics are corrupt. People use religion to spew hate. Hell, then there's the whole earth turning against us; climate change should pretty much kill off what's left on the planet at some point, and you can't even really argue that we wouldn't have it coming."

"But we can still do something about all of that stuff. We don't have to accept it," I argued, leaning forward on my cart.

His smile widened. "And that's why I liked you. It doesn't seem to matter how shitty things look; you find something good in all of it. I want to think the world can be a good place, but you believe it. It's more than that: I need to believe that the world isn't all bad, and I think you might be able to help me with that."

I thought about what he said. "I do believe it. But it's different now. Things aren't as clear as they used to be. It's like I want to have faith everything will work out, but I don't see how."

"Some things won't work out." He looked around, and when he saw we were alone in the aisle, he touched my arm. "I'm not saying things with your dad are going to turn out bad, just that not everything turns out with a happy ending. But some things do. That's what hanging around you taught me."

"And what are you going to teach me?" I asked.

"That it's possible to get through the bad stuff."

I stared at him and then leaned forward.

Neil pulled back. "I thought you didn't want—"

"I want," I said. He didn't pause again; we both leaned forward and kissed.

chapter twenty-six

The first few moments of kissing Neil, every sense in my body reported back how it was different from kissing Josh. Neil smelled like clean laundry and fresh air. Josh smelled like a mix of rubbing alcohol from the labs, Zest soap, and the woodsy cologne he liked. Josh was lean with angles. Neil was larger, his body firm. He was also hot. It was like he had an internal generator cranking out the heat; I felt the warmth from his hands burning through my clothes. It burned thoughts of Josh out of my head.

I felt as if there were a cable that ran from my chest to his, tethering us together. It pulled me toward him, connected us. The blood in my ears made a rushing noise, and the sound of our breath coming faster excited me. Neil pushed me so we were pressed against the shelves and hidden by a display of chocolate syrup. I pushed his T-shirt up so I could feel his bare skin. My index finger traced his ribs under a layer of muscle. It felt as if his body was all that was holding me down and that if he weren't there I would float up and away.

"Wait." Neil pulled back. "Give me a second." He closed his eyes.

My insides had turned into molten metal, and I felt as if I could ooze onto the floor and melt through the tiles. "You okay?" I whispered.

He chuckled. "I'm doing a bit more than fine." He held on to the handle of his cart and took a deep breath. "I don't want this to happen too fast."

"I'm not confused about you, if that's your worry. This isn't some rebound thing. I've been thinking about you for a while, since the bike ride. Probably before that, but I wasn't ready to do anything. I'm ready now."

He smiled. "So you've liked me since the bike ride, huh?"

I rolled my eyes. "Don't fish for compliments."

He looked up and down the aisle. "I want to go out with you. On a real date."

"As opposed to all the pretend dates we've been on."

"I want to take you out to dinner," he insisted. "I want to get to know you. Have you come over, watch movies. I want you to meet my friends. I want to see you ride a horse, but I don't see that happening."

I swallowed. I'd assumed he wanted to go out with me

too, but now I wasn't sure. Did he think he would embarrass me? Or that I would make some random comment that would make me sound like a snobby society girl in front of his friends? He hadn't always seen me at my best, but I was capable of basic social interaction. "Pick a place for dinner and we'll go."

He shook his head clearly frustrated. "You're missing the point. I'm not supposed to see you at all. The police told me to stay away from you, or else," he said. He gestured around the grocery store. "Look at us—we're hiding behind a display of chocolate syrup so we can make out. We're meeting places where we hope no one recognizes us. Does this seem like a normal dating relationship to you?"

My stomach dropped. I tried to picture Neil and my dad sitting in my living room watching a football game together. It was like trying to imagine keeping a mini Godzilla as a home pet—an interesting image, but impossible.

Neil sighed. "Don't you get it? Your dad is the one who sent the cops to my place."

I crossed my arms over my chest. "That's not possible. My dad doesn't know anything about you. This is something that the security detail has focused on. They've seen you protest the company and somehow they found out you were poking into my dad's past." I hated the expression in his eyes. I could tell he didn't believe me. "You don't know these guys. They rely on my dad for their jobs. They'd do anything to protect him. They don't tell him stuff they think would upset him or distract him from what they think he should be doing." I tried to find a way to explain it. "It's not just work—my mom and I have always done it too. We arrange everything so nothing gets in the way of him doing what he does best. My mom makes sure he never has to use his brainpower on repairing the roof, or worrying that we're out of milk, or helping me if I'm struggling in chemistry. My dad isn't going to spend his time on my love life. I'm sure he doesn't know about you. The warning came from someone else."

"This isn't just about who you're dating. It's about him," Neil said. "It's about whatever he did to cover up the lie of your real mom. The reason he doesn't want me around is that he doesn't want to know what I might find out."

I wanted to cover my ears. "What else is there to find out? She died. Most likely I couldn't handle it, or he couldn't handle a nine-year-old obsessed with grief, and he wiped my memory. Should he have done it? No."

"What if it's more than that?" He took a deep breath. "I did some more checking into your real mom."

"I didn't ask you to do that," I pointed out. I didn't want to hear what he found out.

"She was a scientist like your dad, but she was really focused on ethics. She wrote an article about the importance of transparency in the development of new drugs and procedures. She did her PhD thesis on the importance of informed consent." He pulled his backpack out of the cart. "I downloaded a copy of it if you want to read it."

I shook my head. "What's the point of all of this?"

"What if your mom knew that the procedure had major side effects?"

His words hit me, and then their meaning exploded into brittle shrapnel. "You think my dad did something to my mom?" I felt sick. "No, not something. You're saying that she uncovered what the procedure could do and he killed her to keep it quiet." I wanted to run down the aisle away from him. I needed more air or there was the very real risk that I'd vomit. My dad was clearly lying to me, but this was going too far. Neil hated my dad and he was willing to think the worst of him, but that didn't mean I was willing to make this leap. My brain scrambled to go through my memory of Robyn: Had she fallen down the stairs, or had she been pushed?

Neil reached for my hand, but I stepped back, knocking a few boxes of cereal off the shelf. "I don't know if that's what happened—" he said.

"No, you don't know." I cut him off. "I know you think you understand my dad, and I'll admit he's not perfect and he's made some huge mistakes, but he's not someone who would kill someone. Kill my mom, his wife." I hated the feeling of uncertainty in the center of my stomach and was mad that Neil had put it there.

Neil held up his hands in surrender. "I shouldn't have said anything, but I thought you should know what I found out."

"No, you told me because you want to prove to me you're right. You think the world is shit, but I'm telling you not everyone in it is. It might seem like my dad has it all and is some kind of dictator at Neurotech, but he's not God. If he killed someone, the police wouldn't let him off." I pushed down the thought in my head that if it looked like an accident, he might just get away with it.

"There are a lot of people who protest Neurotech. Even if the security staff investigated me because of what I've been checking into, how did they find out that I knew you? Someone told. Who of your friends knows about me?" Neil asked.

I spun around and pushed my cart down the aisle, my hands shaking. I could hear Neil trailing after me. I turned around and hissed at him. "So it's not enough that my dad's a murderer? One of my friends also must have betrayed me too, huh?" Josh's face flashed in my mind. *Would he?*

"You're only mad at me because you don't want to hear this. You don't want to believe that your faith in your family and friends might be misplaced."

"No, I'm mad at you because what you're saying is wrong." *And mean,* I wanted to add, but even in that state I knew that saying it would make me sound like a toddler.

"Look at the facts. Someone from Neurotech warned me to back off from the company *and* you. They might try to protect your dad, but they have no reason to worry about his daughter. The most likely thing is that your dad asked someone to scare me off. How did he know about us? Either he's spying on you, or someone told him."

"It could have been one of your friends," I said.

"The only one who knows anything about you is Trey. Why would he tell on me? There's nothing for him to gain."

"Why would my friends tell on me?"

"Because they think they're protecting you? Maybe because they don't want you going out with me." Neil's voice was getting louder, and a woman glanced at us as she made her way down the aisle. We were attracting attention. He lowered his voice and looked over his shoulder.

I couldn't stop thinking about Josh. How far would he go to protect me? "I need to go." I grabbed my bag out of the cart and abandoned everything else in it. "Thanks for all the information. I'll consider what you said." I forced my voice to come out calm and rational.

"Harper, wait."

I started walking toward the door, but he was right behind me. He sped up and walked around, getting between the door and me. "Get out of my way," I said.

"Let me explain," Neil said.

I felt panicked. I stepped to the right, but he moved so he was still in front of me. "Let me go," I repeated louder. The cashier closest to us looked over. I could tell she was considering calling a manager.

Neil took a quick step to the side and the automatic door whooshed open. "I'm sorry. I don't want to scare you. I just want you to listen."

I stood in the doorway, half in the store and half in the parking lot. The sun had gone down, and the night was cold.

"I'm not saying these things to hurt you. I'd change it if I could. I wish I'd met you in a coffee shop, or at a party, or just about any way other than because I was protesting your dad's company. If I could go back and not know all this stuff, I would, but I do. You know it too. You can't pretend to ignore it," Neil pleaded with me.

"You might be surprised what I can ignore when I set my mind to it." Even as the words came out of my mouth, I knew they were a lie. I had to have answers, but more than anything I wished I could walk away and never think of it again.

chapter twenty-seven

I didn't want to go home, and both Win's and Josh's places were out. One of the best things about animals is that you can trust them. Horses don't lie. They don't say things to hurt your feelings. You don't have to worry about what they really mean, or if they have an ulterior motive. They just are. They might shit on your boots, and if you aren't careful they might nip you, but that's about the worst that will happen. When I turned on my car after the confrontation with Neil and had no idea where to go, the first safe place that came into my head was the stable.

Hampton Mews might have looked like an eighteenth-century barn, complete with quaint details, but it also housed over twenty horses and equipment that added up to hundreds of thousands of dollars. No way were they going to go with old-fashioned guard and just throw a padlock on the door. The security system was as elaborate as Fort Knox with alarms, motion sensors, and for all I knew ninjas that could be lowered from the ceiling in an emergency. I punched in my personal security code number and heard the alarm beep its acceptance.

The main barn had motion sensor lights set up, so as I walked down the hall, the lights flicked on. The horses nickered and neighed in their stalls. They were interested in the change in their routine. The barn wasn't a typical party place; the last groom would finish up and go into his apartment above the stable by eight. A few of the horses tossed their heads over their stall doors to check out events. I grabbed a handful of alfalfa treats from the bag. Dallas gave a nicker of recognition when he saw me. He tossed his head, which I took to mean, *Hey, girl, what's up?* I held out the treats, and his soft velvet mouth took them gently, barely tickling the palm of my hand.

"Things are pretty fucked up," I admitted.

Dallas snorted. I suspected he was a horse who had heard many tales of woe. He butted my head softly with his nose. I gave him another handful and then petted his forelock. There was something about the soft, bristled fur that was soothing.

The next stall over had been Harry's. His brass nameplate was still on the door. The stall had been washed and cleaned, and someone had stacked a few bales of clean hay in the corner, using the space as storage. It looked empty without Harry. I waited for a wave of sadness to come over me, but there was nothing.

I wanted to feel again. The black void where he'd been threatened to consume me. I stepped in and touched the various ribbons on the wall. Some were events I could remember and others were vague. There had been so many over the years that they blurred together. My forehead pressed against the wooden wall, and I thought about Harry. I could picture him, a mental image of me sitting on his back, but I felt nothing. I strained to reconnect with those memories, but they were gone. It was like riding him had been something that happened to someone else. I couldn't even feel sad about losing memories of him; I'd given them away. Traded away all the good memories to get rid of the bad.

I sat on the hay bale and took a bunch of deep breaths to try to clear my mind. Wasn't this supposed to be some kind of Zen thing? Millions of Buddhists couldn't be wrong, but it wasn't working for me. I couldn't stop thinking about everything. I'd push one thought away, and six others would rush to fill the space. My own skin didn't seem to fit anymore. I couldn't get comfortable. Was this how people felt before they finally snapped and went crazy? I wondered if this was how Neil's brother had felt—like his life was unraveling. I jumped up. I needed to do something or I'd start screaming.

I clicked on the light to the tack room. Every owner had a locker for his or her things. I opened the black-stained wooden door. I had a Devoucoux saddle. One of the grooms had cleaned it after my last competition and put it away on the saddle rack.

I pulled it out and placed it on the blanket on the center table. With the exception of Harry, my saddle was the single most expensive thing I'd ever owned. It was a work of art. As far as I was concerned, it could have been propped up on a marble pillar in the house like a piece of sculpture. I caressed the dark mahogany leather and breathed deep to pull in the smell, a mix of leather, horse, and saddle soap.

I dusted the saddle with one of the soft cloths from the equipment room. You had to be careful when you cleaned a saddle so you didn't rub dirt into the leather; you could scratch and scar it that way. I used a paintbrush to clean any dirt under the skirt and around the pommel. I opened a tin of saddle soap and inhaled the familiar smell. I rubbed it on the leather the way Laura had taught me, with tight small circles.

As much as I tried to focus on something else, anything else, I kept cycling back around to what Neil had told me. And to kissing him. That was another memory that I couldn't shake. I was off-balance— part of me wanted to go back to making out with him and the other part wanted to hit him for telling me things I didn't want to know. It didn't seem possible to want both of these things at the same time, but somehow I was managing it.

I polished the saddle harder. How dare he say I was too scared to face real life? It was normal to want to avoid unpleasant things. That was why people didn't go strolling through broken glass or drink milk that smelled off. I picked up the tin of saddle soap and hurled it against the wall. The horses shifted uneasily in their stalls at the loud noise.

Chucking the tin didn't make me feel any better. It also left a small black mark on the wall. I had to do something that would make a difference. Throwing a tantrum like a toddler wasn't going to do it. I pulled out my phone. Did I really think my dad would have done anything to my mom? There was no reason not to confront him. No reason to be scared. If I really wanted answers, I had to stop fishing around and go directly to him. He picked up on the first ring.

"Dad?"

"Hey, Harper, where were you tonight? Your mom expected you home for dinner. When she found the note you left in the hall that you'd gone out, she was on the warpath." He lowered his voice. "Not that I blame you; she made that vegan fake macaroni-and-cheese casserole thing. If there's proof of Satan, it's that fake cheese. What the hell do they make that stuff out of, anyway?"

"I need to talk to you."

He was silent. I pictured him sitting in his office staring up at his action figures. He knew I didn't want to talk about something like the origins of vegan cheese. "Okay. You come home and we can have a family meeting."

"Not Mom." My mouth soured even saying the word "mom." I couldn't stand these lies one more second. "Just you and me." My stomach had gone into high acid production mode. If this kept up, I was going to develop an ulcer by the end of the day. "I have some things I want to ask you."

"I see." His voice had lost the joking tone; now he sounded like he did on one of his conference calls with the Neurotech board. Calm and all business. "When can I expect you?"

"I'll be home in twenty minutes."

"Drive safe. I don't want anything to happen to you."

I clicked off the phone and dropped it on the table. It was too late to back out now. I'd put things in motion. I debated calling Neil to tell him what I'd done, to show him that I wasn't nearly as scared as he made me out to be, but I was afraid he'd hear the tremor in my voice.

I know I should wash the saddle soap off and condition the leather, but I didn't want to take the time. I'd do it later. I gave the saddle a quick wipe and hefted it back onto the rack.

Dallas watched me shut up the tack room. He neighed softly. I grabbed another handful of alfalfa treats and held them out for him. When he finished them, I patted him on the nose.

"Wish me luck," I said. I pulled open the door and reset the alarm.

Dallas neighed again, which I took to mean *You're going to need it.*

chapter twenty-eight

There was no sign of my mom, or at least the woman I'd thought of as my mom, when I got home. I'd expected her to jump on me for missing dinner, but the house was quiet. I wondered if my dad had asked her to leave. The house was perfectly clean, everything put away, tidied up. It could have been cut out of a Pottery Barn catalog. There wasn't anything that made it ours. Even the framed family photos on the mantel looked staged, like the pictures that came with the frame when you bought it.

I grabbed a bottle of water out of the fridge. I wasn't thirsty, but I thought it would be good to have something to keep my hands busy. I stood outside his closed office door. My dad was a master at negotiation and getting people to do what he wanted. He always said he wished he could focus on the science of Neurotech and ignore the business side, but the truth was he liked it. "Business is war" and all that. It gave him a chance to feel like he was living out one of his strategy games. He could be a five-star boardroom general. I noticed that he'd shut his office door, which was a power play. It meant I would knock, letting him be the one to give me permission to enter.

I lowered my hand. Screw it. Neil said he thought I was brave. It was time for me to live up to that. I opened the door without knocking. My dad looked up, surprised. Point one of the game went to me. He glanced up at the clock on the shelf.

"You're early."

"Not a lot of traffic."

I could tell he wanted to ask me where I'd been, but didn't want to waste a question on something that didn't matter. He motioned for me to sit across from him. As soon as I sat, I realized that my chair was lower than his. Point to Dad.

He sat silently, waiting for me to talk. I knew this was a power play too. I tried to hold out, but the silence was stretching my last nerve. "Have you been checking on me?" I finally asked.

"What do you mean, checking on you?"

He wasn't going to make any of this easy. "I mean, have you been having me followed, making notes of who I see and what I do? It's Josh, isn't it?" I put into words what I knew had to be true. "You have him running and reporting to you like some kind of spy. He tells you all about every detail of my life."

"He's concerned about you." Dad leaned back, lacing his hands together over his belly.

My heart sank. I'd known it, but it was still hard to hear. "He wants to make you happy," I spit out. "It's not about me. It's about his desire to make you proud of him." How long had Josh continued to date me because he was really in love with my dad? With the idea that someday he could be just like him? He'd asked me questions, acted interested in my life, and then told my dad everything. It made me sick.

Dad sighed as if the entire conversation tired him. "I think your anger at Josh is misplaced."

"Don't worry, I'm not saving all my anger for Josh. You have no business trying to scare off my friends. Threatening them. Telling them to stay away from me."

"You consider this Neil fellow to be a friend?" His face gave away nothing.

He admitted he knew about Neil. A mix of feelings flooded in, relief that he'd told the truth and disappointment that he'd done it. I hadn't wanted to believe he was capable of it, but now there was no running from it. "Yes. Neil is one of the few friends I have left."

He sighed. "You're not going to believe me, but he's not."

"You're right; I don't believe you." I made myself meet his eyes. "I know about my mom. My real mom."

Dad let out a long breath through his pursed lips.

"Aren't you going to say anything?" I asked, trying to keep

my voice under control. My entire body shook, like an electrical current was running through every nerve.

"First off, I don't think it's fair to imply Louise isn't your 'real' mom. She's been there for you day in and day out since you were nine." He brushed me off before I could cut him off. "I'm aware I owe you an explanation, but I'm going to request that you not interrupt until I've shared the entire story."

I realized I was squeezing the water bottle too tightly and relaxed my grip before it exploded. "Fine."

"I'll admit mistakes were made. However, I won't apologize for doing what I thought was best."

"Erasing my childhood was the best?"

He tapped the desk with his Waterman pen. "I thought we agreed you were going to be quiet until I had a chance to finish."

I clenched my jaw and nodded.

"You and your mom, Robyn, were close. She called you Shadow. As a toddler you'd cling to her legs. If she got up, you got up. She went into the kitchen; you were a step behind her. You had a connection, I guess you'd call it. I suppose lots of moms and daughters do, but it seemed even more than that. You were two peas in a pod. She rode horses too."

I wondered if he knew I'd already found that out. Mentioning Harry was on the tip of my tongue, but I managed to choke it down.

"You know she died." He waited for me to nod. "It was a horrible accident. Stupid. Just a missed step and she fell. It shouldn't have happened, but it did. Losing a mother at a young age isn't easy for anyone. It was more than that for you. You were devastated. Your mom was your bedrock; when she had the accident, it was as if your world bottomed out. You stopped talking. You were hardly eating. You started sleepwalking. One night you let yourself out of the house. You were walking down the center of the road at two in the morning in bare feet. I had to bungee-cord the door shut to keep you from getting out. I used a bell so I could hear you and wake up before you got too far.

"I took you to counselors. God, all sorts of counselors: someone who did play therapy, and another who did art therapy, and another guy who was all about pets; he'd have you playing with bunnies and dogs." Dad snorted. "At least you seemed to sort of enjoy that, but it wasn't making any difference. You weren't any better. I wasn't sure what to do. Everyone kept saying to give you time, but you kept wandering off in the night. Or I wouldn't be able to find you and it would turn out you'd crawled into the closet and cried yourself to sleep. It was like the grief was going to kill you." He looked at me. "Do you remember any of this?"

Nothing. My brain wasn't even giving me a hint. I had a sense what he was telling me was at least partly the truth. There was a nagging feeling that what he was saying was on the border of what I could remember. "No."

"I thought I might lose you." Dad's voice cracked, and he stopped to pull himself together. "I'd lost my wife, and I didn't know what I would do if I lost you, too. All those fancy doc-tots? They didn't know what to do either. What if one night I didn't catch you? What if you got hit by a car and died? What if you wandered off on a cold night and fell asleep in the woods and never woke up?"

I stared at him. I couldn't escape the feeling that he wasn't telling me everything. That there was more, but I wasn't able to find it in the haze of my mind.

"Your mom was the one who had the original idea for Memtex. We were through with the clinical trials around the time she died. We had a green light to move forward. Investors were lining up to give us money. I'll admit I was excited. I knew it was going to be big. It was going to change our lives. But your mom wasn't as excited about the business aspects. She would have been happy signing over the idea and staying in the lab; what made her happy was that the procedure was going to make a difference for other people. People were going to get their lives back. When she was gone, and when I thought I was going to lose you, too, I thought, 'There's nothing she'd want more than to save her own daughter.' Her accident didn't have to end your life too."

A band of tension around my chest loosened. No matter how bad this was, at least he hadn't killed her. It might have been irrational, but I believed him. It had been an accident.

"Why did you take all of her away from me?" I'd planned for the words to come out as a firm question, but my voice made it pleading. "You could have softened things, but instead you wiped them altogether."

Dad rubbed his eyes. "I tried. I took you into the lab and gave you the procedure, but it didn't seem to stick. You have to realize that the procedure wasn't anywhere near approved for use with kids, and certainly not kids as young as you were. The brain at that age is growing and changing, making new neural connections almost fast enough to see. I softened the memories, but as soon as I did, your brain would find another route."

"So you just wiped it out all together. Wiped her."

He nodded. "If I'd thought there was another way, I swear to God, I would have done it. I'm not making excuses, but you have to understand I wasn't in the best place. I'd lost my wife. I was working these crazy hours trying to get the company off the ground, not sleeping well. I didn't have a lot of support; both your mom's family and mine were gone. I wanted to make things better, and at the time it seemed like the only solution."

"Did you love her?"

He looked up shocked. "Your mom? Robyn was . . . everything."

"Then how did you move on so quickly? I get that you needed me to forget, but it's like you forgot too," I said.

Dad pulled his lower desk drawer out and rummaged through, pulling out all the folders. Then he pressed on the bottom of the drawer, and it popped up, showing a shallow hiding space below. Clearly, I should have spent more time when I broke into his office. He pulled out a file and passed it over to me. It was a folder stuffed with photos. I picked through

them: a wedding picture showing my dad and real mom looking impossibly young. My breath caught in my throat. There
was a picture of my parents holding me as a toddler, all three
of us in front of a straggly Christmas tree. Our faces had huge,
matching smiles.

"I never forgot, but I did make a decision to move forward.
I knew staying in our home was a bad idea. There were too
many things to remind you of the past in the house. I didn't
want to take the chance of your memory flooding back. It
made sense to live closer to Seattle for Neurotech's start-up, so
I decided we'd start over. It wasn't that I wanted to erase Robyn,
but it was easier to make a clean break. I told myself I was
doing it for you, but I can admit now it was for me, too." He
stared down at his hands. "It might have been a poor decision,
but I made it for the right reasons."

He tried to smile, but it was brittle. "I've never been good
with emotions and feelings. I've always had an engineering brain.
So I handled this the same way. I couldn't deal with my grief, so
I boxed it up and refused to think about it. Louise worked with
your mom and me. She'd stepped up after your mom died. She
offered to come with me to help. You liked her. You always had.
She moved into the house as sort of a nanny and assistant."

I couldn't meet his eyes. It seemed slimy and wrong no
matter how he tried to package it.

He shrugged. "You already saw her as sort of a mother figure. She was the first woman you saw after the procedure. She

was around and took care of you. It seemed easiest to let her take that role for real." He cleared his throat. "I came to care for Louise. I don't want to make it sound like some kind of business relationship. It evolved into love."

"Did you think I'd never find out?"

"I hoped so. Later, I wondered if I'd made a mistake, but the decision was done. There was no way to go back. I wanted to make the best of things so you could have a good life." He reached for my hand across the desk and squeezed it. "You have had a good life, haven't you? You've been happy."

"Yes, but it hasn't been real," I protested.

"What's real? Life is about experiences and what we remember. I took away a horrific moment in your life and gave you a foundation to build on that led you to this point. What might have happened to you if I'd left things? What if you'd stayed depressed? Would you have done as well in school? Made friends? I don't know, but I wasn't willing to risk it when I had a way to make it better. Am I sorry I lied to you? Yes. Would I do it the same way again? I think so."

I sat silently in the chair. I'd had thousands of questions, but now they'd dried up and blown away. "When you realized I was remembering, you could have told me. You left me twisting, not knowing what to believe."

He fussed with the papers on the desk. "I should have. My only excuse is that I thought it might go away. Or I hoped it would go away. That was why I wanted you to come in for an appointment.

I thought I'd be able to tell how far things had gone. I shouldn't have let you find out all of this from that fellow."

I didn't like how he referred to Neil. "It's not his fault. I asked him to help me."

Dad sniffed dismissively. "I'm sure he's been a great help."

"You can't be mad at him because he told me the truth."

"He's not telling you the whole truth. He hates Neurotech. He wants to use you to take down the company. He's acting as if he's your friend, like he cares about you, but this is all about his misguided desire for revenge." With every word his finger stabbed down on his desk, as if he were pinning the words into place.

"I know about his brother," I said. "He told me the very first time we met. He hasn't been hiding it."

He leaned back in his seat and crossed his hands over his belly. "Did he tell you about his sister?"

I took a slow breath in. It seemed that suddenly I'd turned around and discovered that I was on the very edge of a cliff. That I'd danced right up to it without having any idea how close I was to falling. He knew something. Something that I wasn't going to want to hear.

"She's that reporter," Dad spit out. "The one who's been hounding the company, calling for investigations and trying to sniff out trouble. The one who showed up at your school."

"That's not his sister." Even as I said it, I knew I was wrong. My dad wouldn't be mistaken about something like this. He'd done his homework and was about to make me regret not having done my own.

He tossed a sheet of paper across the desktop. It drifted to a stop in front of me. It was some type of report from a private investigation company. "It's all there. Gambel is her married name."

I stared at the paper, but the words were blurring together. That was when I realized I was crying. No loud sobs, just tears running silently down my face.

"He's using you to help his sister. The two of them are looking to get some kind of revenge for their brother. Don't get me wrong, what happened to his brother is a tragedy, but four doctors and a team of lawyers have been over his case. Neurotech isn't to blame. They can't prove a thing, so they're looking for another way to take me down, and they planned to do it through you. He sucked up to you, pretended to be your friend, pretended to like you so that he could get the justice he thinks he's owed. The whole thing is a setup." His voice dripped disgust.

"I didn't know," I whispered. My eyes stayed on the paper, trying to rearrange the letters so they would say something else, so things would make sense again. I'd known it was a risk to trust him, but I hadn't really believed he would betray me. *Everyone in my life lies.*

"If what happened to you as a child comes out, we could lose everything. This house, the company, our family. I'd go to prison," Dad said.

I looked up, surprised.

"How do you think the police would view me using experimental treatment on a child, on my own child? It wasn't approved for children at that time. They're not going to believe it was about doing the best for you. It will destroy the company. There's no coming back from that kind of public relations nightmare. Not to mention what the federal regulators would do. We'd be buried under red tape for years." He sighed. He suddenly looked tired to me, and older, as if he'd aged ten years during the conversation. "I know you're mad at me and I understand why, but I can't believe you honestly want to destroy this family and everything I worked to build my entire life."

I felt hollowed out. I'd been so sure Neil liked me, but it had all been a lie. My family was a lie. Josh lied. I didn't have the energy to fight anymore. "What do you need me to do?"

Dad leaned forward. "You need to cut off all contact with Neil. Without your cooperation there's a chance this whole story dries up."

"Okay." My voice was barely loud enough to be heard.

He patted my hands on the desk. "Don't worry. We've moved on from worse, and we can move on from this. We'll put this behind us and pretend it never happened."

chapter twenty-nine

I sat in the car trying to convince myself that I had the energy to get through the school day. The cliché would be that I'd been so crushed to discover that Neil was using me that I'd cried myself to sleep. My problem was that while I had done plenty of crying, the sleep part had been a bit harder to come by. I was beyond exhausted when I finally gave up and got out of bed. My brain appeared to be too small for my skull. My eyes felt as if I'd rolled them in sand and grit. When blinking hurts, you know it isn't going to be a good day.

I was mad at myself for never really having questioned Neil or his motivations. I knew he hated my dad's company. He'd told me how much his brother meant to him, and not once had I ever really questioned if he was being honest. I thought I was so clever that I checked on my dad's marriage license, but I'd never checked into Neil's history. I took everything he said as true. It was more than that; I'd wanted what he said to be true, like some little kid lying in bed wanting to know her bedtime story had a happy ending. I wanted him to be my prince, who was going to sweep me up and make everything okay. I was graduating soon. In theory I should have been an adult, and instead I acted like a kid.

There was one more thing to do before I headed into school. I'd spent part of my time awake the night before trying to figure out what to say. I'd practiced different conversations in my head, but couldn't find the right words. Sometime around five a.m. I'd decided that was because there weren't words that would make it right. I'd decided to wing it.

Neil's phone went direct to voice mail. I couldn't decide if I was happy about being able to dodge talking to him, or disappointed to miss hearing what he had to say.

I waited for the beep and then took a breath hoping the words would come. "It's me. Guess what I discovered? That reporter who's been chasing after my dad? She's your sister. 'Course, I imagine you already knew that. I was the only one who didn't know. You should have told me." My voice caught, and I paused to get control. "I thought you were—I thought we—" My voice cut off again. "Guess I'm learning all the time that the world isn't the nice place I thought. I learned that from you, so I guess I did get something out of our relationship. I got the lesson, so you don't need to ever call me again."

I clicked off the phone and rested my head on the steering

wheel. The only thing I wanted to do was sleep. There was a huge band of pressure around my head, like I'd stuffed it in a vise and kept turning the crank. The first bell rang in the distance. Maybe I could miss the first hour and take a quick catnap in the car.

A tap on the window made me jump. Josh stood outside the car, peering in.

"You okay?" he asked.

I stared at him through the window. I grabbed my bag and got out of the car. "Bad night." I headed into the building. I'd checked one thing off my list, but I wasn't interested in tackling this so early in the day. I needed to wake up.

Josh trailed a step behind me. "I was thinking we could maybe grab something to eat after school."

"I'm not really feeling that great." I flung open my locker and grabbed my history text out of it. I wanted him to give me some space, but he was stuck to my side.

"I could come over to your place, make you some of that ginger tea my mom always makes."

"No thanks. I need sleep more than anything else." I slammed my locker shut.

"Tell you what, if you're that tired, why don't you talk to the nurse and head home? I'll talk to your teachers and get any homework and bring it by later." Josh was still one step behind me as I walked down the hall.

My shoulders hunched up around my ears. "Don't make me say it," I said over my shoulder.

He touched my elbow. "Say what?"

I whirled around. "I don't want you to come over." I stepped closer so I was inches from his face. "I don't want you in my house. I don't want to see you."

A few people near us turned to look at us, sensing drama in the air. I spun on my heel and stormed off.

"No you don't." Josh chased after me. "You can't say something like that and not explain yourself."

"Hey, you guys," Win called out. She stopped when she saw our faces. "Whoa. Is everything okay?"

Josh threw his hands up in the air. "I have no idea. You need to ask her."

"You want an explanation, Josh? Why don't you tell Win how you've been spying on me for my dad."

Win's mouth made a silent O.

"I didn't—" Josh started.

I cut him off before he could add to the lies piling up around me, burying me alive. "My dad told me."

Josh's shoulders slumped. He looked smaller. "I was worried about you; I was trying to help."

"I used to think the best of everyone, you know. There was a time that if you said that, I would have been mad, annoyed at you, but I would have accepted that you did it because you care. I want to believe that, but I don't know if I do anymore."

"Why else would I? You've been different ever since you had the procedure." Josh's face was blotchy and red.

"Don't lie to yourself, too. You did it to get in good with

my dad. Maybe he framed it that you were doing it for me. He gave you an excuse to do it, but in your heart you did it because you wanted his approval. Well, congrats. You got it. All it cost you is me."

"That's crazy," Josh said, but he didn't meet my eyes.

"No, it isn't. You always wanted to be like him. I suppose the good news is that you are. My dad isn't a bad guy, but he's really comfortable with making things gray. As long as there's a good reason, a greater good, it means everything's on the table. He can do anything and not feel bad."

Win's eyes darted back and forth between us.

"Win, talk to her. Tell her she's being ridiculous," Josh begged.

Win backed up a step. "Oh no. I don't think I should be mucking about in the middle of this one."

"Having Win talk to me isn't going to make a difference. This is a decision I made myself. It's not up for a group vote. We can't be together. At least not the way we were."

Josh ran his fingers through his hair. It looked like he was going to start grabbing handfuls and yanking it out. "I can't believe you're saying this. We talked about sort of backing off. I shouldn't have pushed you about coming over."

I shook my head. "No. That was before I knew what happened. Now that I know, there's no going back."

"This is so you can date that guy, isn't it?" Josh's face flushed red.

A rush of shame filled my chest. I should have broken it off with Josh before now, but he had no business getting on his high horse. "I don't have to justify myself to you. This is about me not wanting to date someone who lies to me. Who takes my secrets and runs to my dad with them," I spit out.

"You've never liked that your dad and I got along so well." Josh looked ready to cry. I opened my mouth to say something, but he cut me off before I could speak. "You're afraid that I'm more the kid he always wanted. Someone who understands, hell, someone who is at least interested in, what he does. He likes me better than you, and you can't stand that."

Win's eye grew wider.

"Get out of my way," I said, my voice a low rumble. I could feel the rage inside me building. He was right. At some level, maybe, I'd kept Josh around because I knew it was a way to get my dad's approval. I certainly wasn't getting it on my own. It would be a cold day in hell before I admitted it to him.

I could see that Josh wanted to say something else, but I couldn't tell if it would be an apology or another insult. Instead he turned around and marched stiffly down the hall. I slumped against the closest locker. It felt like someone had let the air out and I was going to deflate like a balloon the day after a birthday party. I could picture myself flat and limp, lying on the floor.

"Didn't see that coming," Win said, her voice soft.

"Story of my life." I sighed. "Wanna hear another shocker? Neil's sister is that reporter who has been hunting down the story on my dad's company. He was using me to get info for her."

I was glad Win looked as shocked as she did. It made me feel like I hadn't been a complete loser for not suspecting him.

"How did you find out?"

"My dad told me." I managed to pull up a small smile. "I ended up confronting him the way you wanted."

"Based on how this turned out, I guess this means you're not going to take my advice anymore," Win said.

"I'm going to take some of your original advice and give love a pass for a while. No more guys. No more dating. Instead I'll hang around you and Kyle and make fun of the two of you for being all lovey-dovey."

Win tossed her hands in the air. "We should skip class and go to Walmart to load up on bottled water and canned goods. If I'm the optimist who believes in love, then it has to be a sign of the end of the world. It's just a matter of time until there's famine, volcanoes, maybe some zombies."

"Religious statues flinging themselves from their alcoves to take people out."

Win threw her arm around me. The vanilla smell of her Tom Ford perfume filled my head and made me feel slightly better. "Stick with me. There's no reason to lose faith in the world. Our buddy Saint Tom blessed me, and I'm going to pass it along. Besides, I happen to be an excellent zombie killer. I've got your back," she said.

I felt better for the first time in over a day. Life might be full of lousy things and people who'll stab you in the back, but never underestimate the value of a good friend. It gives you something to believe in.

chapter thirty

S pecial delivery," Laura called out.

I stopped inside the barn door. "What?"

"You got some mail." She waved an envelope back and forth.

I walked toward her carefully as if I expected it to blow up. "Who sent me something?"

Laura laughed. "How would I know? I'm nosy, but not so nosy that I'd open your letter." She nodded toward the door. "You come by to take one of the horses out? Dallas was out earlier, but Star could use a run."

"I came in to condition my saddle. I started to clean it the other day, but didn't finish."

Laura frowned. "Did one of the grooms not do a good job?"

I shook my head. The last thing I needed was to get someone

in trouble. "No, I just felt like giving it a good clean." She nodded. Laura understood I needed a project.

Laura passed me the envelope. I saw my name on the front. There was no address or stamp; it must have been dropped off personally. "Use the Amerigo conditioner. That saddle is worth it. Take care of it and it will last you a lifetime," she lectured me.

I saluted. Laura was rabid about taking care of your equipment. I was glad there was no one else in the tack room. I wanted to be alone. Win had offered to come with me, but I'd told her to go out with Kyle instead. I suspected she needed a break from my sad sighs and the fact that I broke into tears over anything from songs on the radio to what was on the menu for hot lunch. She'd stuck by my side for the past two days like my own personal emotional bodyguard. She'd done everything possible to make me happier. She brought Krispy Kreme doughnuts when she picked me up for school and blasted only upbeat music in the car. She lent me one of her pashmina scarves that she knew I loved. She made sure Josh and I stayed far apart and must have talked to our bigger circle of friends, because no one asked me about what had happened between Josh and me.

I pulled the saddle down and put it on the rack. I turned the letter over in my hand. I knew who'd sent it. Neil was the only person I knew who still wrote letters, other than someone's grandparents. Just because he sent a letter didn't mean I had to read it. There was no law against chucking unopened mail in the trash. It wasn't like angry postal workers were going to sweep in and hold me down until I read it. I rubbed conditioner into the saddle with firm strokes.

He had no business sending me a letter. Sure, I'd told him not to call me, but the implication was clear: I didn't want to hear from him. I shouldn't have had to send a twenty-page contract outlining that not only did I not want to hear from him by phone, but I didn't want to hear from him in person or by letter, sign language, or smoke signal either. I put down the rag, crumpled the letter, and tossed it into the trash.

I turned the saddle so that I could work on the other side. I found myself glancing up to look at the trash can as if I thought the letter might pop up over the edge and start crawling toward me like a zombie. Unless you take those things out with a head shot, they keep coming back. I stormed over to the trash can and picked the letter back out. One edge had an oily smear from the conditioner, which made the envelope almost translucent. I held it in my hands, ready to tear it into two.

Shit

I tore the envelope open and pulled out the letter. Just because I read it didn't mean that I had to talk to him, or even tell him that I'd read it. I could read it and then tear it up and send him the pieces.

Harper—
I've started this letter at least a dozen times. I want a way
to say I'm sorry that really shows how much I mean it,

but I don't know the words. I figure you deserve a written apology so that it's more official.

You probably wonder how all of this happened. The first time I met you outside the school, my sister suggested that I try and talk with you. That you might be willing to listen to someone who was closer to your age. I wanted to convince you that Neurotech was evil and needed to be stopped. I didn't know you. You were just this extension of your dad's company to me. I'm not saying that made it right to lie; I'm just explaining how I viewed it. How I excused it. Then it got more complicated as I got to know you. I thought about telling you about my sister, but I didn't know how to start. I knew if I did, you'd never want to see me again. I wanted to go back in time and start over, but I couldn't. I couldn't go back and I didn't know how to go forward.

I want you to know that I haven't told my sister about your mom and I won't. That was never about getting a story. I really wanted to help. I still want to help. I want to be a part of your life. I know you have no reason to forgive me, or even believe that I'm telling the truth, but I hope you will. I've given you no reason to trust me, but I can't help but hope you'll give me a chance to earn your trust back.

I miss you—
Neil

I stood there shaking. It felt like my skin was too small to hold in all my emotions. I didn't know how it was possible that part of me wanted to scream and hit him for lying to me and another part wanted to skip around the room because he missed me.

I folded the letter and put it in my pocket. I had no idea what I wanted to do with him, or with the letter, but until I decided, I didn't want to throw it away. I could feel the weight of the letter in my pocket as if it were made of lead instead of paper.

I picked up a rag and tackled the saddle again. I put all my frustration into rubbing the conditioner into the leather. It would be as soft as a baby's butt by the time I was done with it. I might not be able to fix things with Neil, but I could fix this.

As I rubbed, my ring caught on the stitching on the bottom of the cantle and I felt something pop. Shit. I dropped the rag, my hand cramped. I should have taken off my ring. I was going to kick myself if I'd put a deep scratch in the leather. It was like I couldn't touch anything lately without making it worse. A piece of the stitching was pulled slightly up near the back panel. I ran my thumb along where it joined. I'd have to get Laura to look at it to see if I needed to take it to a saddler for repair or if she would know how to even the stitches back out.

Something was wrong. I leaned in closer. The nylon thread seemed to be just a slight shade lighter on this part of the saddle, as if it had been torn and repaired before. I dragged the saddle over to the light on the desk so I could see it better. The thread was definitely different. It had been stitched up before, but I'd never had it repaired. I picked at the thread until it started to unravel. I pulled out two stitches. I ran my pinky nail into the small gap in the leather. There was something crammed in between the layers of padding.

I pulled two more stitches out so I could hook my index finger inside. I rocked whatever was in there back and forth. It fell out onto the table. It was hard plastic, about an inch long. I turned it over in my hand. It was one of those thumb drives that plug into a computer. I stared at it. What in the world was it doing sewn into my saddle? There was a logo on it from Washington State University, where my parents had met.

My mouth went dry. There was a buzzing in my ears. There were black spots in my vision and I could feel a clammy sweat break out all over.

I took a couple of steps back and sat down hard on a stool. I put my head between my knees and took a few deep breaths. *In through the nose, out through the mouth.* The smell of leather and hay filled my head.

That's when I remembered everything.

chapter thirty-one

I was in a tack room, but not the one at Hampton Mews. I was sitting on a wool blanket on a hay bale. There was a plastic toy horse in my hands, and I was brushing the long mane. I could even remember the name of the horse. Midnight.

My mom—my real mom, Robyn—was cleaning her saddle, whistling a song. She looked over and smiled at me. She had a small pair of nail scissors in her hand and was snipping at the threads on the saddle. My eyes went wide. Even though I was just a kid, I knew this was something that wasn't done. She pulled a thumb drive out of her jeans pocket and slid it into the small hole.

Mom winked at me. "This one's our secret."

I remembered the rush of warmth I felt. I liked having a secret with my mom.

Memories of my mom flooded in, tumbling over one

another, each one pushing for attention. I remembered her teaching me to ride my bike, holding on to the back of my seat and running along the street next to me. She was laughing and her hair was blowing around. I thought I was flying.

I remembered how she smelled like vanilla, and how she would crawl into bed with me in the mornings as part of waking me up for school. She'd start off rubbing my back, but if I didn't get up, she'd tickle me until I would giggle and tumble out of bed.

Some memories were just images. Her laughing. Her coming home from work and falling asleep curled up in the corner of the sofa. Her and my dad kissing in the kitchen when they didn't know I was watching.

I held the sides of my head. I felt like my skull was going to explode. There wasn't room inside for all the new memories. I was squeezing the thumb drive. She'd hidden it for a reason. My stomach tightened as another memory clicked into place.

I'd stayed home from school because I was sick. I'd thrown up that morning, spewing brightly colored Froot Loops onto the white linoleum kitchen floor. I felt better after I'd thrown up, but I didn't protest when my mom called the school and said I couldn't make it. It meant she would stay home with me.

We'd watched a movie and somewhere in the middle I'd fallen asleep. My mom had carried me upstairs and tucked me into my own bed. The slam of the kitchen door woke me up.

My dad was yelling. I could smell the meat loaf my mom must have put in the oven while I napped.

I pulled the blanket up to my chin. My parents were fighting. They'd been fighting a lot lately. They tried to do it when I wasn't around, but I still knew. My stomach hurt again. I didn't know what was wrong, but I knew it was about their work. Things in the house were different. Even when they weren't fighting, there was a tension underneath everything, as if we were all waiting for a bomb to go off.

"It's not up to just you. We need to take the information forward!" my mom yelled. "It can't stay a secret."

"You bring that forward and everything will be ruined," my dad fired back.

I stood in the doorway, uncertain. I could hear my mom coming up the stairs with my dad right behind her. I wasn't sure if I should say anything or not. If they saw me, they would stop arguing or at least stop yelling. I wondered if the secret my mom was talking about had anything to do with what she'd hidden at the barn the day before. I could smell the meat loaf starting to burn. Meat loaf had always been one of my favorites—she made it with the ketchup crust—but now the smell made me nauseated again. I stepped softly into the hall. My mom stood at the top of the stairs ready to go back down and rescue dinner from burning further.

"This isn't up for discussion. If you won't bring forward the information, I will." Her voice was cold.

"You aren't the one who gets to decide if this conversation is over," Dad said.

Mom whirled around to say something, but her foot slipped on the laminate wood floor. She reached out and grabbed for the bookcase, her hand knocking the shelf. The globe that sat on the top rocked back and forth. Everything slowed down. She fell backward. My dad reached for her, but she was already gone, tumbling down the stairs. Her body hit the landing with a loud, wet thump. The globe exploded next to her on the tile floor.

She never screamed, but I did. My dad turned and saw me standing there.

I realized I was crying. The tears carved hot trails down my face. My memory was a blank after my mom's fall. I wanted to believe my dad had made the decision to wipe my memory because I saw her die and it changed me in some way, but I feared the truth was he hadn't wanted me to tell anyone what I'd heard. He wouldn't have wanted anyone to know they'd been fighting, that things in our house were anything less than perfect. Maybe he was simply afraid that if people knew they'd fought, he might be suspected of something. But I knew it was more than that. If he'd been hiding information on side effects that my mom had discovered, I would be the only other person who knew. Any side effects were a problem with his plan. That made me a problem. I turned the thumb drive over again in my hand. I rubbed my face with the back of my hand. The time for crying was over.

I tapped on Laura's office door. The door swung open. She wasn't there. This made it easier. I crossed the room and jiggled her computer mouse to wake up her monitor. I slid the thumb drive in and held my breath. It was almost nine years old and had spent that time jammed in a saddle. It was a really expensive saddle. My dad probably couldn't bear the idea of getting rid of something so valuable, but he'd had no idea what was still inside it. I wasn't even sure the drive would work anymore, but the small icon appeared on the desktop. I bit my lip, said a small prayer, and clicked on it.

For a second nothing happened. Then a document opened. It was an Excel spreadsheet. I scrolled up and down trying to make sense of the numbers. It had to be the data on side effects. My mom had made a copy and hidden it where she knew my dad would never look. I pulled the drive back out and then slid it back in and quickly e-mailed a copy of the documents to myself so I'd have an extra just in case. My mom might not be able to do anything about the situation anymore, but I could.

chapter thirty-two

It might have been a Saturday, but there would still be people working at Neurotech. The clinic side was closed for the day, but there was always a small group working in the labs. Progress didn't take a break.

Mr. Epstein, the security guard, smiled when he saw me. He buzzed open the door. There was a rush of cold air. It made the thin sheen of sweat on my arms ice over. The air conditioner was set up too high.

"What are you doing here on the weekend?" I asked, rubbing my arms to warm them up.

"Regular weekend guy has the flu. Figured I better pick up the extra hours; one of these days that little girl of mine is going to go away to college, and I'll be glad of the money. That reminds me—I've been meaning to thank you for the advice."

My mind drew a blank.

"You sent me places I could take my little girl for her birthday. The trail ride places." He mimed galloping along.

"She had a good birthday?"

"She just about busted her buttons when she saw what we had planned for the party. Girl is horse crazy." He shook his head like it drove him nuts, but I could see in his eyes how much he loved her.

I managed a smile. "I was too at that age. Careful, some of us don't outgrow it."

"Can't say which of us enjoyed the day more. It's not often I get to be that much of a hero just for renting a couple of old nags. I figure I've only got a few more years where she believes I'm the bee's knees and then she'll be all grown up. Maybe if I play it right, she won't outgrow thinking her dad is the best guy she knows, huh?"

His words felt like a sucker punch to the gut. "She shouldn't," I said. Mr. Epstein looked pleased. The guy worked extra hours to give his daughter everything. I wonder if she knew how lucky she was.

"Your dad's down in the big conference room. You want me to buzz him?" he said, bringing me back to reality.

"No, thanks. I want to surprise him."

Mr. Epstein hit the buzzer that unlocked the door to the hall. He had no idea just how surprised my dad was about to be.

The halls were quiet; the building felt empty. My shoes

made a squeaking sound on the white tile. The big conference room was in the very corner of the building, where the floor-to-ceiling glass windows commanded the best view. I didn't bother knocking. I pushed open the door. My dad sat at one end of the table with stacks of paper spread out in front of him and Josh. Josh looked like a mini version of my dad, right down to his lab coat with his name stitched on the lapel. They both pushed their glasses up on their face at the same time. No other CEO would spend time with an intern, but I knew my dad couldn't resist having Josh around hero-worshipping him. Josh's internship was more for my dad than anyone else. I should have seen it all along.

Dad leaned back. "Well, what do we owe this unexpected surprise to? Couldn't keep away from your two favorite guys, huh?"

Josh shifted uncomfortably in his seat, not meeting my eyes. Apparently he told my dad everything I was up to, except for the fact that we'd broken up. He must have been afraid he might lose his precious internship if my dad knew.

"I remember everything," I said. "It all came back to me."

My dad's jawline tightened. "Maybe we should go home and talk about this."

"You want Josh to tell you every little detail—shouldn't you return the favor?" I crossed my arms.

Josh looked like he wanted to crawl under the table to avoid the entire conversation.

"My real mom did find data to prove there were side effects. You didn't want any bad press. Wiping my memory was never about helping me. Maybe that is what you told yourself to feel better about it, but you know that's not true. It was about helping you." I swallowed hard to keep myself from crying. My mom would want me to be strong. "She died, and you never brought her worries forward, and to make sure I wouldn't, you blocked everything. Wiped it clean."

"Harper—"

I cut him off. "You got your business, your big house, and if a few people got sick, then it didn't matter. Guess the end justifies the means."

Dad pushed back from the table. "Honey, I know all of this probably seems very real to you."

"Seems real?" I sputtered.

"Memory is fragile. Things slip away." His hands waved vaguely. "This is why I wanted you to come back for that appointment."

"Slip away? I think you meant wiped away."

He sighed. "Yes, or wiped away. I've explained what I did and why. What you need to be aware of is that whatever you think you remember, you can't trust it."

I snorted. "That's convenient for you."

Dad rubbed his eyes. "Trust me, nothing about this is convenient. Your memory is damaged. Now that you know there are gaps, you're more susceptible to suggestion. Your memories could be a dream, or a snippet from a TV show that your brain is cutting and pasting to fit."

"You think I'm making this up?" The disbelief was clear in my voice.

Josh shook his head. "That's not what he's saying. He's saying that your brain could be making it up. To you it would seem as real as any other memory."

"Especially if you're agitated," Dad added. "I'm worried about you. I think all of this is affecting you. You're not yourself." He looked at Josh for confirmation. "Your friends have noticed."

"This is me. You might not like it, but one thing that all of this has taught me is that just because things aren't pretty doesn't make it right to hide from them."

Dad pressed his lips together. "I think you're having paranoid delusions." He held out a hand. "I know you don't believe me, but that's because you're in the middle of everything." He stood and reached for me. I backed up. He flinched as if I'd slapped him instead of stepping away. "Honey, I'm going to make this okay."

I laughed. "Really? That would be an interesting trick. Your best one ever."

"You need medical treatment. You're not well." He rubbed the bridge of his nose as if all of this were just too much for him.

"You think this is all in my head?" I hated the look on

his face. He was so sure he could sweep this under the carpet too. Keep things just the way he liked them, and anything that didn't fit would be shoved to the side. All he had to do was convince everyone I wasn't quite all there and he'd get away with it again. This time it wasn't going to be that easy. I fished the thumb drive out of my bag and tossed it onto the table. "This isn't in my head. This is real. It's the data Mom collected. It's all here."

My dad paled slightly. Josh looked shocked. It was as if I'd dumped a grenade into the room. I fought the urge to jam my fist in the air in a victory.

"I'm going to get you help," Dad said.

"You should worry about getting yourself a lawyer."

Dad and I faced off. It was a showdown. He crossed the room and picked up the phone. "Evan, can you leave one of the treatment rooms open for me?" He unplugged the phone from the wall and put the receiver in his pocket. No one else was making a call. Black spots appeared in the corner of my vision. I'd made a critical mistake. I'd wanted to confront him so bad I hadn't taken time to consider how far he might be willing to go.

I backed up. "You're going to wipe my memory again."

Josh looked shocked. I saw him swallow hard, his Adam's apple bobbing.

"I'm going to try to help you." My dad held out a hand as if to try and calm me down.

"How are you going to explain that? You got away with it when I was nine, but people are going to ask questions now. People will wonder what happened to me, why I suddenly can't remember months of my life."

"You're sick, Harper. All I want to do is make you better. You're clearly upset. You don't have to feel like this."

I could feel my blood pressure rising. My heart was beating a thousand times a second. Josh looked at my dad. He wanted to believe what he was saying. Why wouldn't he? It made it easier. If I was telling the truth, everything he wanted and believed in was blowing up in front of his face. If my dad was telling the truth, then there was the chance that all of this was just a bad dream. They'd wipe it out of memory and start again.

"How do you explain that?" I pointed to the thumb drive on the table. I hated how my voice came out screechy and desperate. I took a step closer, hoping to pick it back up.

Dad swept it up and put it in his pocket like he was a magician making it disappear. "It's just a blank data key. Your brain is filling in the rest."

My stomach rocketed to the floor. Would the copy in my e-mail be enough proof? "Plug it in, prove it." I hadn't planned to pull it out and show it to him. When Josh didn't believe me, I wanted to make him realize I was telling the truth. Now my showing off was going to cost me. He was going to make the only hard evidence I had disappear, and I'd handed it right to him. The situation was spinning out of control. I wanted to kick myself for being so stupid, for thinking that he wouldn't do it again.

Dad turned to Josh. "I'll be glad to show you there's nothing on here, if you need confirmation. I know this is upsetting, but I need you to be logical. What makes more sense, that there's some conspiracy to keep things hidden or that she's unwell? The important thing is that we do what's needed for Harper. If you need to see it, we'll take the time to go look."

I knew what he was doing. He was manipulating it so that Josh would have to ask to see it, to question him. He was implying that my idea was absurd and didn't even merit checking out any more than checking under the bed made sense when a kid was scared of monsters. Josh never questioned my dad; no one at Neurotech did.

I whirled to face Josh. "You're not going to let him do this, are you?"

"Maybe we should take some time," Josh hedged.

"If we don't treat her soon, I'm afraid the delusions will move into her long-term memory. If that happens, she could have serious long-term psychological problems." My dad's face was serious, his eyes locked onto Josh. He was ignoring me.

"Can't you see what he's doing? Or do you see it and want to agree because it gets you what you want?" I barked out a laugh. "Wow, I guess you're more like him than I imagined."

Dad clapped his hand on Josh's shoulder. "It's okay, Josh. She doesn't mean what she's saying."

Josh's eyes were glassy, filling with tears. "I know."

When Josh wouldn't look at me, I knew I'd lost. "I'll scream," I threatened.

"Go ahead. You won't be the first PTSD patient who had the procedure in a crisis mode." He pressed his mouth into a firm line. "When they were done with the treatment, they were better too. I know you're upset, but hold on to the idea of recovery. You'll be back to yourself in no time." He picked up my purse and pulled out my phone and car keys. He unlocked my phone and started to look at something on there. I wanted to grab it back from him, but I knew he'd pull back before I could reach it. I'd had to give my parents the password to my phone or they wouldn't let me have one. It was their way of making sure I didn't get involved in some sexting scandal. My dad's fingers flew across the screen. He smiled, and my stomach turned; he'd found something. He jabbed at the phone and turned it off. He put both the phone and the keys in his pocket.

"What did you do?" I demanded. Unease rippled up my spine. "Give me my phone."

Dad's expression was impossible to read. "I knew your e-mail password would be Harry's full name."

Josh's face wrinkled up as he tried to understand what had happened.

I felt light-headed. He'd deleted my e-mail copy. I was sure of it. I didn't have any proof. He was going to get away with it. "I hate you," I said.

"I know. But you won't, This will all be behind us soon." Dad gestured to Josh to walk ahead of him to the door. The two of them stepped out, and the door clicked shut behind them.

I yanked on the door. It was locked. I pounded on the door with my fists. Adrenaline was flooding my system. I had to do something. I heard them moving away down the hall. I ran around the table and looked out the tall windows. There was someone crossing the parking lot. I beat on the window. It made a quiet thumping sound, but must not have been loud enough for anyone to hear. My glance flickered over the chairs. If I hurled one at the glass, would it break, or was it some kind of safety glass? Even if I could break the glass, I was up too high to jump.

I heard voices in the hallway, and the door pinged as the electronic lock opened again. I backed up against the window. Josh was standing there, my dad right behind him.

"I thought you might be cold." Josh held out his lab coat. "The air conditioner is on high and you only have on short sleeves. You can take this while you wait."

"I don't want anything from you," I said. I wished there were a glass or water I could throw at his face.

"Come along, Josh, I told you to let her be. Go home and leave this with me. I'm sorry you had to see her like this." Dad motioned for him to walk away from the door. I thought about rushing straight for them, but I knew I wouldn't make it.

"Please let me do this for you," Josh pleaded. He held out

the coat again. I was about to tell him off when I noticed the intensity in his eyes. He was staring at me, his mouth tight. His head gave the smallest of nods.

"Okay." A shiver ran down my spine that had nothing to do with the air conditioning.

Josh put his lab coat on the back of the closest chair.

Dad guided him out of the room without saying another word to me. I waited until I heard their footsteps disappear back down the hall. I carefully picked up the lab coat and slid it on. It was still warm from Josh's body. I might have been wrong. He might not have been trying to tell me anything. There was just a second there when I'd thought that while he might not stand up to my dad, he might still do something to help me. That when my dad had made that comment about my e-mail, he'd known something wasn't right. I slid my hand in the lab coat pocket.

My breath let out in a slow whistle. I pulled it out. It was Josh's key card.

chapter thirty-three

I counted to two hundred to give them time to leave this part of the building. I said a small prayer it would work and wiped the key card over the panel by the door. The lock clicked open. I pulled the door open a few inches and peeked out. The hallway was empty.

I slid out and started walking. I glanced up at the ceiling. There were cameras everywhere. Odds were no one would be watching them on a Saturday—they might not even be on—but I couldn't count on it. As soon as my dad realized I was missing, he was going to raise the alarm. He'd find me on his own if he could to avoid including too many others, but if he couldn't, he'd tell everyone I was crazy. I had to get out of here. I didn't have any car keys, so I wasn't going to get far without a plan.

My footsteps seemed extremely loud to my ears. I swiped

the card by one of the doors in the hall and went inside. It was a large room filled with cubicles, one of the customer service departments. I ducked into the first one. The cubicle was clearly owned by a proud parent. There were pictures of a baby pinned all over the fabric walls. A small teddy bear leaned against the computer monitor.

I picked up the phone and waited to see if hordes of security would race down at me, but nothing happened. I pushed for an outside line and dialed. I thought about calling the police, but I was afraid they wouldn't believe me. My dad was right; what I was saying wasn't an easy story. By the time they got there, he would have already swapped out the thumb drive for a blank one. He'd tell them I was unwell, that I was some kind of trauma victim who'd snapped. They might tell him he couldn't do the procedure, but I wasn't sure. My dad was an important guy in town. The police would want to trust him. There was only one person I could think of who would believe me. Thank God he made me memorize his number so it wouldn't be programmed on my phone. I had no idea what I'd do if he wasn't home.

"Hello?" The sound of Neil's voice washed over me like fresh air after having been underwater too long. "Who is this?" He sounded wary.

"It's me," I said softly in the phone.

"Why are you calling me from Neurotech?" He must have had caller identification on his phone.

"You were right," I said in a rush. "About everything. I remembered."

"Why are you there?"

"I came to confront my dad. My real mom discovered there were side effects. He wanted to keep that hidden. He didn't kill her, it was an accident, but he wiped my memory to keep me from telling anyone about the data."

"You shouldn't have gone there on your own."

I rolled my eyes. "I figured that out already. He's threatening to wipe my memory again. He's going to make all of this disappear."

I heard him mumble to someone in the background. "Okay, write this down." Neil spewed off a number at me. "That's Trey's cell; he's lending it to me. Call me right back at that number. I'm leaving now to come get you."

He hung up. I felt better knowing that he was already on his way. I pressed down the receiver and then called the cell right back. He picked up before the first ring completed. I could hear a car revving up.

"You should call the cops, or I will," he said.

"Don't. If you do, he's going to tell them I'm crazy. That I'm having paranoid delusions."

"Someone will listen," he said.

"Maybe. Maybe not. The thing is, there's proof. There's a thumb drive with the research data on it. There was a copy, but that's already gone. If I know my dad, he's put the drive back in his office. He'll want to check it out for himself and he's got to convince Josh to leave. I'm going to get it."

"No. It's too risky. Get out of there. If you don't trust the cops, then we'll take you away, where he can't touch you until we do make someone believe us." I could hear a car honk through the phone. He must have been racing through traffic.

"They're not going to believe us without proof."

"Then we'll figure out what we need to do to get you out of that house. You're eighteen."

I heard a sound in the hall and froze. "Shhh." Someone was walking by. I slid down the cubicle wall so I was sitting on the floor. The door rattled when someone tried the knob. The industrial carpet gave off a vague chemical smell, and I prayed I wouldn't sneeze. Neil's quiet breathing in my ear was the only thing keeping me grounded. I squeezed the phone. I peered around the cubicle wall. There was another door at the far end. I had no idea if it led into the hall or a storage closet. The person in the hall walked away, their footsteps receding. "They're gone," I whispered into the phone.

Neil let out a gasp. "Jesus, my heart almost stopped. You need to leave now. Get out of there."

"If I get that thumb drive, we can prove all of it. That what happened to your brother wasn't an accident."

Neil was silent on the line for a second. "It doesn't matter. Just leave."

I pulled back the receiver and looked at it as if I could see him and then brought it back to my mouth. "Don't you get it? This is your chance. This is what you've always wanted. A chance to break this open. Prove what you've always suspected. You told me once that you wanted to do something that would make up for your brother being gone. This is it."

"What I learned is that I matter when someone else matters to me. *You* matter. Nothing is worth more to me than knowing you're safe. I put getting Neurotech ahead of you once, when I lied to you. I don't plan to make the same mistake twice. I thought beating Neurotech would make me happy, but it won't. I've been focused on the past and I don't want to be like that anymore." His car squealed again as it rounded a corner. "I'm on the highway now. I'll be there soon. Get out before someone finds you. There's a wooded lot behind the building; go there and wait for me."

"You'd give up proving your brother's death wasn't an accident?" I asked. "Why?"

"How can you be so smart one second and so dim the next? I would do it because I love you."

My mouth fell open.

"Are you there?" he asked. "Please tell me you didn't just hang up on me. I know this isn't the right time or place to tell you."

"You do have a flair for the inappropriate," I managed to say.

He laughed. "I promise to work on it if you give me another

chance. Next time I'll do it over a romantic dinner, or by the ocean. Or at the very least not while you're hiding somewhere and we're talking on the phone."

"I'd like that," I said.

"Then give us that chance. Leave." His voice was urgent.

"I want you to know that I want to more than just about anything, but I have to do this. It's the right thing to do. I lost my way recently, but I believe in this. That this is the right thing to do."

"Harper—"

"Meet me in the parking lot. I'll get there as soon as I can."

"No! What if you're caught? He'll wipe your memory."

I took a deep breath. "Then I better tell you now that I love you too, just in case. I'm going to get the thumb drive."

I hung up the phone before he could say anything else.

chapter thirty-four

I sat on the floor of the cubicle for another minute and let myself enjoy the fact that he loved me. I wanted to do what Neil had told me, to just run away, but I couldn't. I needed to do the right thing, even if it wasn't easy. I had to prove to myself that I was more like my mom than my dad. She hadn't backed down, and I wasn't going to either.

"Mom?" I whispered. "I'm sorry I forgot about you, but I remember now. All of it. And I'm going to make sure it all comes out." I made myself get up before I was too scared to move. If she could be brave, then I could. She'd been willing to face down my dad, a guy she loved, because she believed in herself. If I'd inherited her eyes, her riding ability, and her inability to cook, then there was a chance I'd inherited her sense of justice too.

I opened the door to the hall and started walking. I wanted to run, but I was afraid if I started I'd panic and not be able to stop until I ran straight out the front door. I counted the floor tiles as a way to slow myself down. Two tiles per step.

A door in front of me opened. My heart froze in my chest. It was one of the lab workers coming out of the bathroom.

"Oh, hey." She smiled when she recognized me. "You probably don't remember me; we met at the summer picnic last year. Volleyball."

I nodded stiffly.

"You here visiting your dad?"

I knew I should say something, but the best I could do was another nod.

"I think I saw him go into the clinic." She turned as if she were going to walk me down there.

I made a strangled cry. She turned back. I swallowed the panic down. "I mean, I'm supposed to meet him in his office," I squeaked out. "I don't want to bother him."

"You sure?" She held up her key card. "I can swipe you in."

"No, thanks." I smiled again, hoping she would stop being so damned helpful. Did she think she was going to win employee of the month? Was she hoping my dad would see her as useful and give her a promotion complete with a corner office? It was just a matter of time until someone else came along, including my dad, and if that happened, I was in deep shit.

"You want me to keep you company while you wait? Knowing your dad, he could be a while." She laughed.

"Um. No, thanks. I'm sure you're busy. Since you came in on the weekend and all." I took a couple of steps down the hall. "I'll let you go so you can finish up and get out of here." I took a few more steps.

"See you again sometime," she called after me.

I waved and then dodged down the next corridor. I stopped and leaned against the wall. I half expected her to still be tailing after me, but she must have taken the hint.

I reached my dad's office and nudged the door, letting it swing open silently. He wasn't there. I shut the door behind me and crossed quickly to his desk. Just like home, his office was a mess. Stacks of files were piled everywhere with papers spilling out. Magazines with dog-eared pages, and what looked like the leftovers from yesterday's old takeout lunch. My hands ran over the stacks looking for the thumb drive. Nothing.

I double-checked the USB port on his computer, but it was empty. As much as I wanted the thumb drive to suddenly appear, it didn't. I yanked the desk drawer open and rummaged through the pens, paper clips, loose change, and, for some reason, M&M's that had spilled out of a bag and were mixed up with everything else.

I ran my hands back over everything again, refusing to believe it. I'd hoped it would be one of those things like sunglasses or keys that go missing, until you realize they're sitting on the counter right in front of you. I was so sure he'd have to check out what was on the thumb drive. My dad was the kind of person who sneaked around the house in December to peek at his presents. He read the last chapter of a book before starting it, so he knew how it would end. I didn't think he'd be able to be patient and wait to see what I'd found. He used to say the reason he was such a great scientist was his insatiable sense of curiosity. Brain itch, he called it.

I stood and walked over to the bookcase, looking over each shelf, hoping to see it, but even as I did, I knew it wouldn't be there. What if it was still in his pocket? What if for once his sense of curiosity hadn't gotten the best of him?

Then it came to me. The lab. If he planned to do the procedure on me today, then he would have gone in there. While he was waiting for the equipment to start up, he would have time to look at the data. It had to be there. I said a quick prayer to Saint Thomas More that I was right. Since his statue had almost taken out my best friend, I figured he owed me. I slipped out of my dad's office and swiped the key card to take me over to the clinic side of the building. The lights were off in the hall. I could hear someone in the medical clinic. It had to be my dad. I slipped off my shoes so they wouldn't make any sound on the tile. I slid down the hall, ice skating on the waxed floors with my socks.

He was whistling. The sound creeped me out. He planned to wipe out my memory and he was whistling like he was doing yard work. The medical lab was open on one side, with a long counter. During the day the nurses would sit at the counter looking out over the recovery room. They could do the needed paperwork while keeping an eye on everyone. Sitting in the center of the counter was an open laptop. From the hall I could see the flicker of light. The screen was on. My dad was just beyond the counter in the treatment room. If I walked past, he'd see me.

I crouched down and crawled along the floor. Whenever my dad would stop whistling, I'd freeze and wait for him to start again. Finally I was directly under the counter. I could even hear the cooling fan from the laptop whirring away.

My guts felt like they'd turned into water. I was pretty sure that if I stood up, every one of my organs would pour out. I'd be like the Wicked Witch in *The Wizard of Oz*, who disappeared into a smoking puddle. I was shaking. I wasn't going to be able to pull this off.

A metal click came from the treatment room. I slid slowly up until my eyes were level with the counter. I could see the shape of my dad moving in the other room. Then I saw it. The thumb drive sticking out of the laptop. Thank you, Saint Thomas More. I reached for it and gave it a small pull. It didn't budge, but the laptop moved slightly on the counter with a tiny squeak.

I dropped back down to the floor, my heart slamming in my chest. My dad rummaged around in the other room. He came out into the nurses' unit. If he rounded the corner, this was going to be quite the surprise. The water cooler gurgled, and he poured himself a glass. Then it was quiet. I couldn't tell if he was still there or had gone back into the other room. I was shaking so hard I was afraid he would hear me.

An image of Harry flashed in my head. The first time I'd jumped a fence, I'd been terrified. I'd been shaking then too. I was convinced that Harry would throw me and I'd end up with a broken arm or worse. In order to jump, the rider had to lean far forward. If the horse balked, I'd go flying over his head and hit the dirt. I would canter toward the jump and then at the last second lose my nerve and sit back quickly, yanking the reins to stop Harry. Laura told me that day that it was okay to be scared; the important thing was to be scared and do it anyway. I took a slow, deep breath, the same way I did before a show. When jumping, you had to focus on the gate in front of you. Not on the ones that would come later—you had to narrow your focus down so you could concentrate. I didn't have to think beyond this next step. One thing at a time.

I slid slowly back up and peeked over the counter. No sign of my dad. There was a part of me that wanted to wait until I knew exactly where he was, but just like in jumping I couldn't hesitate. I had to commit. One hand grabbed the laptop to hold it still and the other yanked out the thumb drive. I shoved it in my bra and dropped back to the floor.

I waited just a beat before crawling for the hall again. I

was certain that if I turned around, Dad would be standing there staring at me. I didn't let myself even look; I had to have faith this would work. I got to the hall, grabbed my shoes, and sprinted for the door. Holy shit. I'd done it. I had the thumb drive. My hands, which had been steady while I grabbed it, went back to shaking. It was as if now that they knew it was going to be okay, they'd given themselves permission to fall apart.

I heard my dad again down the hall in the treatment room. It was only a matter of time until he finished up in there and went to get me from the conference room. I couldn't find Josh's key card. I pulled on the door, but it didn't move. A sick feeling washed over me. What if the key card had fallen out of my pocket when I was crawling along the floor? I'd had it when I opened the door, so it had to be between here and the lab. Keys don't disappear.

"Harper?"

My head shot up. Dad was standing down the hall, looking at me in shock. I swallowed. He couldn't figure out what I was doing there. I must have seemed like a hallucination to him. My hands were sweating, and I rubbed them on my jeans. Then I felt it. I shoved my hand back in my pocket and pulled out Josh's key card. I must have missed it in my panic. I swiped it against the door and pulled it open.

"Harper, wait," Dad called out.

I stared him down and slowly shook my head. Then I

turned and ran. I bolted down the main hall without waiting to see if he was coming after me. I skidded around the final corner, still in my socks. Sunshine poured through the glass front doors. I hit the panic bar and spilled outside. I blinked, trying to focus in the bright light, and then I saw him.

Neil ran toward me and pulled me into his arms. I'd made it. We were safe.

chapter thirty-five

A re bad memories holding you back from doing everything you want and enjoying the life you deserve?"

The commercial cut off midstream and the camera returned to a close-up of the news anchor, her hair perfectly coiffed and looking like it was encased in a layer of clear plastic.

"Pharmaceutical giant Neurotech has its now controversial Memtex treatment in recall, pending investigation by both the Food and Drug Administration and the Seattle Police Department."

The footage on the TV showed my dad walking out of the office building, holding his hand up to avoid the glare of the cameras.

"Neurotech president Peter Bryne has stepped down from his position. Current industry insiders say that the leaked information brought to light by a local journalist proves that he was aware years ago of possible side effects and hid them. As a result, he will likely face criminal charges. Anyone who's had the treatment and is concerned about their health is encouraged to see their regular physician. We can tell you that the number of impacted individuals does appear to be low and that the FDA is giving this investigation their full attention.

"Given the low incidence rate and overall positive impact of Memtex treatment, it's possible the treatment will be approved again, although guidelines regarding who is a candidate for treatment may be changed." The anchorwoman smiled at the audience. "After all, most of us have something in our past we'd like to forget."

Win came into the room and clicked off the TV. "You shouldn't watch that stuff."

I'd been staying with Win since everything came out. There were only a few weeks until graduation, and I couldn't face going home. The official version for Win's parents was that there was too much stress in the house with the investigation and I couldn't focus on finals.

Neil had told me to wait a day before making any decision, but the moment I'd decided to get the thumb drive, I'd known I was doing it to make things public. The next morning he'd called his sister, who met us at the coffee shop, and I handed everything over to her. I told her I didn't want to pursue the fact that my memory had been wiped. I wanted to keep the focus on the data about the side effects. She promised to do her best to keep my name out of it, to call me an anonymous source. My dad was in enough trouble without us dredging up what he did to me.

While the press might not have known who was behind the disclosure, my parents did. You can't imagine awkward family dynamics until you've spilled your guts to a reporter, knowing all the while that your own dad would have wiped your memory before losing his house. There was no way I could ever go home. They knew it and so did I. I hid out at Neil's until everything came out, but once it was public, I knew they couldn't do anything to me anymore.

I'd gone back to the house to get a bunch of my stuff. The day I went home, my mom—technically my stepmom, I guess—was sitting in the kitchen, crying.

"I didn't want to lie to you," she said.

"But you did." I wanted to believe her. I'd always wanted a closer relationship with her, but I realized now we never could have had it. Everything we had was built on a lie. I couldn't look at her without seeing her part in the betrayal. She wasn't the worst person in the situation, but she had her own share of the blame.

"You have to know he did what he did because he was worried about you," she said.

I didn't answer and she looked away. Maybe she'd believed that initially, but now she had to know that wasn't the full truth. She still wasn't willing to face it. What I'd learned was that many people were more than happy to rearrange reality if it meant they didn't have to deal with the ugly facts.

She wiped her eyes, trying to pull it together. "You don't have to move out. If you would feel more comfortable, I can ask your dad to stay somewhere else."

"I feel like I do." I tried to find the right words to explain everything. I wasn't even sure how much my dad had told her. I suspected he'd either left out the part where he was going to wipe my memory again, or he'd downplayed the whole thing. He had a way of making stuff he didn't want to face disappear. What I did know is that I wouldn't be able to stay there. It wasn't my home anymore. I wasn't safe there.

"Did you feel bad? About any of it?" I asked her.

Her eyes looked haunted with dark circles. "I wanted to do what I could for you."

"And the fact that you got this house, the vacations in Europe, not having to ever work again—the whole package. Was that part of it?" I asked.

Her lower lip trembled. "I don't know. I want to say no, but I don't know anymore."

"Me either."

Neil wanted me to file charges for what my dad did to me, for wiping my memory as a kid and for threatening to do it again, but I didn't. There was nothing to be gained from a big court case. I wasn't even sure how much could be proved. He'd lost his professional reputation and his job and was still facing the chance of jail. That was enough for me. I'd lost what was left of my family. I didn't want to hash it all out while the whole world watched it on truTV.

"It might be a small comfort, but I never saw acting like your mom as a job or a duty," she said. "It started as a lie, but somewhere along the way it felt like the truth."

She crossed the room and hugged me. I could tell she was about to cry again. I pulled back. I wanted to forgive her, but it wasn't going to be easy, and I wasn't even sure it was possible. "I need to finish packing."

I went upstairs. I had just a few more boxes to pick up. I grabbed one and passed by my dad's office and saw him sitting at the empty desk.

"I want you to know I paid for Josh's first year of college," he said. "I sent the money direct to Stanford."

I stopped. "That was nice." Josh and I had reached an uneasy peace. He'd betrayed me, but when it had really mattered, he'd done what he could to help me. There was a history between us that couldn't be wiped out. We might not ever be close again, but he was a part of my past, of who I was now. I was glad he'd get a chance to start over at Stanford next year.

"I didn't want all of this to blow his chances. He's a good kid." My dad looked pale, almost a green gray, like he had the flu. "He could do some great things."

"He could." I waited to see if he would say anything else,

but he just sat there, looking down at his desk. I took a step away.

"I'll do what I can to pay for your college too," he said.

"You don't have to do that." I didn't want him to know how scared I was about the future. That I'd always been able to fall back on family, on our money, and I didn't feel ready to be on my own at eighteen, but that I also didn't have a choice.

"I want to do it. I'm not sure what will happen long-term, but I talked to my lawyer. He can make sure some funds are still there for your school. I want you to know I'm sorry." Dad cleared his throat. "I know how completely inadequate that is, but I don't know what else to say. I really believed that I was doing the right thing, that the good outweighed the bad."

My throat was tight. I wanted to say that I forgave him— you don't give up years of being a daddy's girl without a hitch— but I couldn't. "I know you're sorry," I said. That was the best I could do. I picked up my box and headed toward the stairs.

"Harper?" I paused, waiting to hear what he would say. "Your mom would have been so very proud of you."

That was the only time I cried.

I pushed away the memory. I took the remote back from Win and clicked the TV back on. "I can't ignore what's happening."

"I just don't think you need to know all the negative stuff." Win stood in front to the TV.

"Pretending the world doesn't have bad things happen in

it doesn't make them go away." I smiled at her. "But thanks for acting like my mom."

She flopped onto the sofa. "How did I get to be the overly perky one in this relationship? I thought you had dibs on being Mary Poppins."

"I don't know." I turned my head to the side as if I was trying to make something out. "I can sort of see you dancing around singing 'A Spoonful of Sugar.' It suits you."

She poked me hard in the side. "Bite me."

"Oooh, Mary Poppins is getting some gangster street cred." I laughed.

"Trust me, Poppins could cut a bitch if she had to. You don't get to be an English nanny without being tough." Win threw her arm around me. "Lots of people are tougher than you might think."

chapter thirty-six

There are few things in life that can't be made better by fancy iced coffee drinks on a hot day. I tilted my face up toward the sun and let it beat down on me while I waited. It was one of the first really hot days of the year.

"Here you go." I squinted into the sun. Neil put down three drinks on the table and sat next to me. "I got her a latte like you said, but I didn't know if she'd want sugar, or fake sugar, or honey, so I brought a couple of each." His hands spilled out a buffet of sweeteners on the table.

"Are you nervous?"

Neil fidgeted with one of the sugar packets, turning it over and over. "No."

I raised my eyebrows.

"Yes," he admitted.

I pulled the sugar packet out of his hand before it exploded all over the tabletop in a sticky mess. "She's going to like you."

"She's your best friend," Neil pointed out. He and Win were meeting for the first time. Unless you counted the time she almost decked him when I met him in the parking lot the real first time, and we had all decided to forget that.

"You'll like Win. You guys remind me of each other, in a way." Neil looked at me like I was crazy. "I'm serious. You guys are both very determined, driven, talented."

"Is there a chance you and I will become best friends one of these days?" Neil asked.

"Just friends?" I teased him.

Neil pulled me close and nuzzled into my neck. "Friends with benefits." He kissed my ear, his breath warm on my skin. "Benefits like this." His mouth continued down my neck. "And this, too."

I giggled and acted like I was going to pull away, but actually snuggled in. I never got tired of his touch.

"Love's a benefit too," Neil added.

"I like that one."

Neil pulled back as if he were insulted. "What, you didn't like the other benefits?"

I pulled him close again. "I'm not sure. You might have to practice some more."

Neil kissed the top of my head. "It's a dirty job, but I guess someone's got to do it."

We sat together letting the sun warm us. "This is nice," I mumbled, feeling almost sleepy from the heat despite the caffeine infusion.

"I wish things between us didn't start the way they did." Neil admitted. "It would be easier if the first time I met your friend I wasn't hoping that she didn't hold it against me that I lied to you at the start. Or that you got dragged into all the ugly business with your dad."

"Win doesn't blame you. More importantly, I don't blame you. Look at it this way—if it hadn't been for everything, we wouldn't have met at all."

"Now, that would have been a tragedy."

"Exactly." I kissed him. "We'll always have an interesting story when people ask us how we started dating."

Neil laughed. "Good point."

The fellow next to us got up, leaving his newspaper on the table. The headline spread across the front page was on Neuro-tech. "Did you hear they might still approve the treatment?" I asked. "After everything, it may not even matter."

He shrugged and tossed the paper in the recycle bin. "It matters. People may still go through with the treatment, but at least they'll know the risks they're taking. Truth is, I suspect my brother would have gone through with it even if he'd known what he was risking. Sometimes people just want to forget." He managed a smile. "With everything you've been through in the past couple of months, it will be a miracle you don't go in for the treatment again."

"No way. There's not a chance in the world I'm forgetting a second with you."

He leaned forward and we kissed.

"Not a single second," I repeated.

ACKNOWLEDGMENTS

Writing is a lonely occupation. The bulk of your time is spent huddling in your office in yesterday's yoga pants, drinking gallons of tea, and wondering just how much trouble you can get your imaginary friends into. Publishing, however, takes a team of people. I am hugely fortunate to have a great team in my corner.

Thanks to my previous agent, Rachel Coyne, who represented me yet again with her endless energy and humor. Kudos also goes to my new agent, Barbara Poelle, who has taken me on despite my many writer oddities.

Simon Pulse is full of amazing people to work with, most importantly Liesa Abrams, who edited this book with her trademark grace and calm. She's my superhero and truly deserves a Batman belt of her very own. Thanks also go out to Michael Strother, who always jumps in to help. Karina Granda deserves applause for a great cover, and as always, big thanks to the Pulse crew for copy edits and support with promotion. I also have to give a shout-out to the Simon Pulse Canadian team, in particular Amy Jacobson, who always seems to have a new great idea.

I owe my family and friends endless gratitude. You can't choose your family, but if I could I would choose the one I have. For my friends, I have no idea why you all put up with me, but I am grateful.

To my husband, Bob, thank you for listening to endless

hours of me trying to sort out this plot. I also have to thank my dog, Cairo, who is my fearless writer companion and snores under my desk while I write.

Lastly, huge thanks to all of my readers. Your e-mails and notes make my day over and over. I promise to keep writing if you promise to keep reading.